Fantastic Four

WORLD'S GREATEST

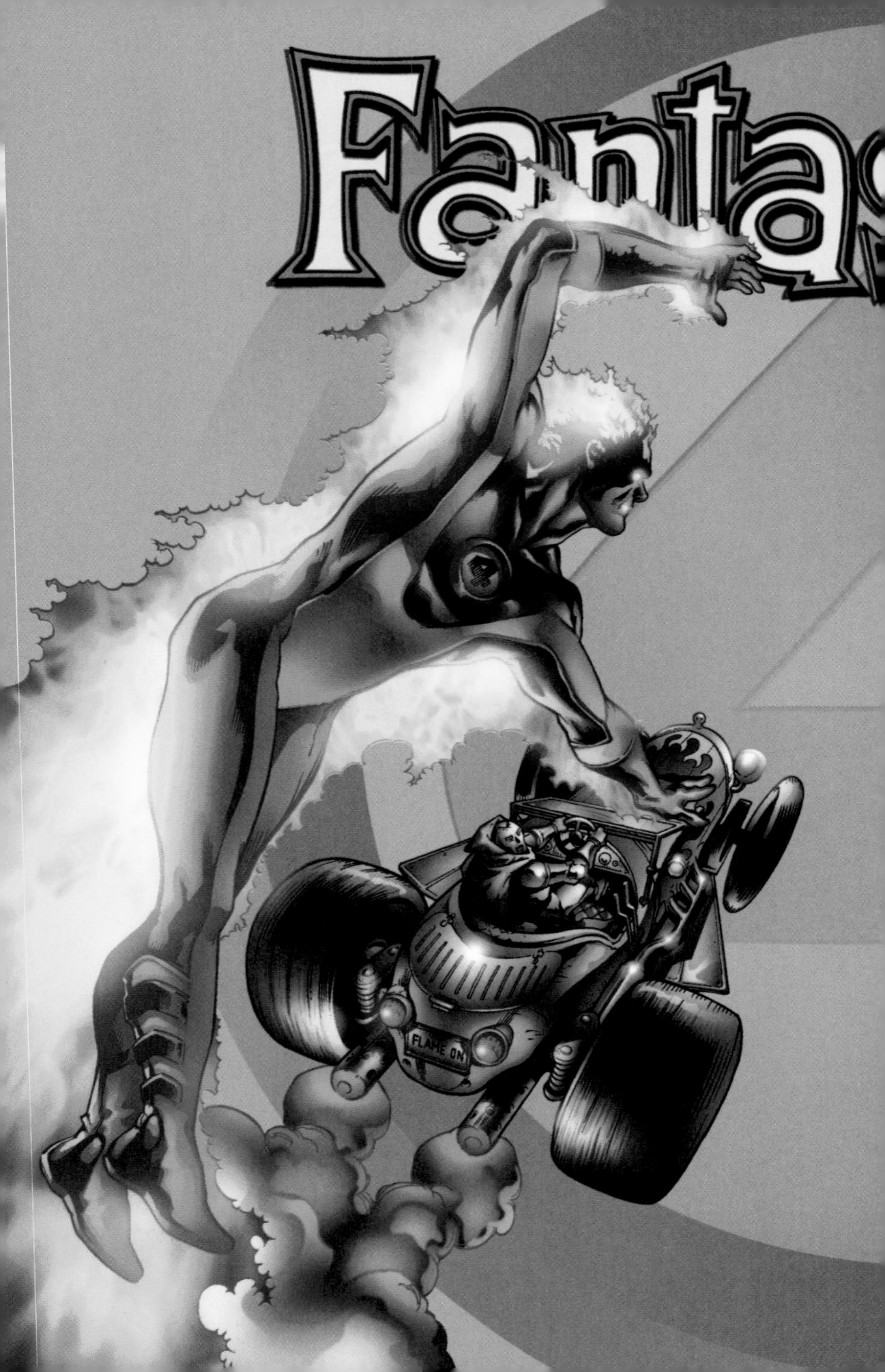

Fantas
FLAME ON

tic Four

WORLD'S GREATEST

Writer:
Jeff Parker
Pencils:
**Carlo Pagulayan, Manuel Garcia &
Juan Santacruz**

Inks: **Jeffrey Huet, Scott Koblish &
Raul Fernandez**
Colors: **Sotocolor's A. Crossley**
Letters: **Dave Sharpe**
Assistant Editor: **Nathan Cosby**
Consulting Editor: **MacKenzie Cadenhead**
Editor: **Mark Paniccia**

Collection Editor: **Jennifer Grünwald**
Assistant Editor: **Michael Short**
Senior Editor, Special Projects: **Jeff Youngquist**
Vice President of Sales: **David Gabriel**
Production: **Jerron Quality Color**
Vice President of Creative: **Tom Marvelli**

Editor in Chief: **Joe Quesada**
Publisher: **Dan Buckley**

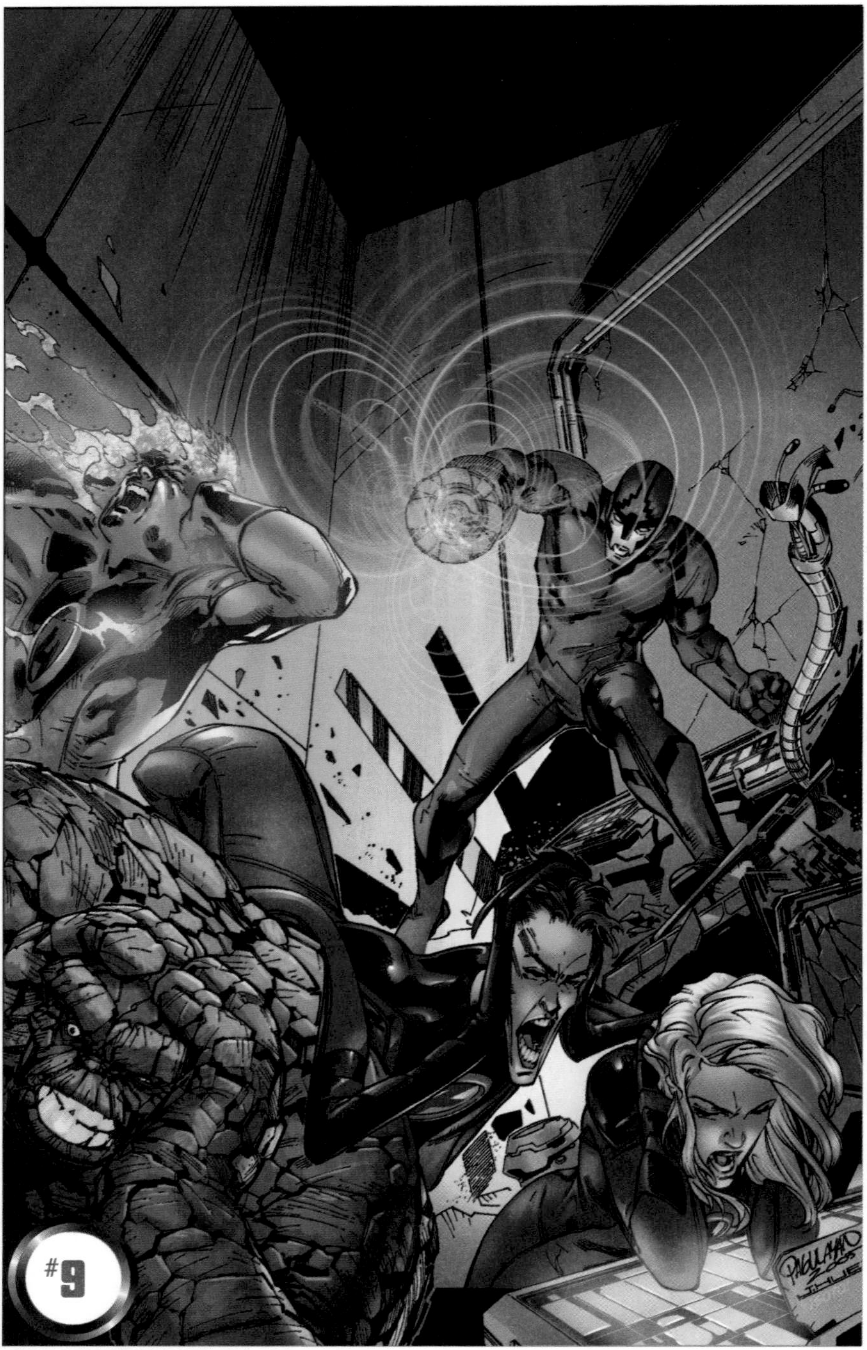
#9

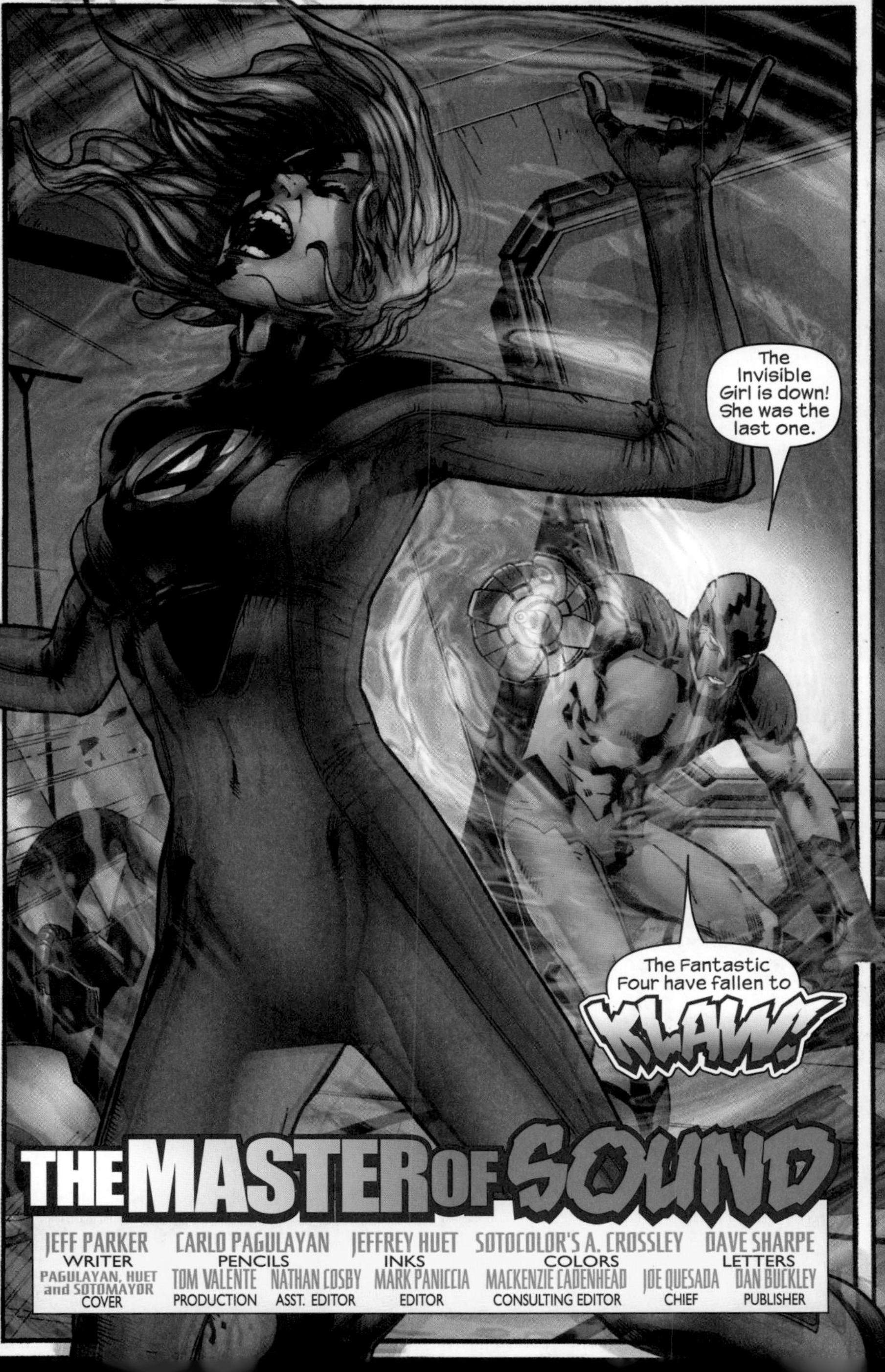

The Invisible Girl is down! She was the last one.
The Fantastic Four have fallen to KLAW!
THE MASTER OF SOUND
JEFF PARKER WRITER
CARLO PAGULAYAN PENCILS
JEFFREY HUET INKS
SOTOCOLOR'S A. CROSSLEY COLORS
DAVE SHARPE LETTERS
PAGULAYAN, HUET and SOTOMAYOR COVER
TOM VALENTE PRODUCTION
NATHAN COSBY ASST. EDITOR
MARK PANICCIA EDITOR
MACKENZIE CADENHEAD CONSULTING EDITOR
JOE QUESADA CHIEF
DAN BUCKLEY PUBLISHER

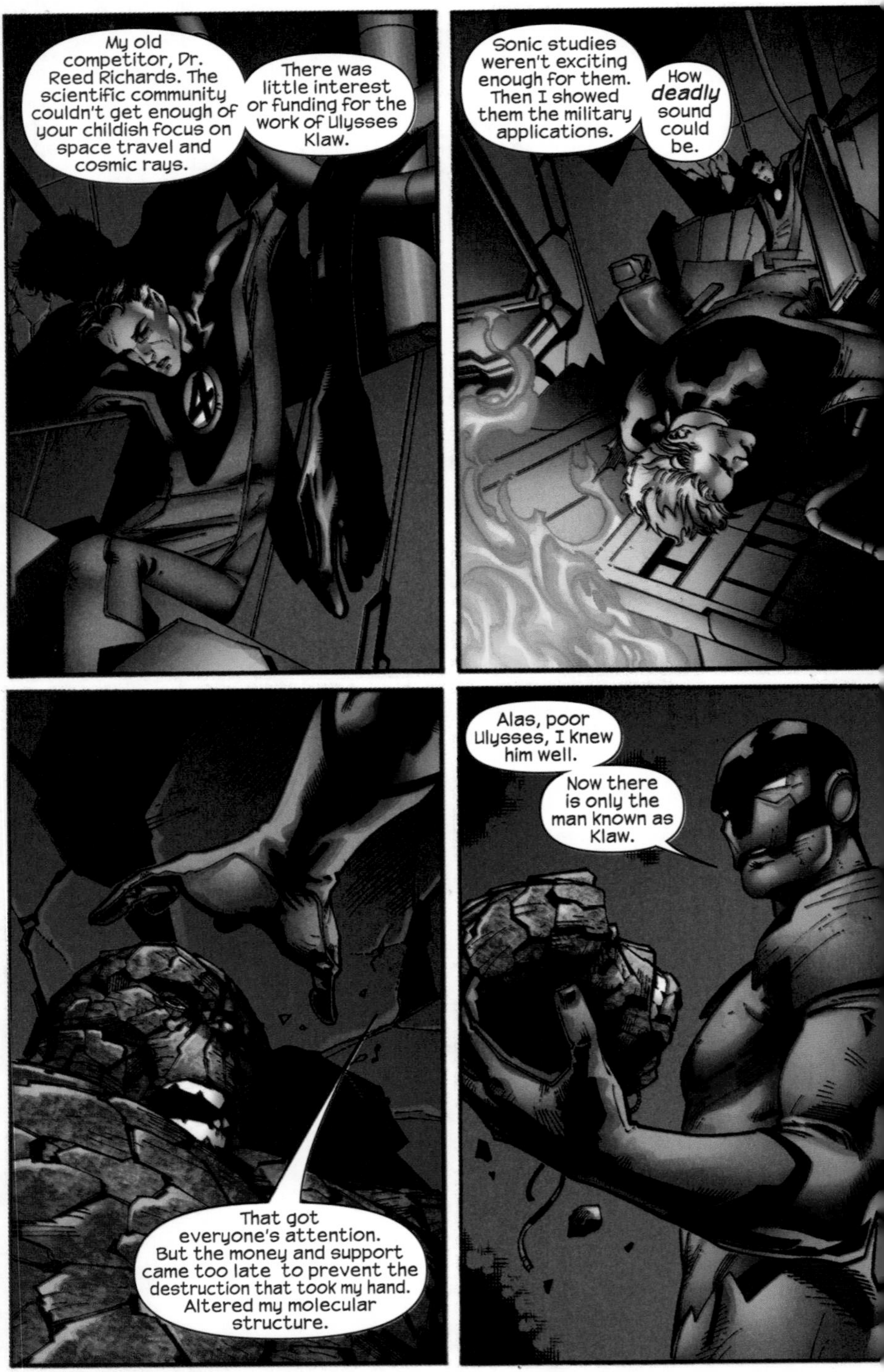
My old competitor, Dr. Reed Richards. The scientific community couldn't get enough of your childish focus on space travel and cosmic rays.
There was little interest or funding for the work of Ulysses Klaw.
Sonic studies weren't exciting enough for them. Then I showed them the military applications.
How *deadly* sound could be.
That got everyone's attention. But the money and support came too late to prevent the destruction that took my hand. Altered my molecular structure.
Alas, poor Ulysses, I knew him well.
Now there is only the man known as Klaw.

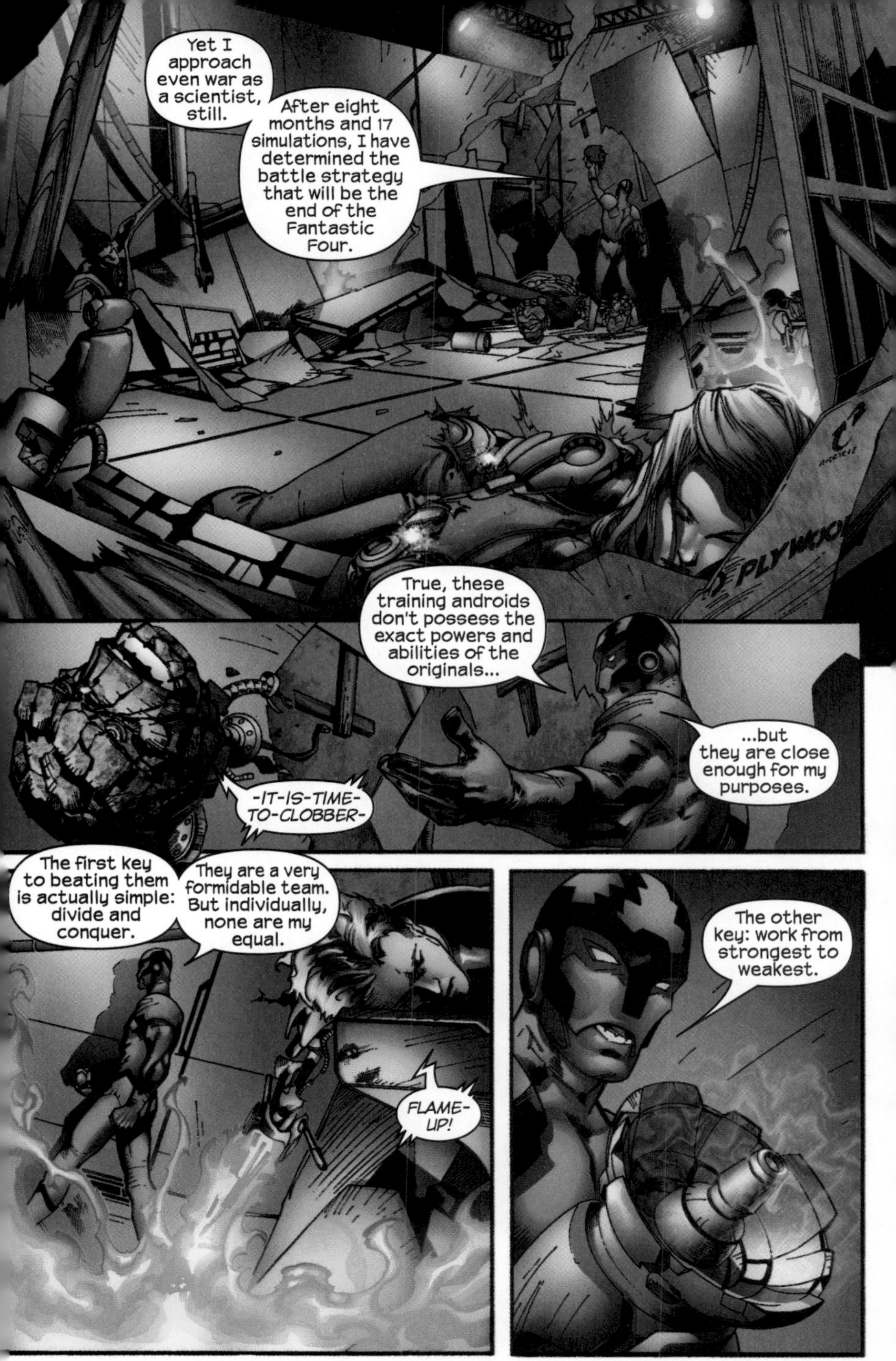
Yet I approach even war as a scientist, still.
After eight months and 17 simulations, I have determined the battle strategy that will be the end of the Fantastic Four.
PLYWOO
True, these training androids don't possess the exact powers and abilities of the originals...
...but they are close enough for my purposes.
-IT-IS-TIME-TO-CLOBBER-
The first key to beating them is actually simple: divide and conquer.
They are a very formidable team. But individually, none are my equal.
FLAME-UP!
The other key: work from strongest to weakest.

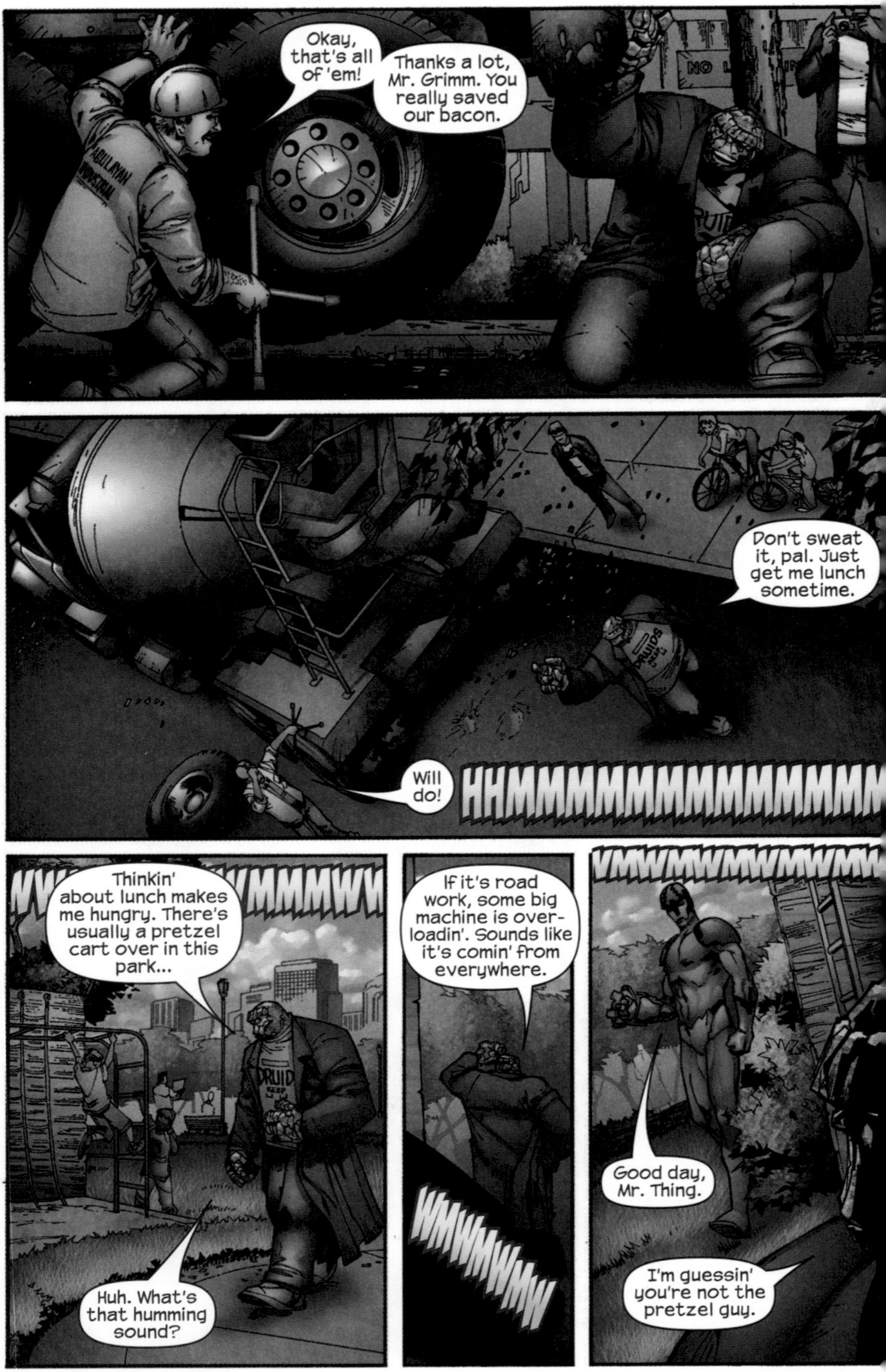

Okay, that's all of 'em!
Thanks a lot, Mr. Grimm. You really saved our bacon.
NO L
ABULAYAN INDUSTRIAL
DRUIDS
Don't sweat it, pal. Just get me lunch sometime.
Will do!
HHMMMMMMMMMMMMMM
VWMMMWVWMMMMWW
Thinkin' about lunch makes me hungry. There's usually a pretzel cart over in this park...
Huh. What's that humming sound?
If it's road work, some big machine is over-loadin'. Sounds like it's comin' from everywhere.
WMWMWMW
VMWMWMWMWMW
Good day, Mr. Thing.
I'm guessin' you're not the pretzel guy.

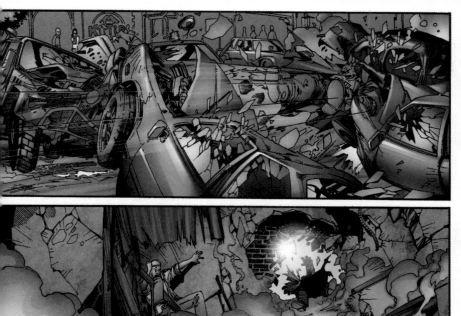

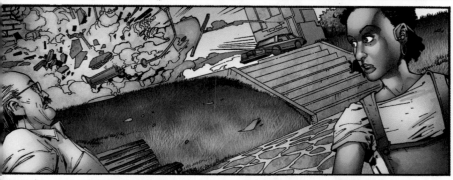

ESTABLISHMENT

CONDEMNED

CITY ENGR OFC
MANHATTAN

OFF
LIMITS

ANG LAMOK

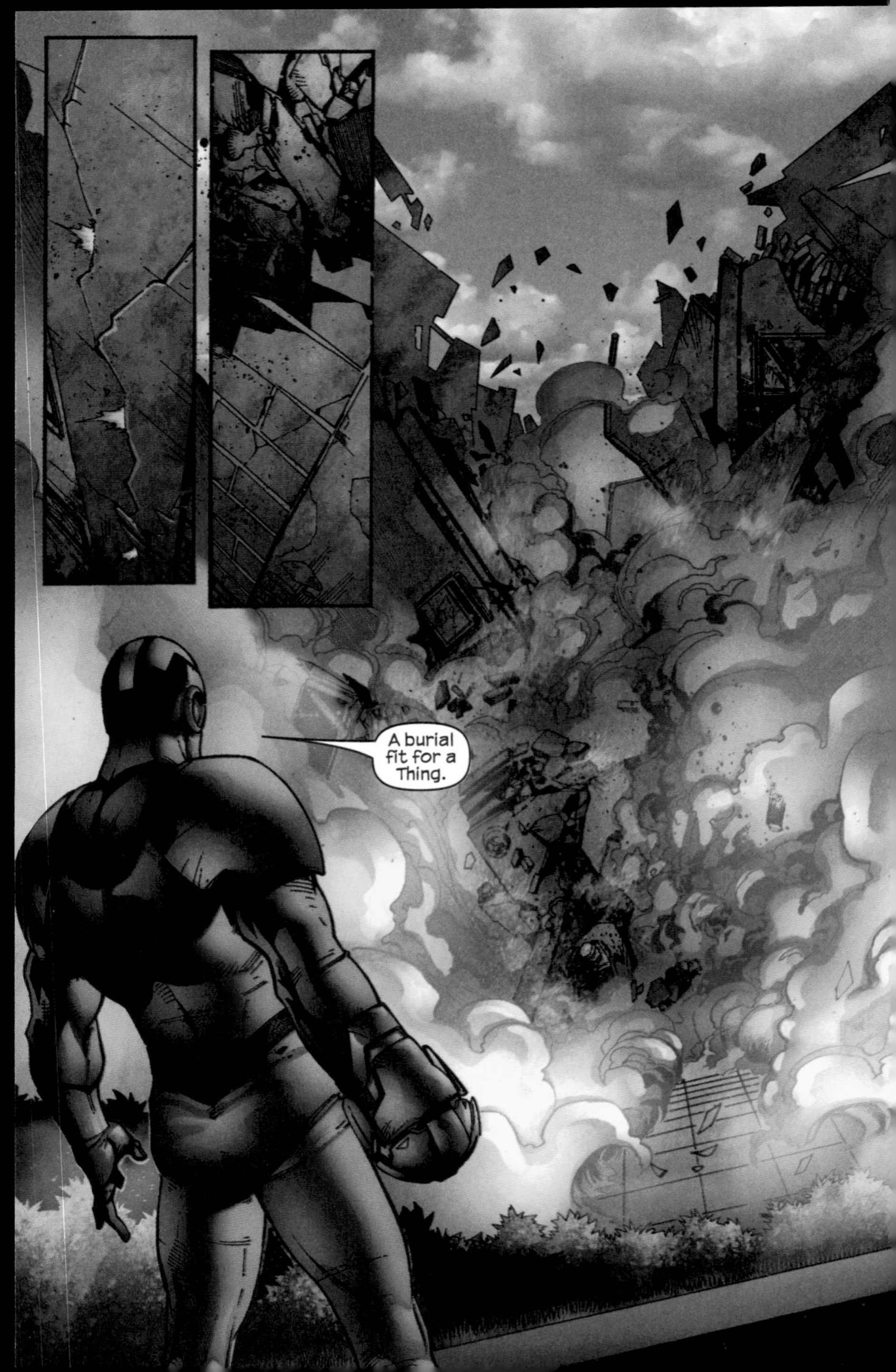
A burial fit for a Thing.

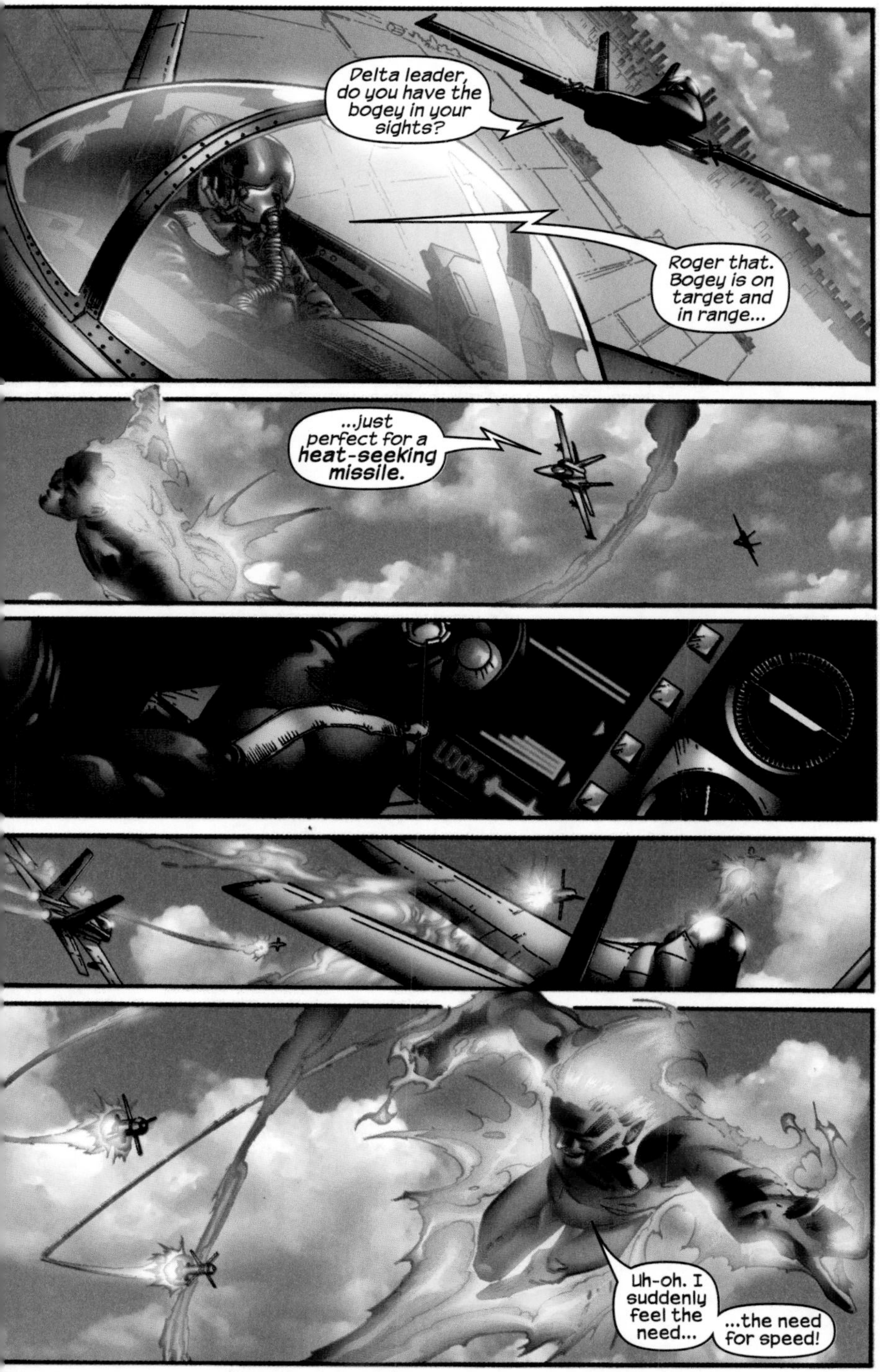
Delta leader, do you have the bogey in your sights?
Roger that. Bogey is on target and in range...
...just perfect for a heat-seeking missile.
LOCK
Uh-oh. I suddenly feel the need...
...the need for speed!

Hoo-Whee! These things don't want to be ditched!

Now we'll see what has the greater ability to maneuver...

The AIM-9 Sidewinder missile...

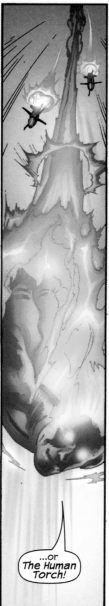

...or The Human Torch!

BENNETT FIELD

C-1-3

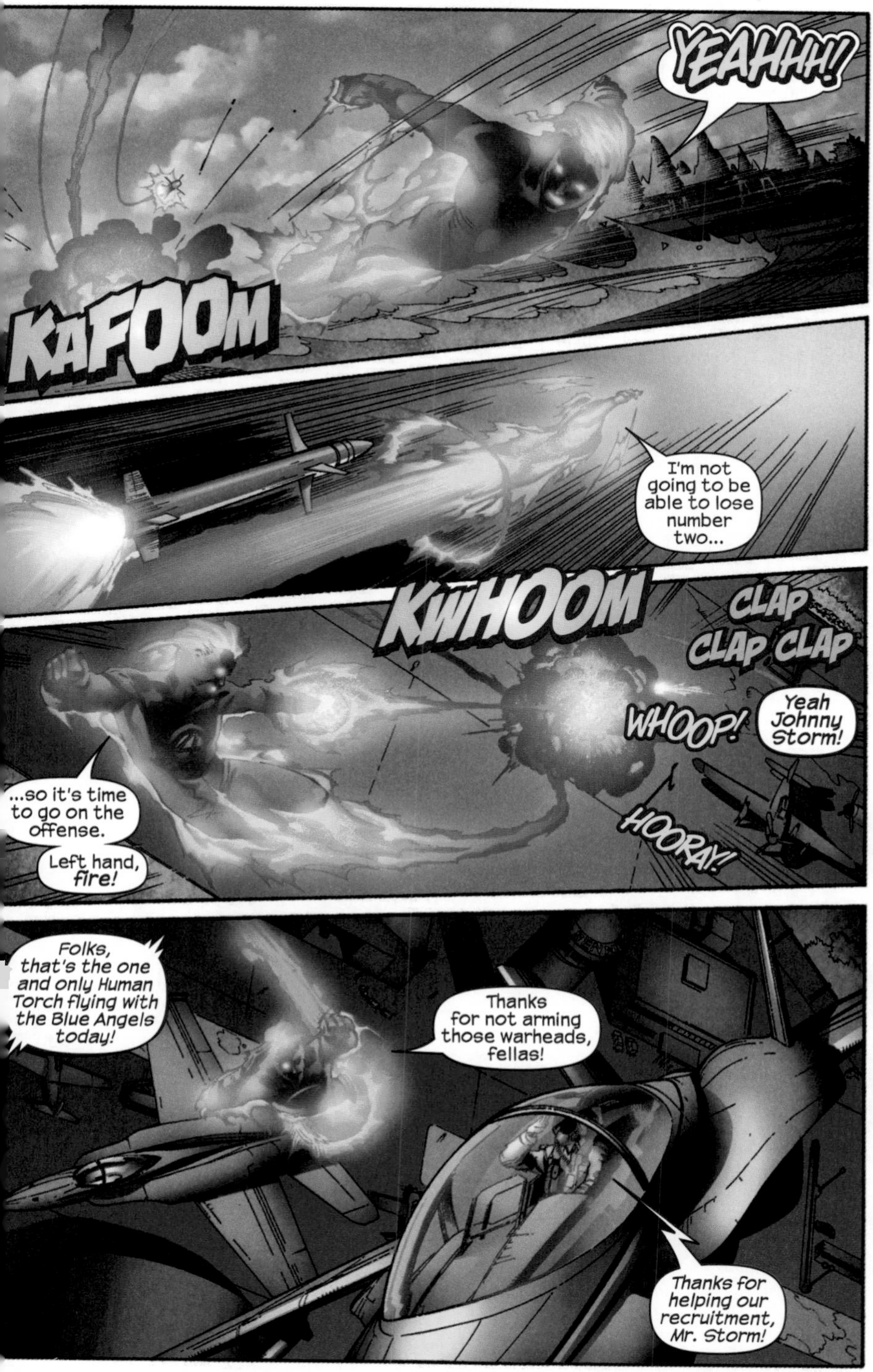
YEAHHH!
KAFOOM
I'm not going to be able to lose number two...
KWHOOM
CLAP CLAP CLAP CLAP
WHOOP!
Yeah Johnny Storm!
HOORAY!
...so it's time to go on the offense.
Left hand, fire!
Folks, that's the one and only Human Torch flying with the Blue Angels today!
Thanks for not arming those warheads, fellas!
Thanks for helping our recruitment, Mr. Storm!

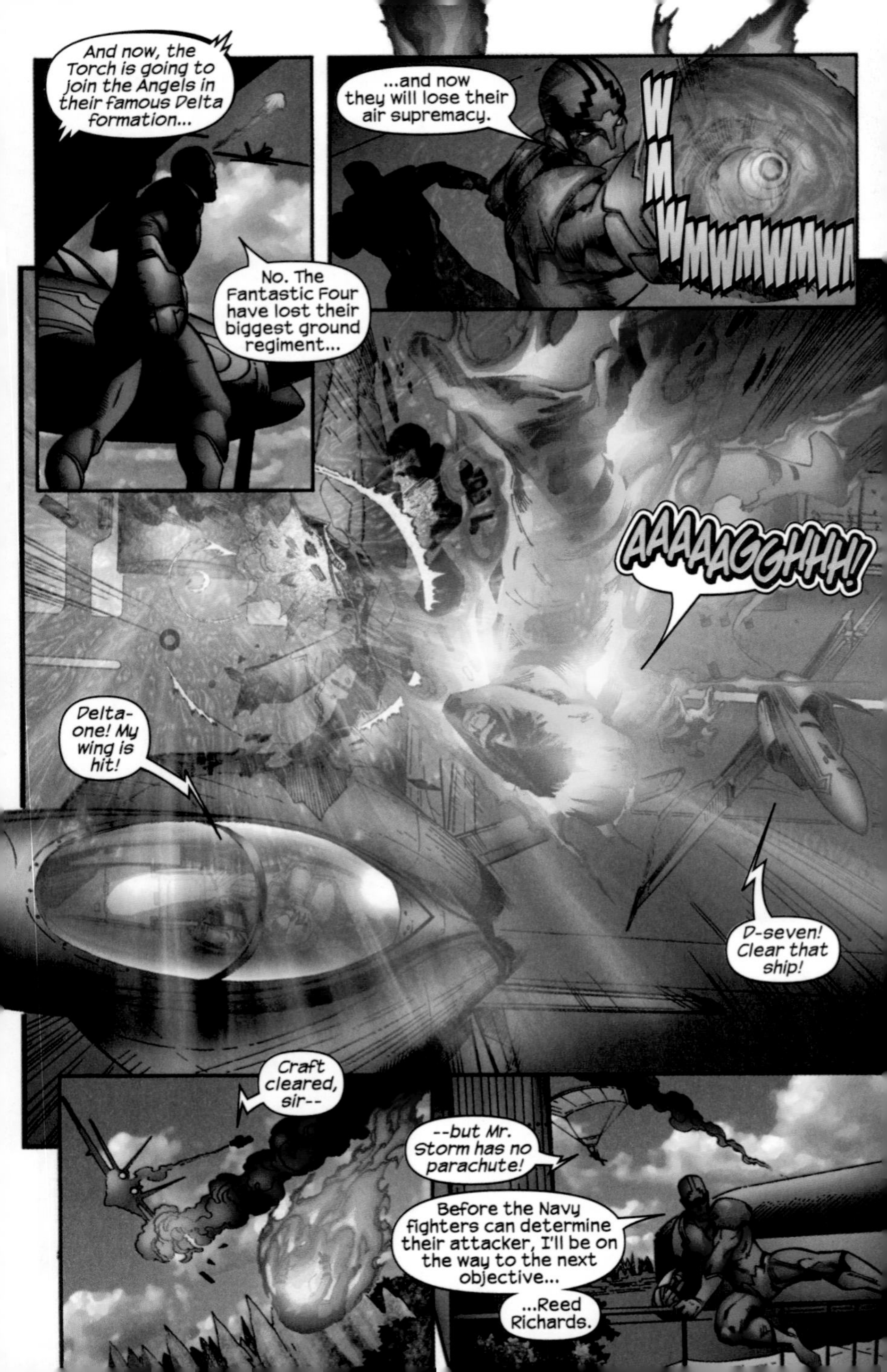

And now, the Torch is going to join the Angels in their famous Delta formation...
...and now they will lose their air supremacy.
WMWMWMWMWMWMW
No. The Fantastic Four have lost their biggest ground regiment...
AAAAAGGHHH!
Delta-one! My wing is hit!
D-seven! Clear that ship!
Craft cleared, sir--
--but Mr. Storm has no parachute!
Before the Navy fighters can determine their attacker, I'll be on the way to the next objective...
...Reed Richards.

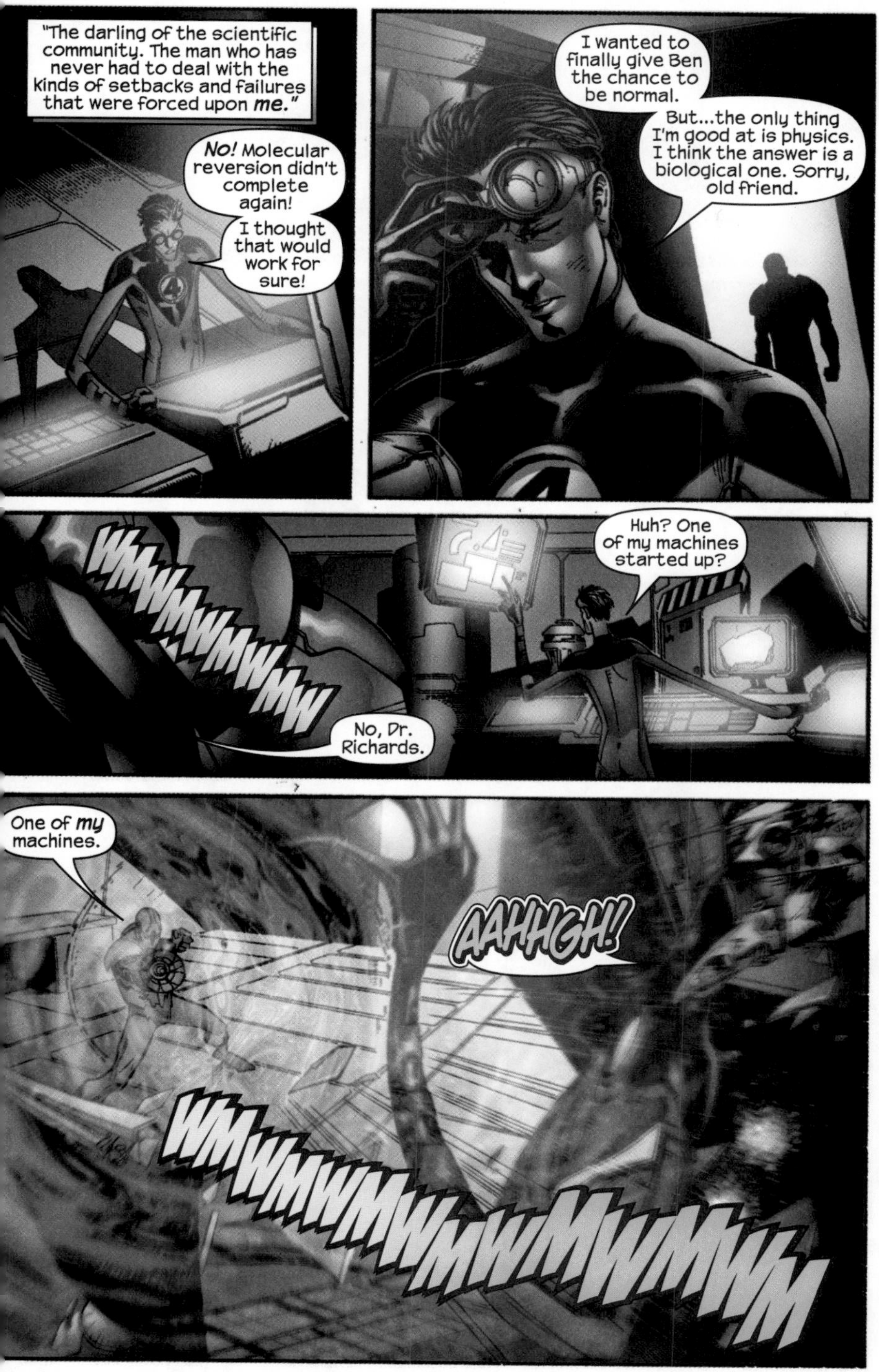
"The darling of the scientific community. The man who has never had to deal with the kinds of setbacks and failures that were forced upon *me*."
No! Molecular reversion didn't complete again!
I thought that would work for sure!
I wanted to finally give Ben the chance to be normal.
But...the only thing I'm good at is physics. I think the answer is a biological one. Sorry, old friend.
WMWMWMWMWMW
Huh? One of my machines started up?
No, Dr. Richards.
One of *my* machines.
AAHHGH!
WMWMWMWMWMWMWMWMWM

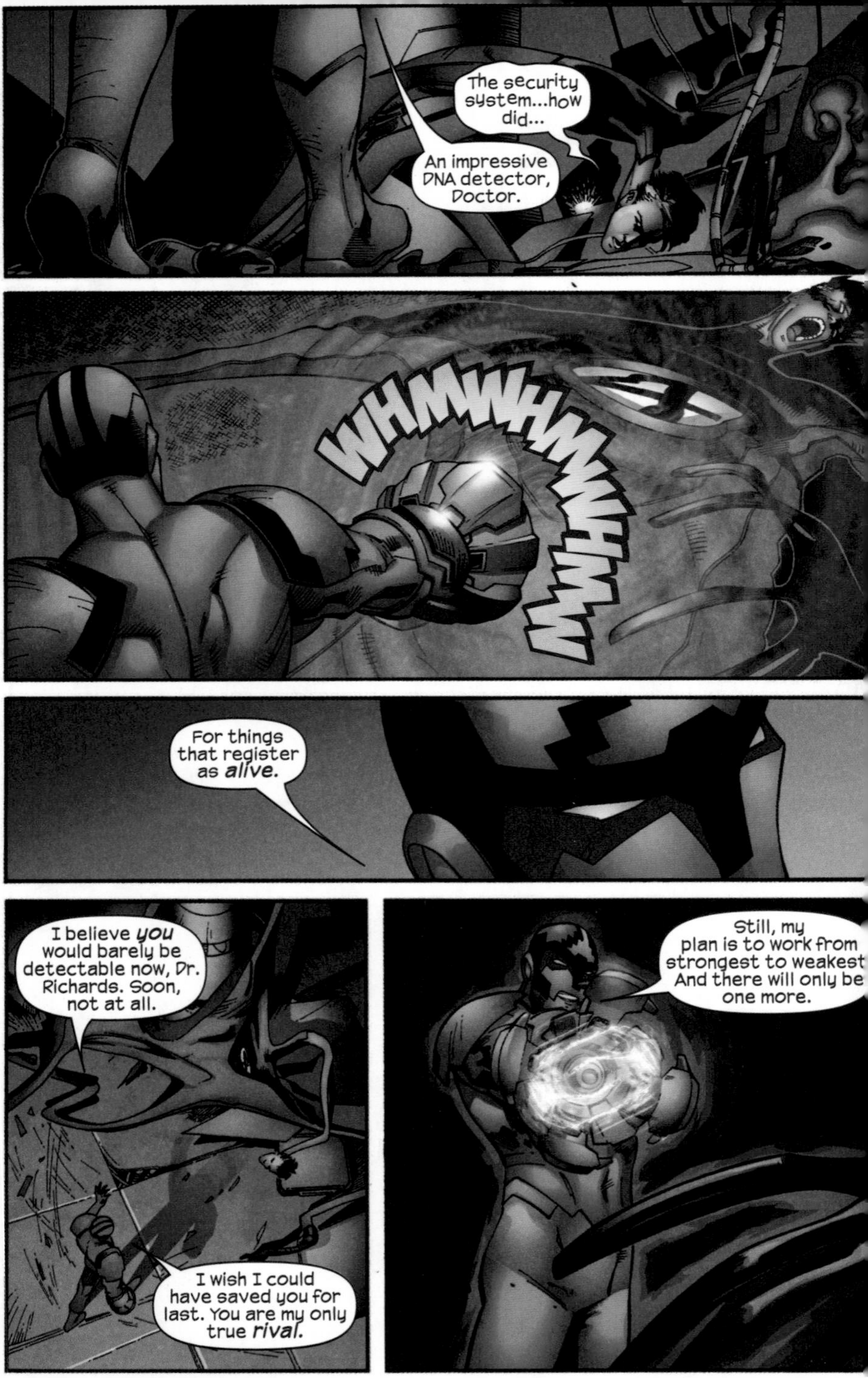

The security system...how did...
An impressive DNA detector, Doctor.
WHMWHMWHMWHMWHM
For things that register as *alive.*
I believe *you* would barely be detectable now, Dr. Richards. Soon, not at all.
I wish I could have saved you for last. You are my only true *rival.*
Still, my plan is to work from strongest to weakest And there will only be one more.

You'll...never...get...Susan...

You each have very distinct sonic signatures, Doctor.

It will take me no time to--

--find her?

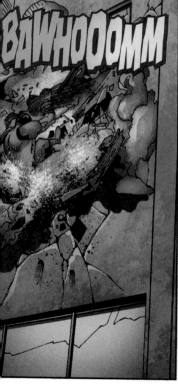

BAWHOOOMM

What was that about the weakest?

Guess I better break his fall with a force cushion.

...his body is now a strange combination of matter and sound waves.

...don't bother... ≶cOff≶...

You don't have to worry about hurting him.

Oh really?!?

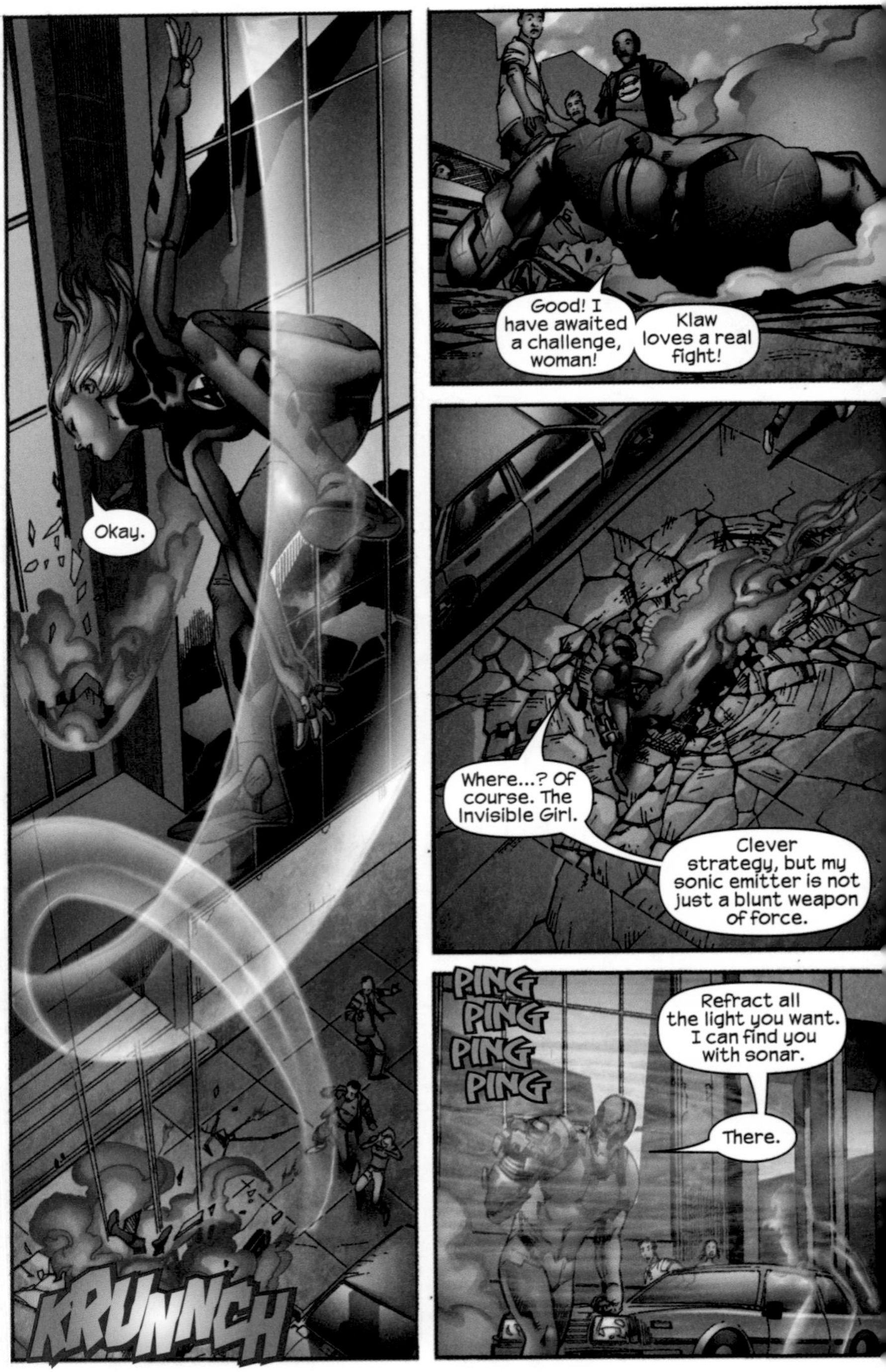
Okay.
KRUNNCH
Good! I have awaited a challenge, woman!
Klaw loves a real fight!
Where...? Of course. The Invisible Girl.
Clever strategy, but my sonic emitter is not just a blunt weapon of force.
PING PING PING PING
Refract all the light you want. I can find you with sonar.
There.

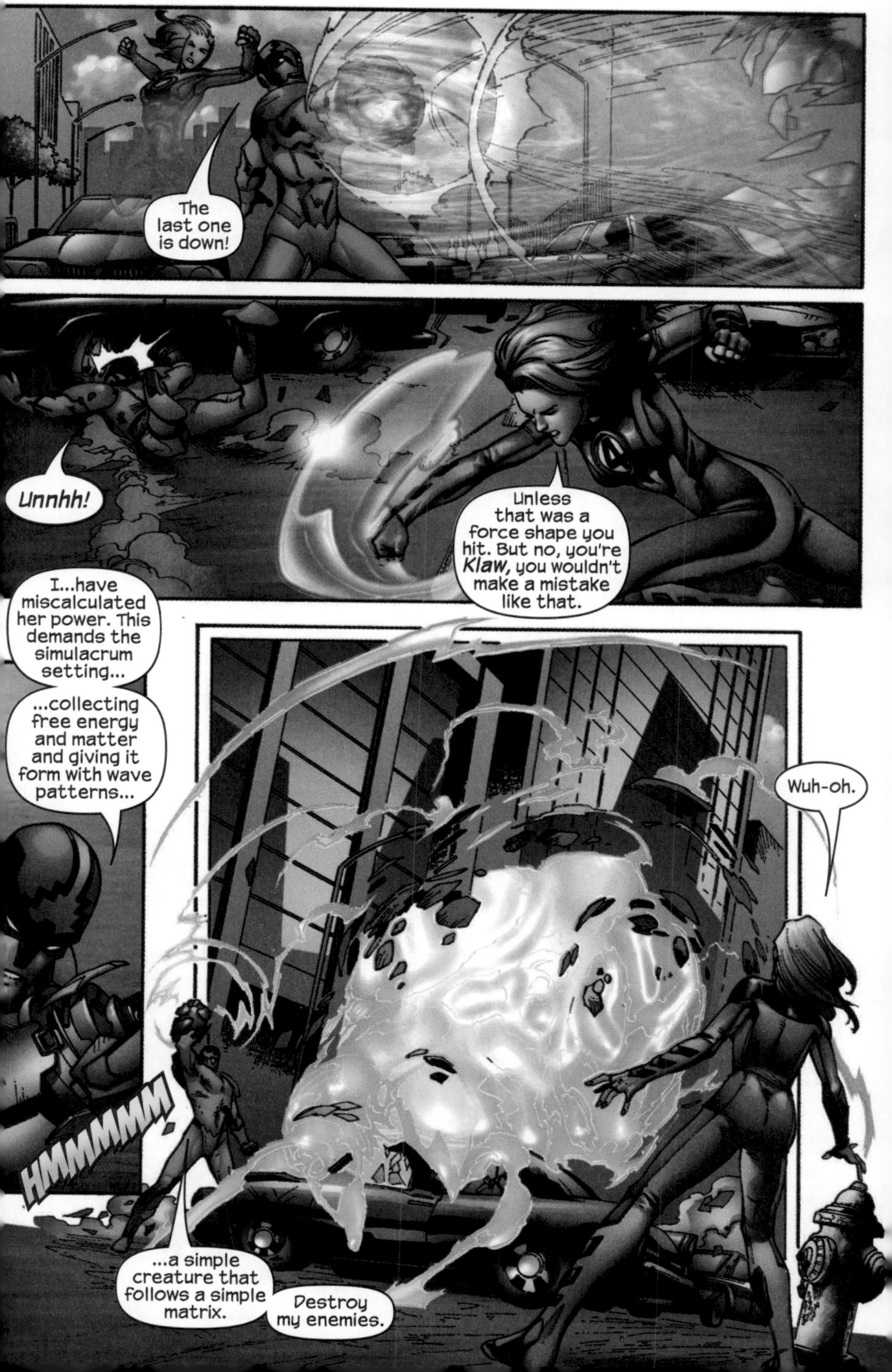
The last one is down!
Unnhh!
Unless that was a force shape you hit. But no, you're *Klaw,* you wouldn't make a mistake like that.
I...have miscalculated her power. This demands the simulacrum setting...
...collecting free energy and matter and giving it form with wave patterns...
Wuh-oh.
HMMMMM
...a simple creature that follows a simple matrix.
Destroy my enemies.

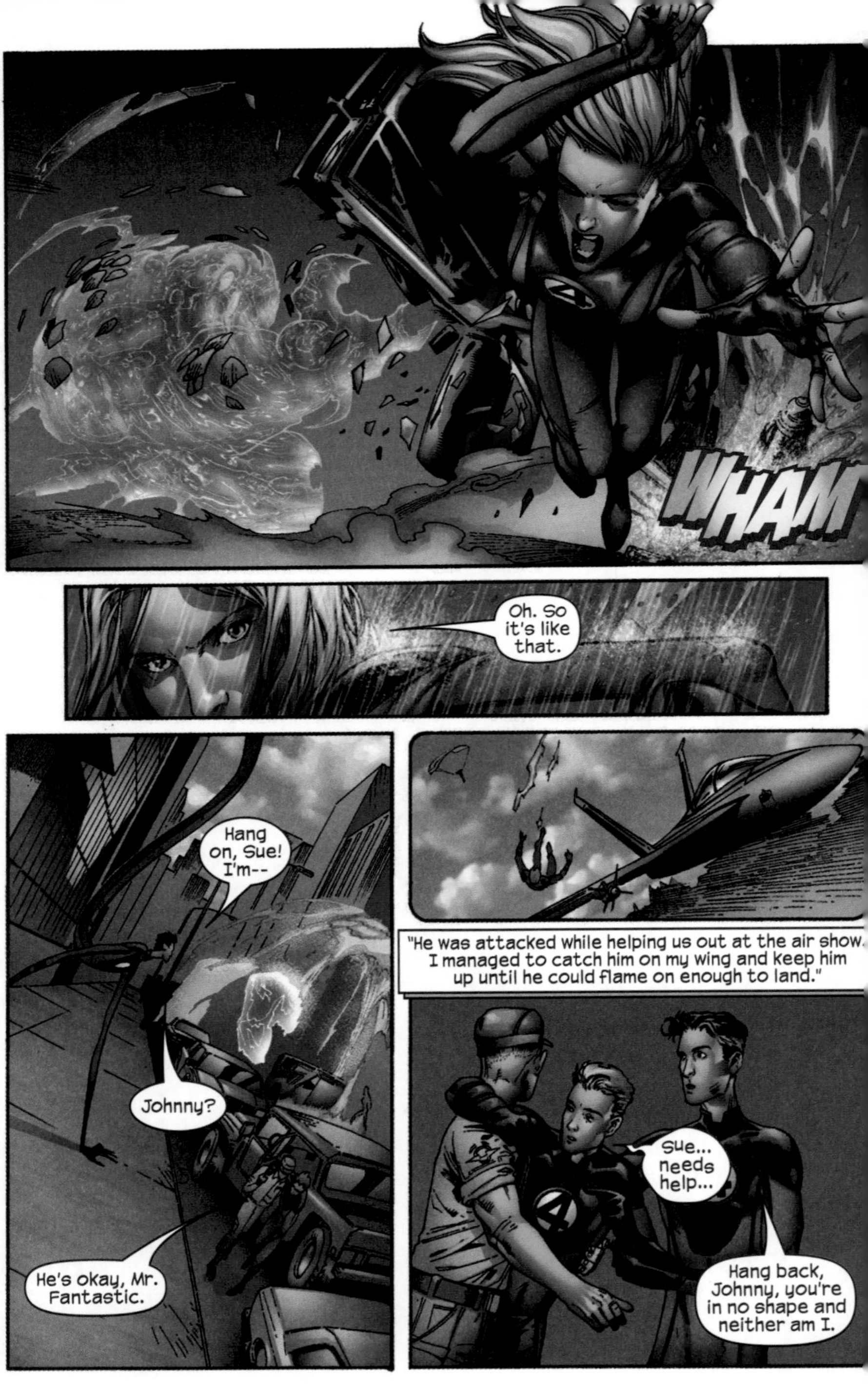
WHAM
Oh. So it's like that.
Hang on, Sue! I'm--
Johnny?
He's okay, Mr. Fantastic.
"He was attacked while helping us out at the air show. I managed to catch him on my wing and keep him up until he could flame on enough to land."
Sue... needs help...
Hang back, Johnny, you're in no shape and neither am I.

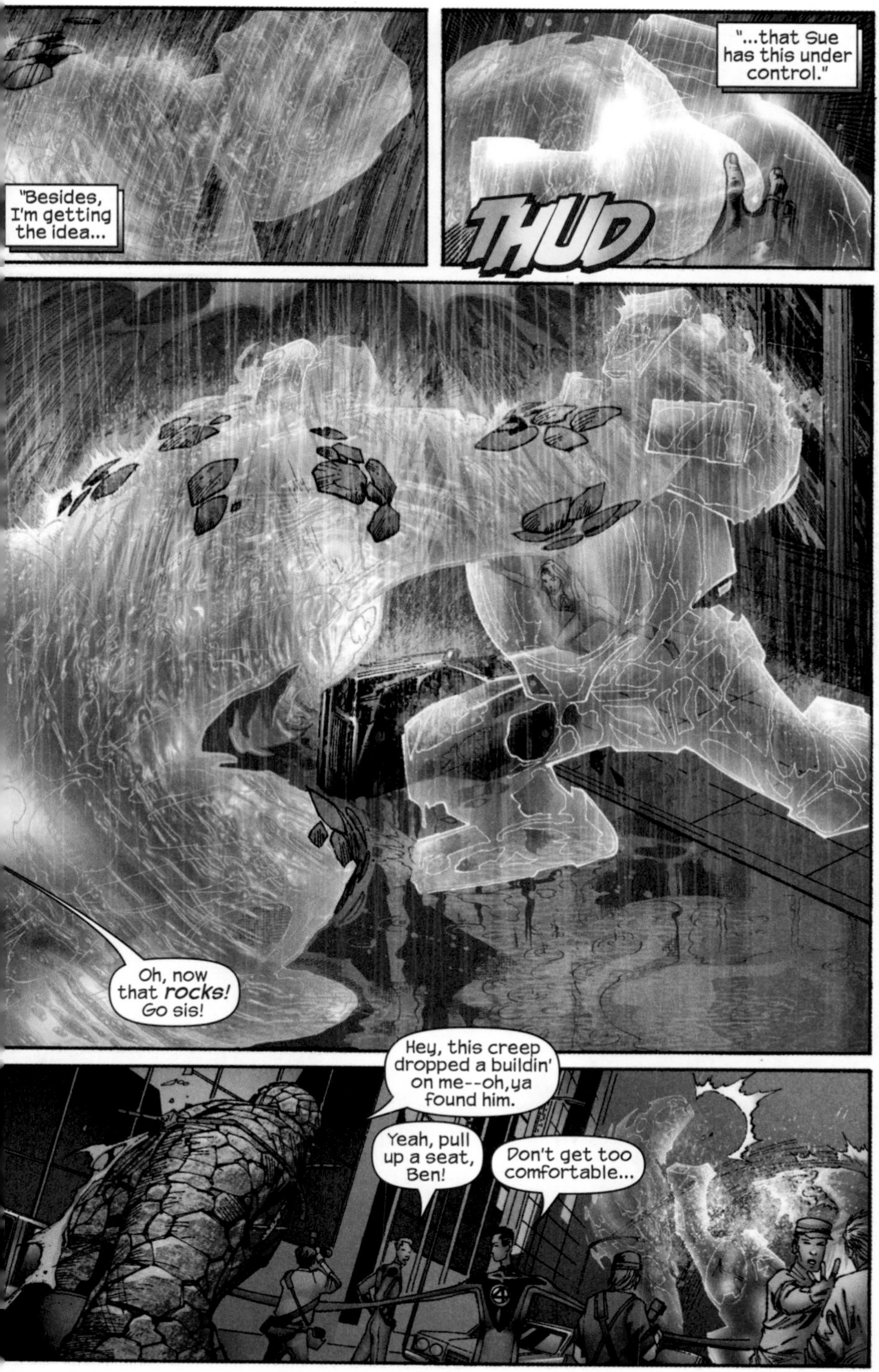
"Besides, I'm getting the idea...
"...that Sue has this under control."
THUD
Oh, now that rocks! Go sis!
Hey, this creep dropped a buildin' on me--oh,ya found him.
Yeah, pull up a seat, Ben!
Don't get too comfortable...

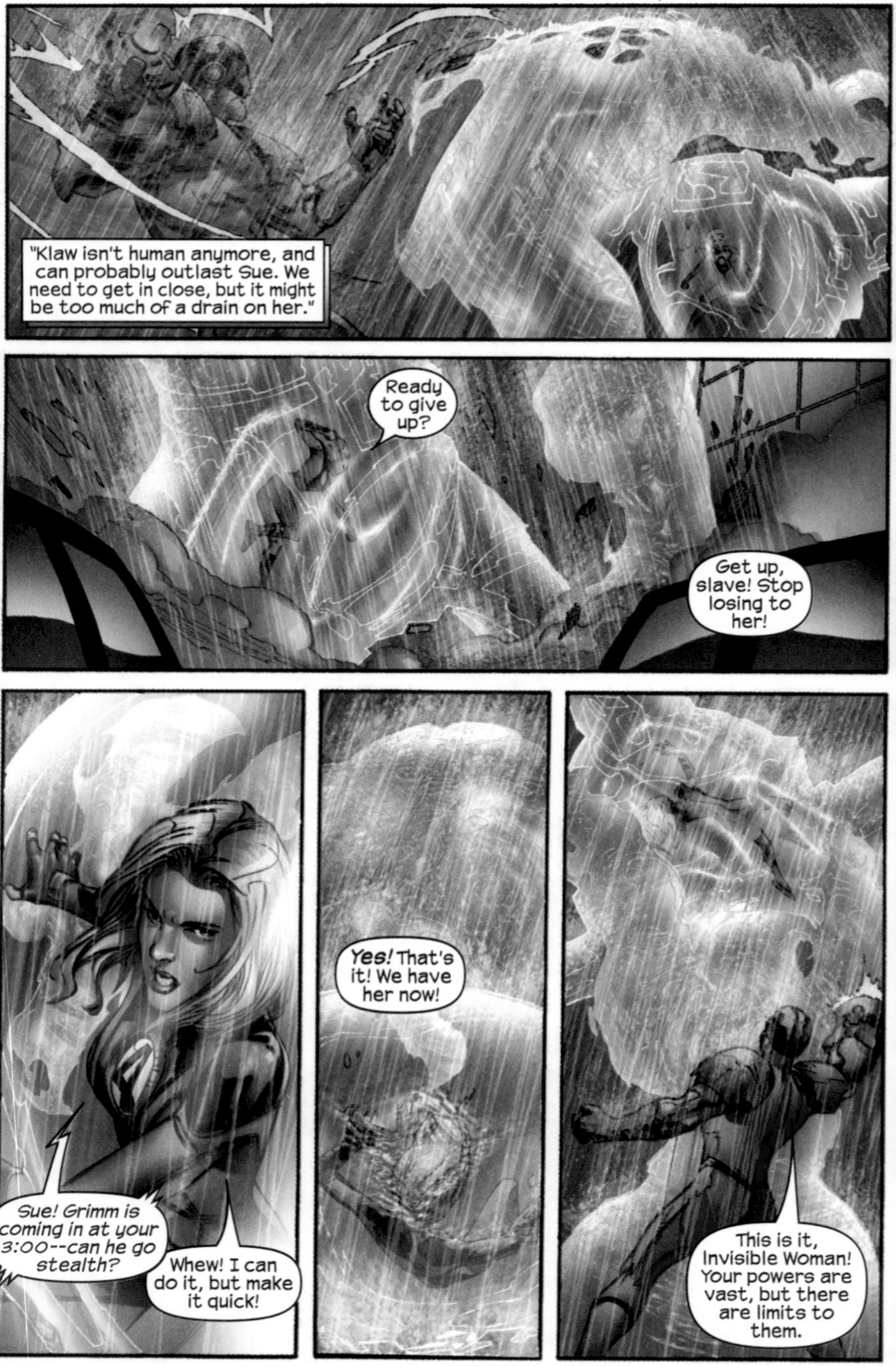
"Klaw isn't human anymore, and can probably outlast Sue. We need to get in close, but it might be too much of a drain on her."
Ready to give up?
Get up, slave! Stop losing to her!
Sue! Grimm is coming in at your 3:00--can he go stealth?
Whew! I can do it, but make it quick!
Yes! That's it! We have her now!
This is it, Invisible Woman! Your powers are vast, but there are limits to them.

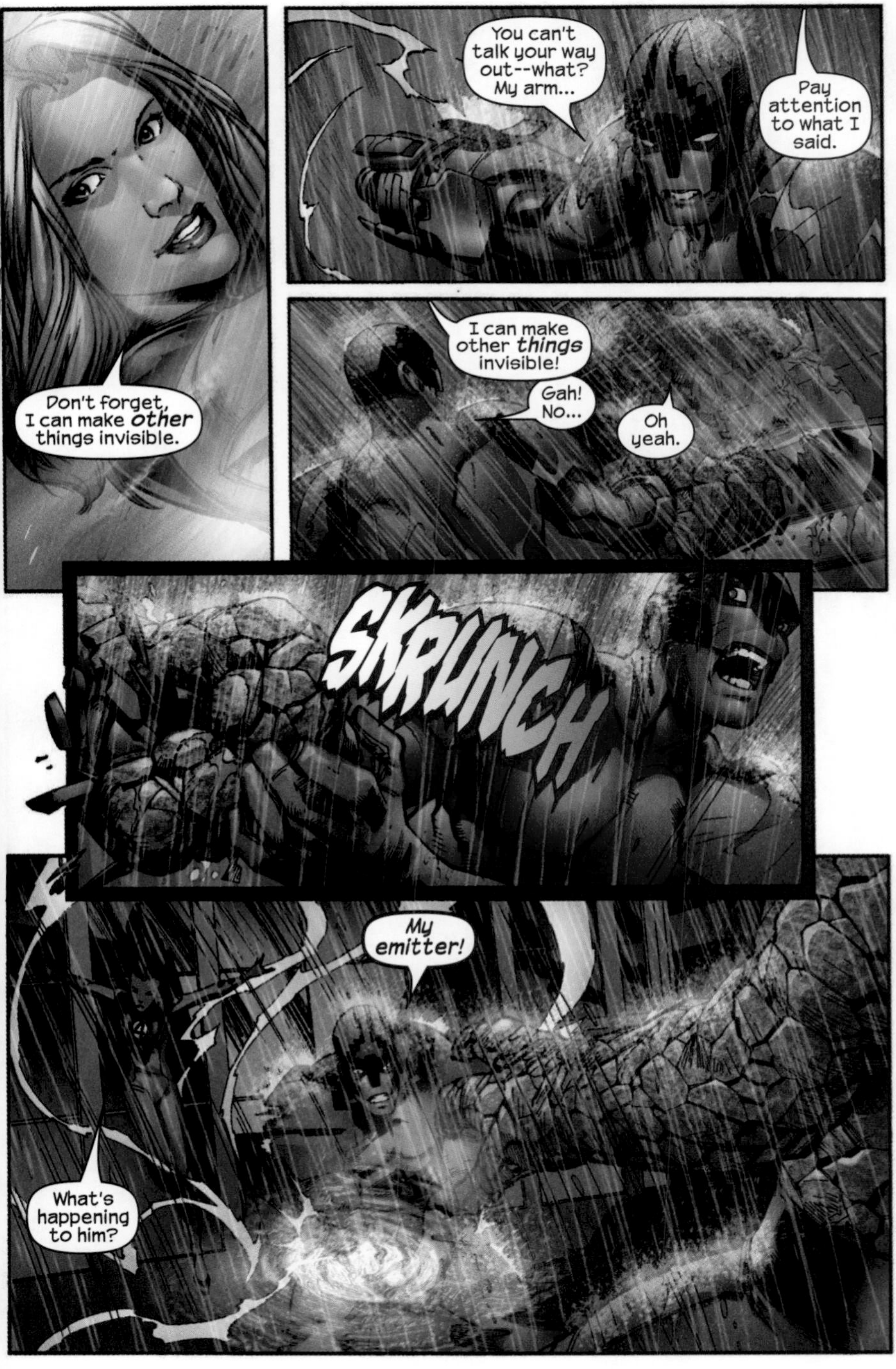
You can't talk your way out--what? My arm...
Pay attention to what I said.
Don't forget, I can make *other* things invisible.
I can make other *things* invisible!
Gah! No...
Oh yeah.
SKRUNCH
My emitter!
What's happening to him?

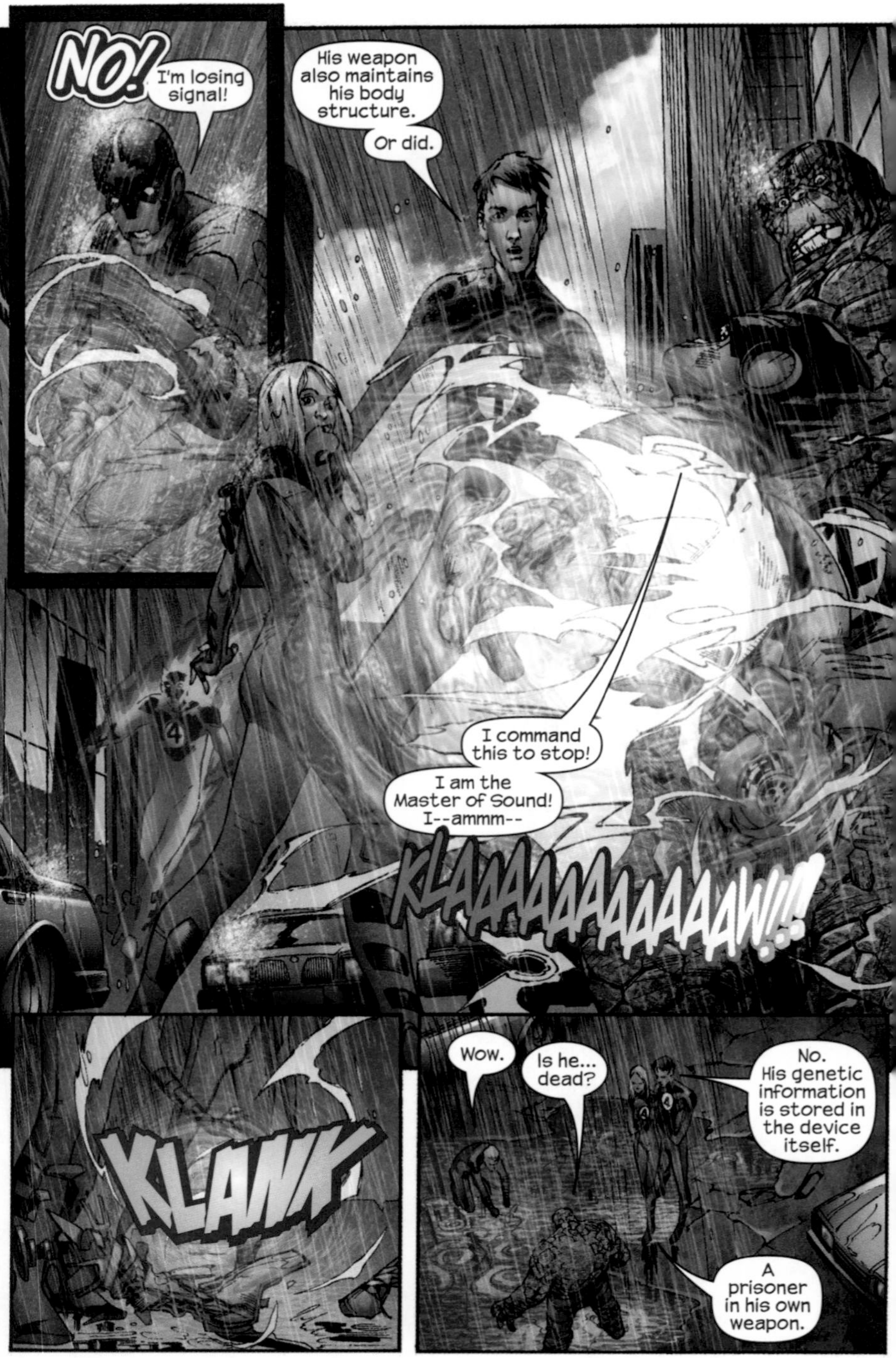
NO! I'm losing signal!
His weapon also maintains his body structure.
Or did.
I command this to stop!
I am the Master of Sound! I--ammm--
KLAAAAAAAAAAAAW!!!
KLANK
Wow.
Is he... dead?
No. His genetic information is stored in the device itself.
A prisoner in his own weapon.

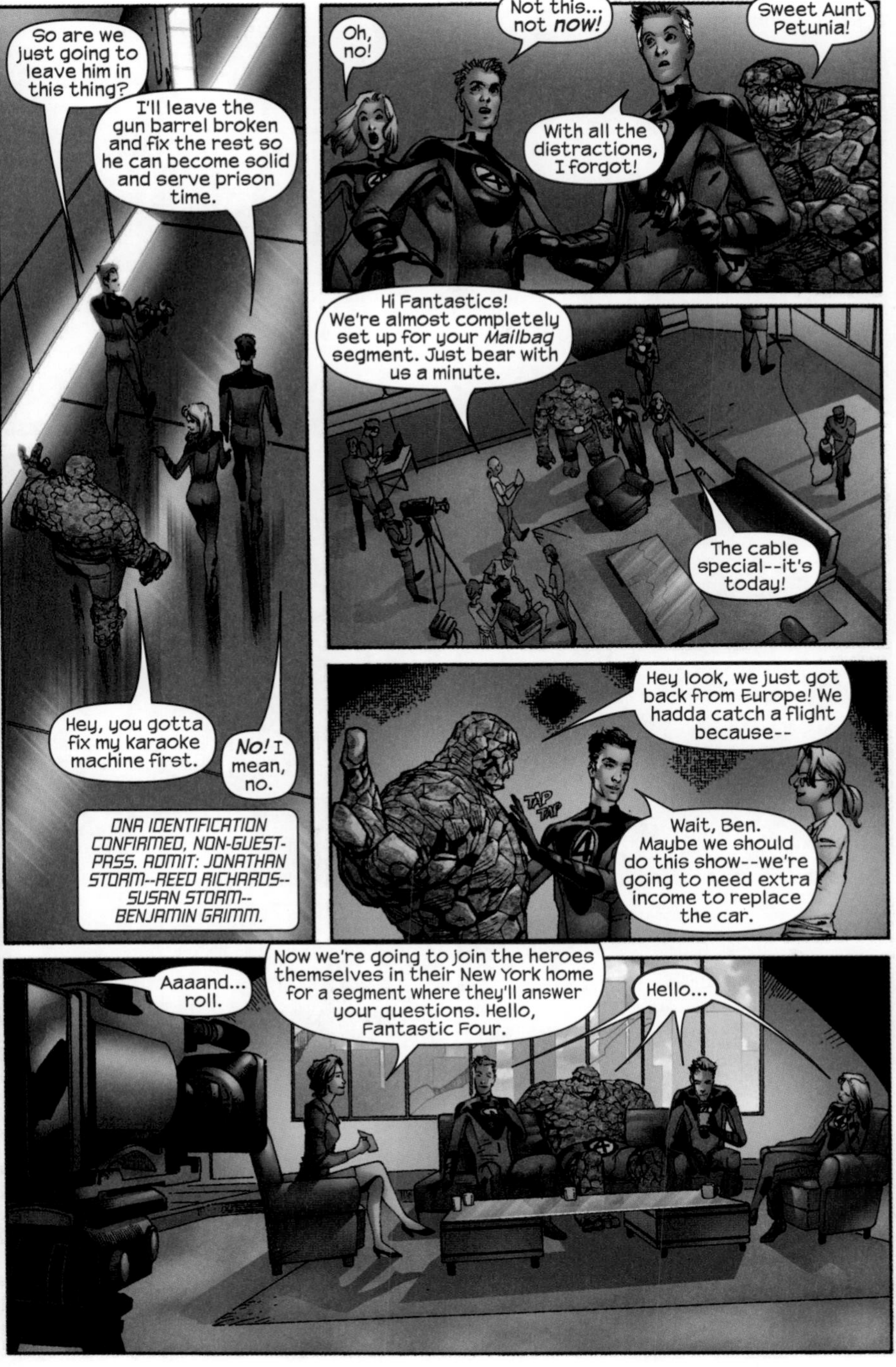
So are we just going to leave him in this thing?
I'll leave the gun barrel broken and fix the rest so he can become solid and serve prison time.
Hey, you gotta fix my karaoke machine first.
No! I mean, no.
DNA IDENTIFICATION CONFIRMED, NON-GUEST-PASS. ADMIT: JONATHAN STORM--REED RICHARDS--SUSAN STORM--BENJAMIN GRIMM.
Oh, no!
Not this... not now!
Sweet Aunt Petunia!
With all the distractions, I forgot!
Hi Fantastics! We're almost completely set up for your Mailbag segment. Just bear with us a minute.
The cable special--it's today!
Hey look, we just got back from Europe! We hadda catch a flight because--
TAP TAP
Wait, Ben. Maybe we should do this show--we're going to need extra income to replace the car.
Aaaand... roll.
Now we're going to join the heroes themselves in their New York home for a segment where they'll answer your questions. Hello, Fantastic Four.
Hello...

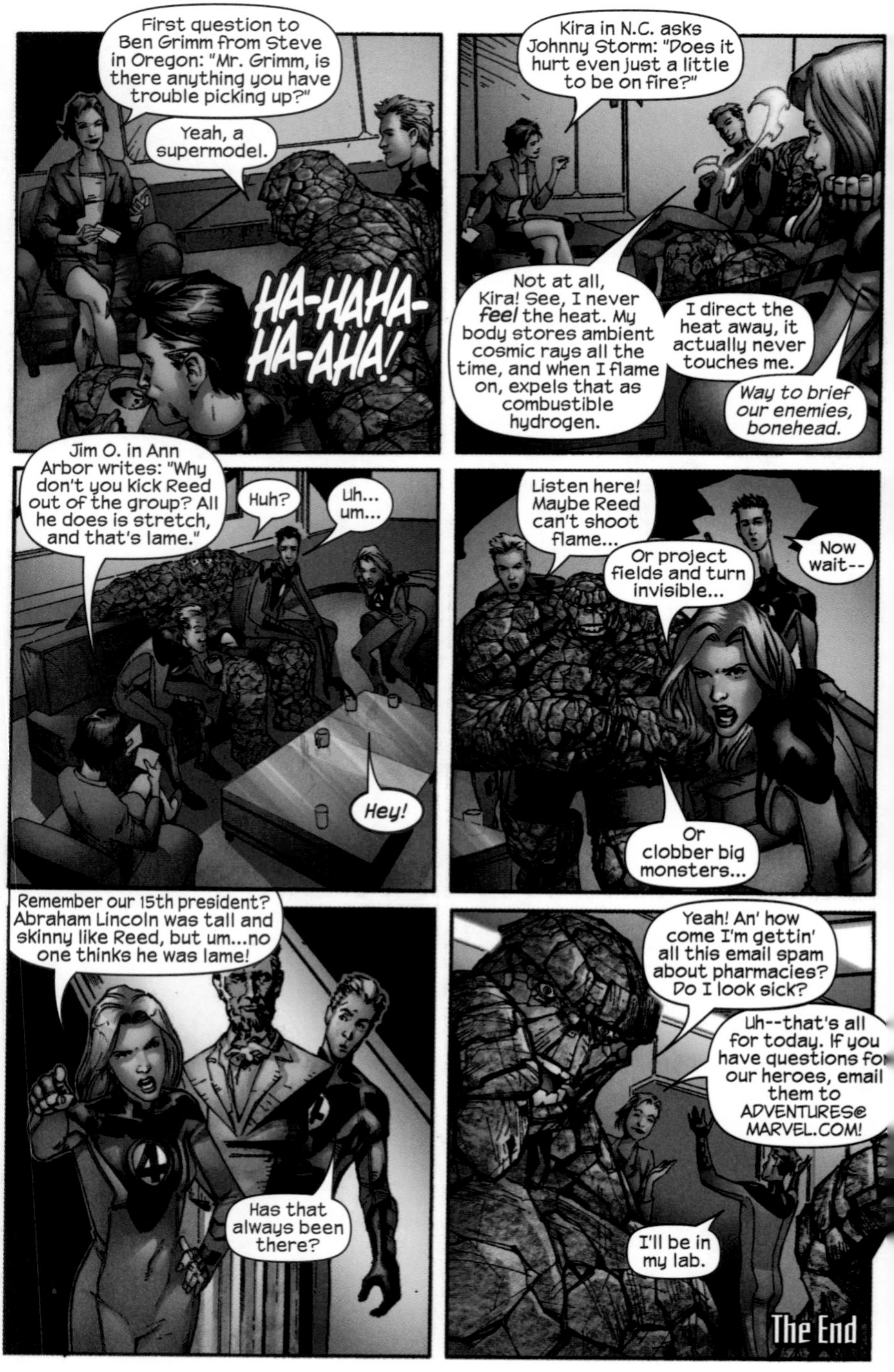
First question to Ben Grimm from Steve in Oregon: "Mr. Grimm, is there anything you have trouble picking up?"
Yeah, a supermodel.
HA-HAHA-HA-AHA!
Kira in N.C. asks Johnny Storm: "Does it hurt even just a little to be on fire?"
Not at all, Kira! See, I never *feel* the heat. My body stores ambient cosmic rays all the time, and when I flame on, expels that as combustible hydrogen.
I direct the heat away, it actually never touches me.
Way to brief our enemies, bonehead.
Jim O. in Ann Arbor writes: "Why don't you kick Reed out of the group? All he does is stretch, and that's lame."
Huh?
Uh... um...
Hey!
Listen here! Maybe Reed can't shoot flame...
Or project fields and turn invisible...
Now wait--
Or clobber big monsters...
Remember our 15th president? Abraham Lincoln was tall and skinny like Reed, but um...no one thinks he was lame!
Has that always been there?
Yeah! An' how come I'm gettin' all this email spam about pharmacies? Do I look sick?
Uh--that's all for today. If you have questions for our heroes, email them to ADVENTURES@ MARVEL.COM!
I'll be in my lab.
The End

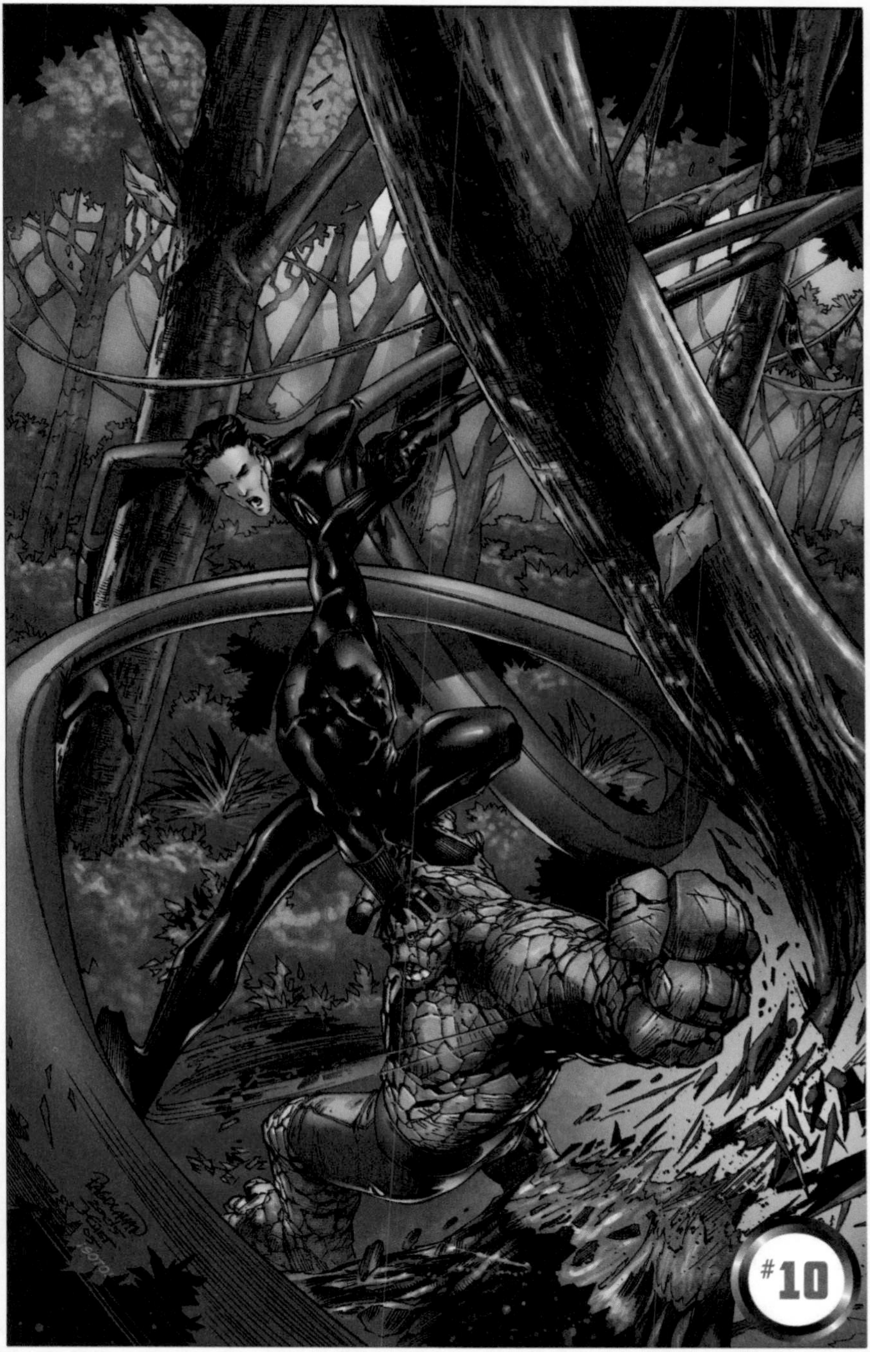
#10

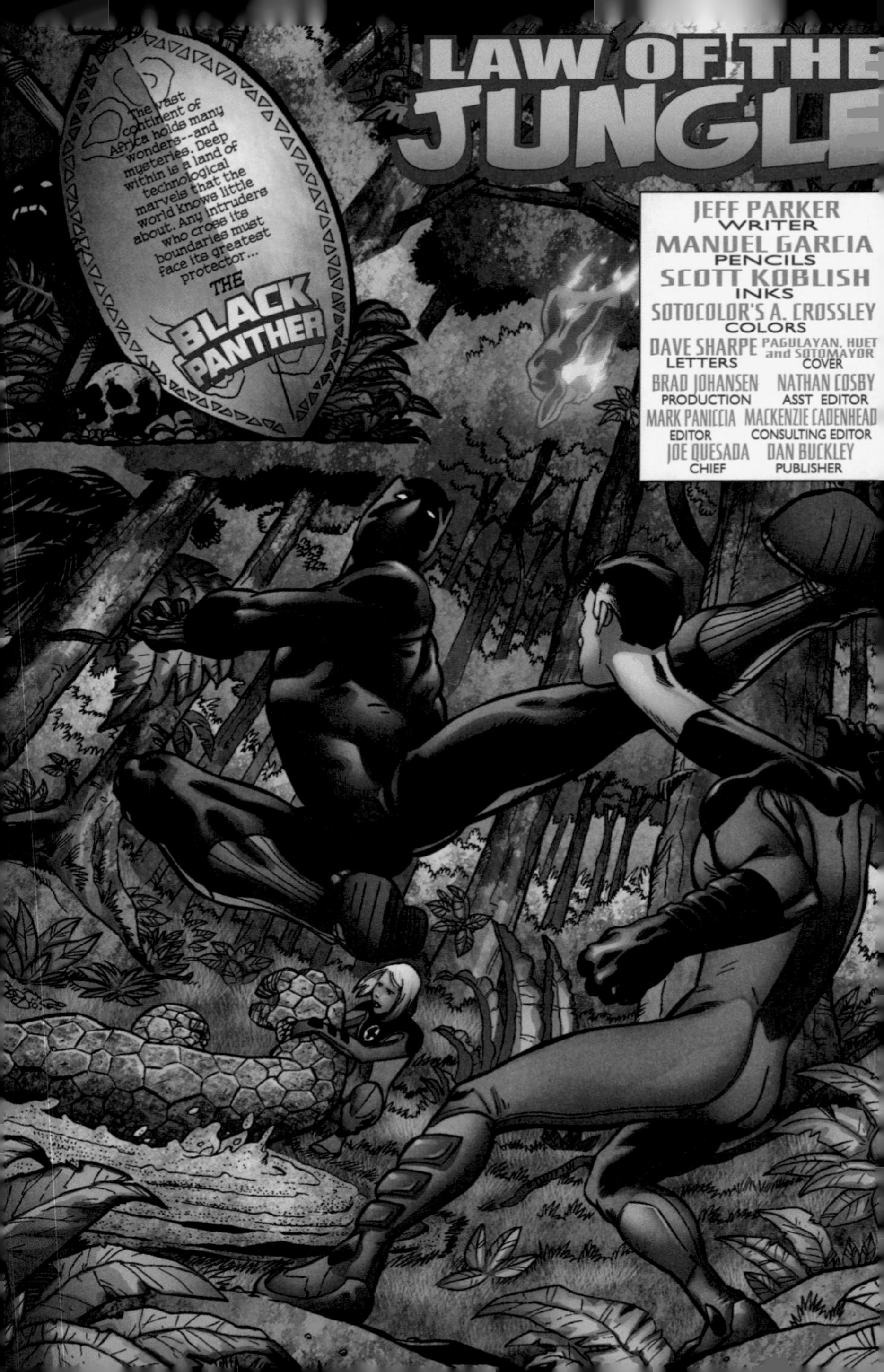

LAW OF THE JUNGLE
The vast continent of Africa holds many wonders--and mysteries. Deep within is a land of technological marvels that the world knows little about. Any intruders who cross its boundaries must face its greatest protector...
THE BLACK PANTHER
JEFF PARKER WRITER
MANUEL GARCIA PENCILS
SCOTT KOBLISH INKS
SOTOCOLOR'S A. CROSSLEY COLORS
DAVE SHARPE LETTERS
PAGULAYAN, HUET and SOTOMAYOR COVER
BRAD JOHANSEN PRODUCTION
NATHAN COSBY ASST EDITOR
MARK PANICCIA EDITOR
MACKENZIE CADENHEAD CONSULTING EDITOR
JOE QUESADA CHIEF
DAN BUCKLEY PUBLISHER

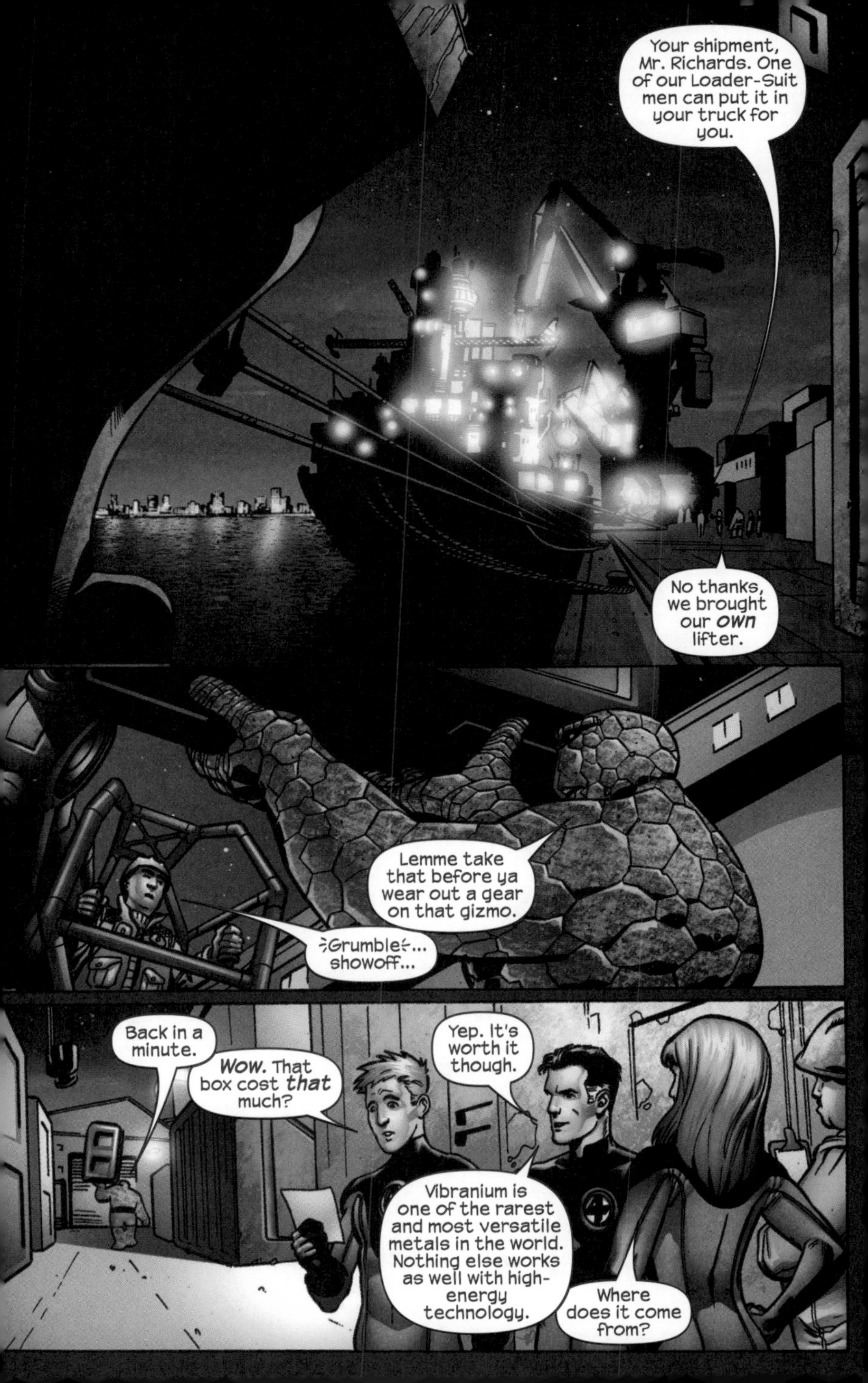
Your shipment, Mr. Richards. One of our Loader-Suit men can put it in your truck for you.
No thanks, we brought our *own* lifter.
Lemme take that before ya wear out a gear on that gizmo.
Grumble... showoff...
Back in a minute.
Wow. That box cost *that* much?
Yep. It's worth it though.
Vibranium is one of the rarest and most versatile metals in the world. Nothing else works as well with high-energy technology.
Where does it come from?

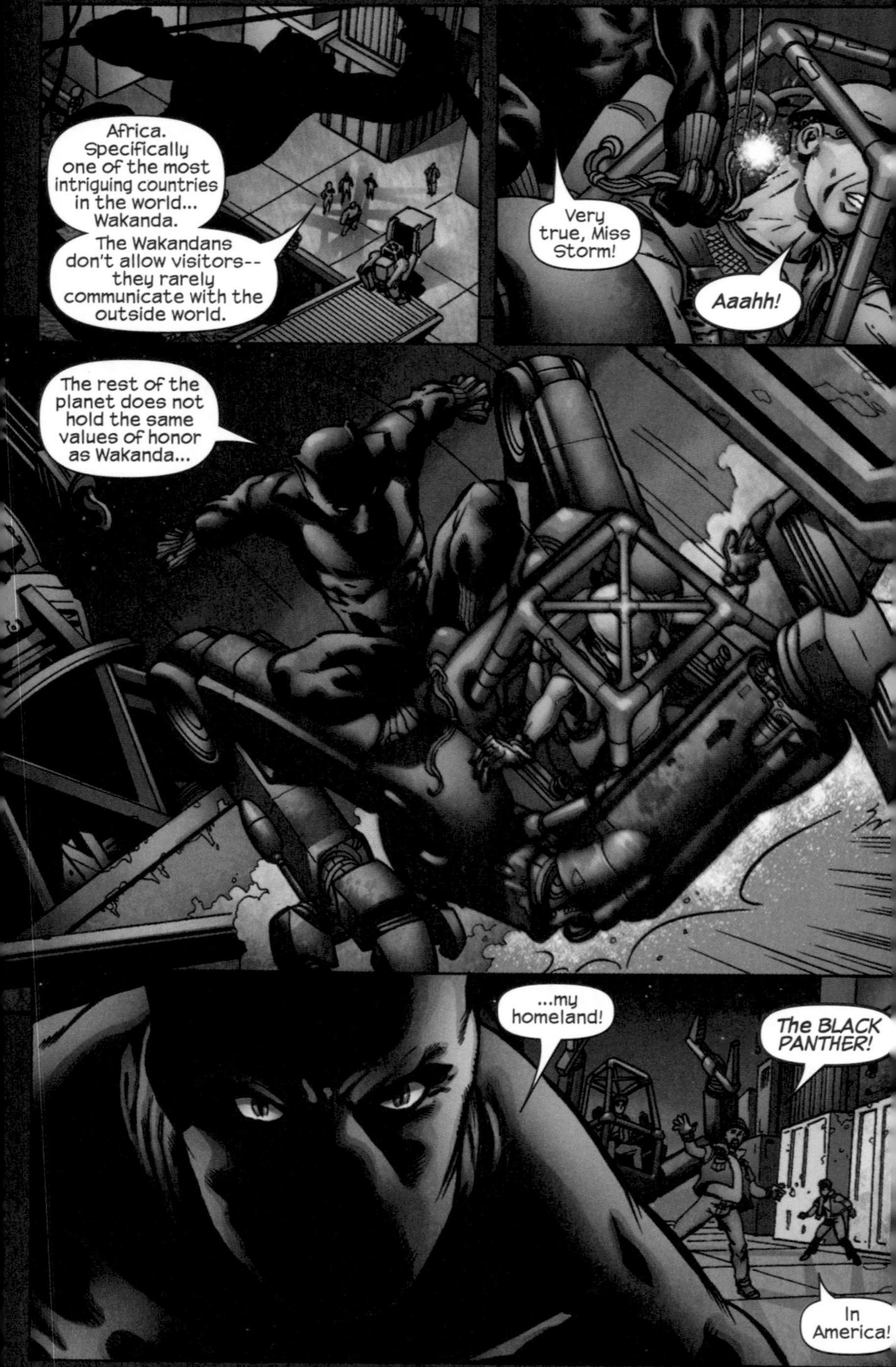
Africa. Specifically one of the most intriguing countries in the world... Wakanda.
The Wakandans don't allow visitors-- they rarely communicate with the outside world.
Very true, Miss Storm!
Aaahh!
The rest of the planet does not hold the same values of honor as Wakanda...
...my homeland!
The BLACK PANTHER!
In America!

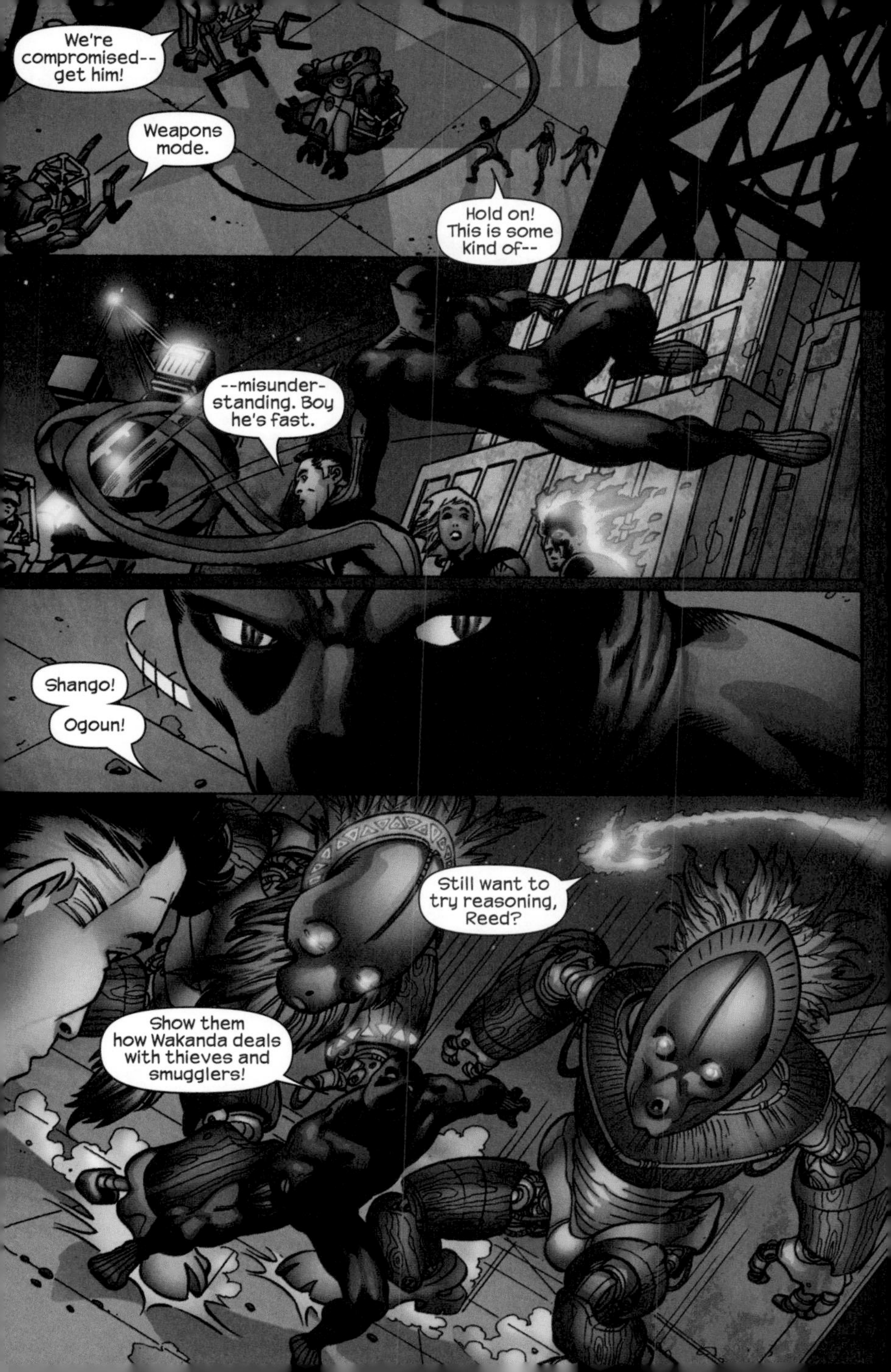
We're compromised-- get him!
Weapons mode.
Hold on! This is some kind of--
--misunder-standing. Boy he's fast.
Shango!
Ogoun!
Still want to try reasoning, Reed?
Show them how Wakanda deals with thieves and smugglers!

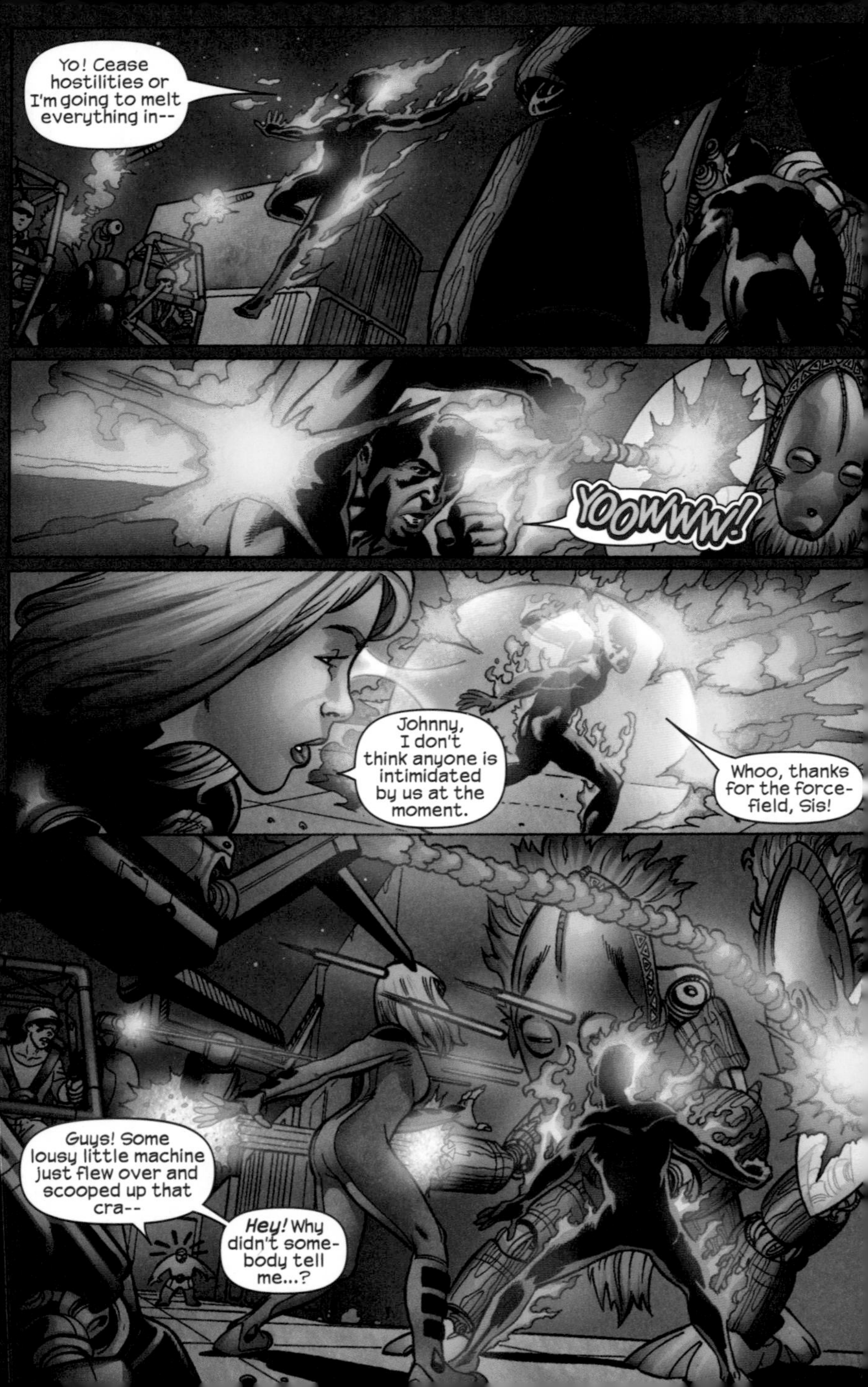
Yo! Cease hostilities or I'm going to melt everything in--
YOOWWW!
Johnny, I don't think anyone is intimidated by us at the moment.
Whoo, thanks for the force-field, Sis!
Guys! Some lousy little machine just flew over and scooped up that cra--
Hey! Why didn't some-body tell me...?

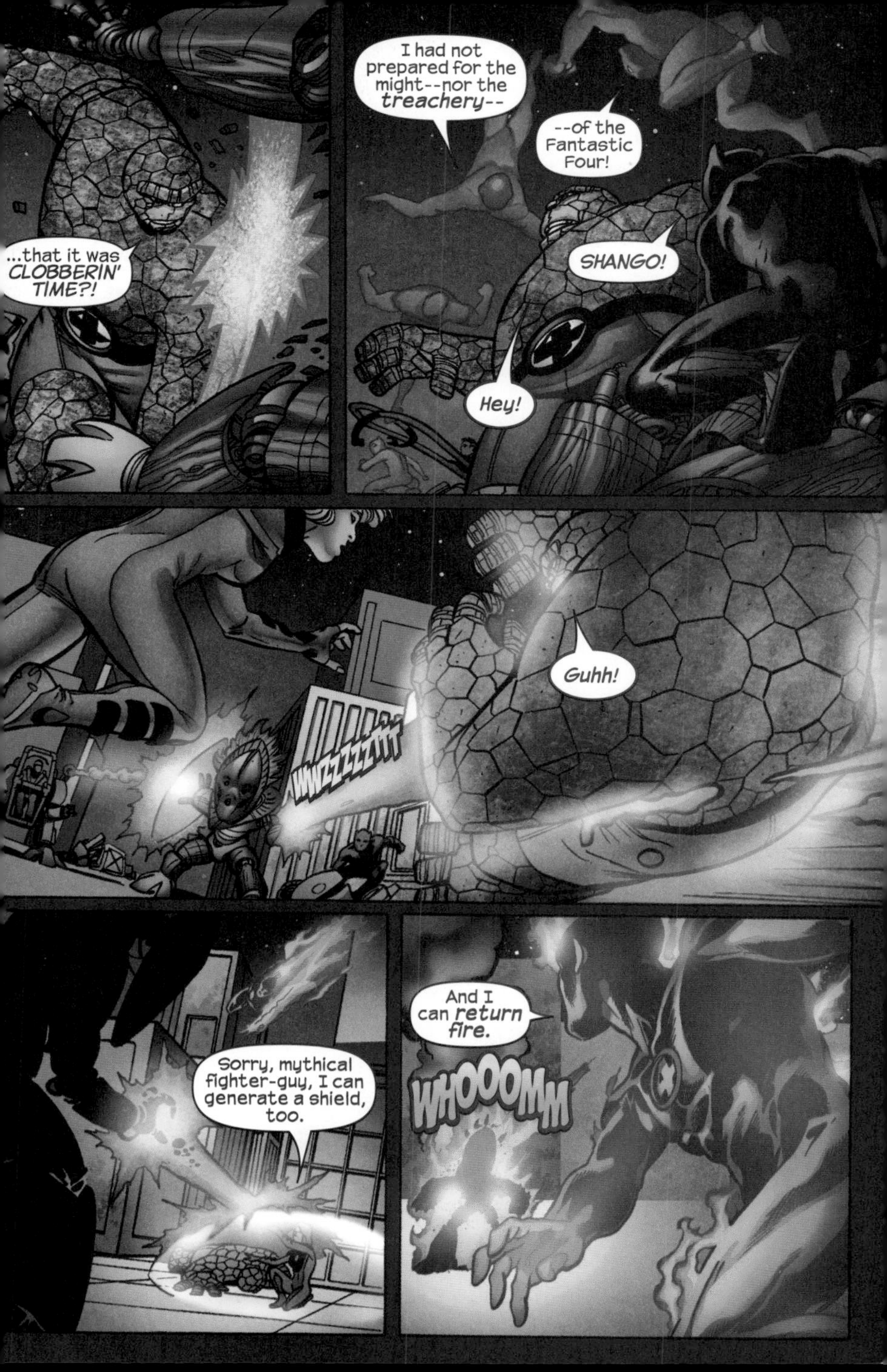
...that it was CLOBBERIN' TIME?!
I had not prepared for the might--nor the treachery--
--of the Fantastic Four!
SHANGO!
Hey!
Guhh!
WWZZZZZTTT
Sorry, mythical fighter-guy, I can generate a shield, too.
And I can return fire.
WHOOOMM

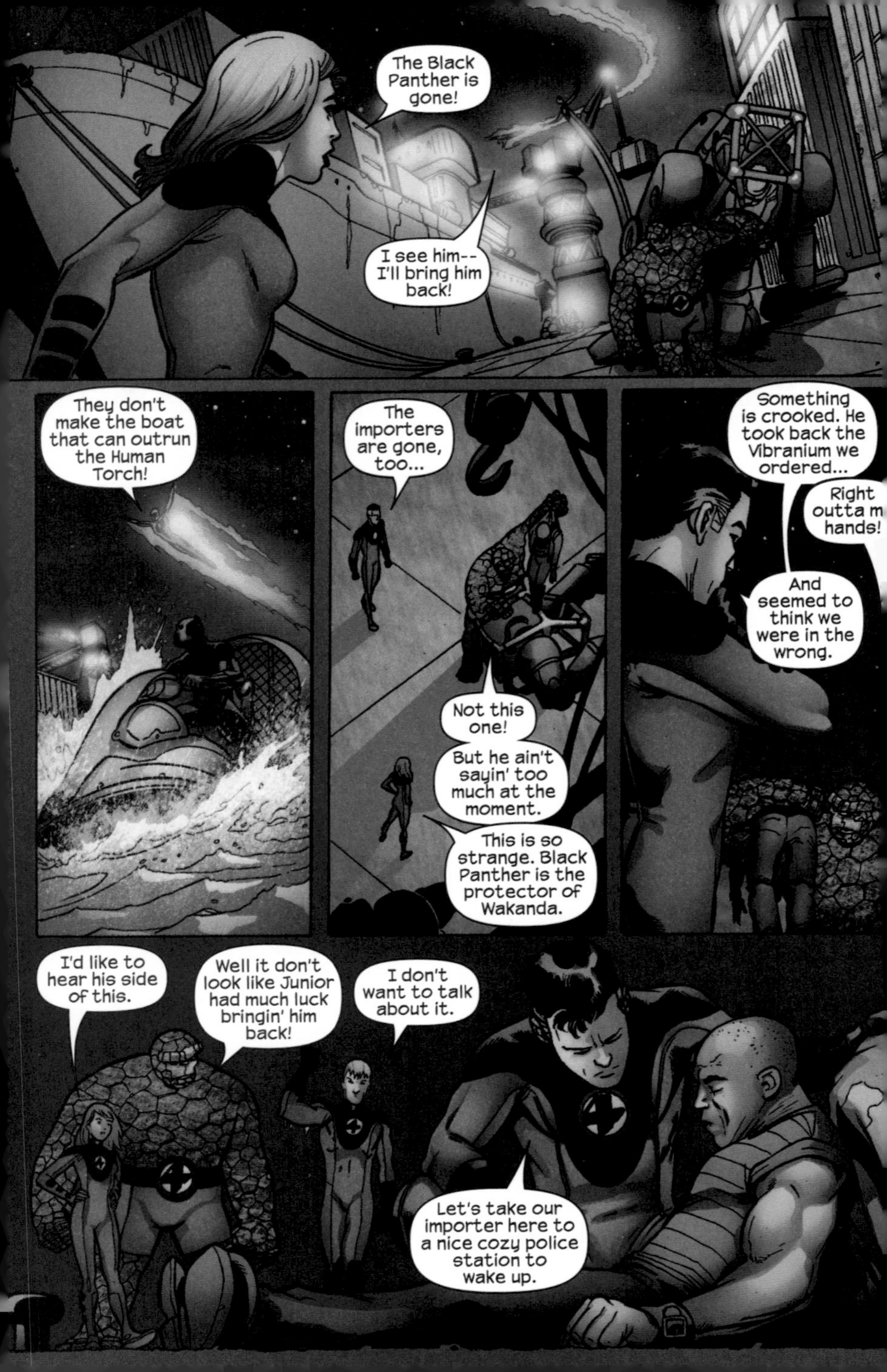
The Black Panther is gone!
I see him-- I'll bring him back!
They don't make the boat that can outrun the Human Torch!
The importers are gone, too...
Not this one!
But he ain't sayin' too much at the moment.
This is so strange. Black Panther is the protector of Wakanda.
Something is crooked. He took back the Vibranium we ordered...
Right outta m hands!
And seemed to think we were in the wrong.
I'd like to hear his side of this.
Well it don't look like Junior had much luck bringin' him back!
I don't want to talk about it.
Let's take our importer here to a nice cozy police station to wake up.

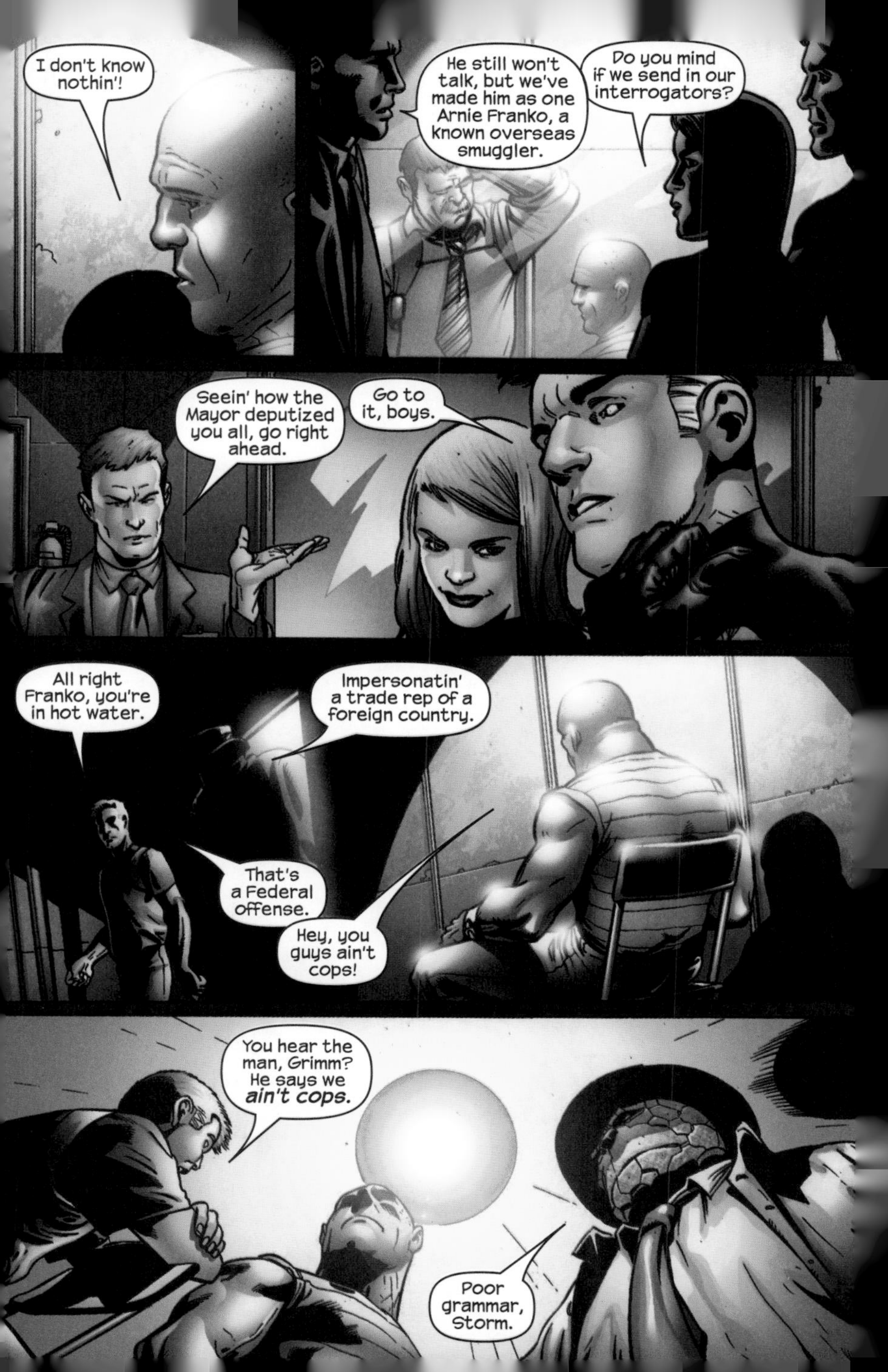
I don't know nothin'!
He still won't talk, but we've made him as one Arnie Franko, a known overseas smuggler.
Do you mind if we send in our interrogators?
Seein' how the Mayor deputized you all, go right ahead.
Go to it, boys.
All right Franko, you're in hot water.
Impersonatin' a trade rep of a foreign country.
That's a Federal offense.
Hey, you guys ain't cops!
You hear the man, Grimm? He says we *ain't cops.*
Poor grammar, Storm.

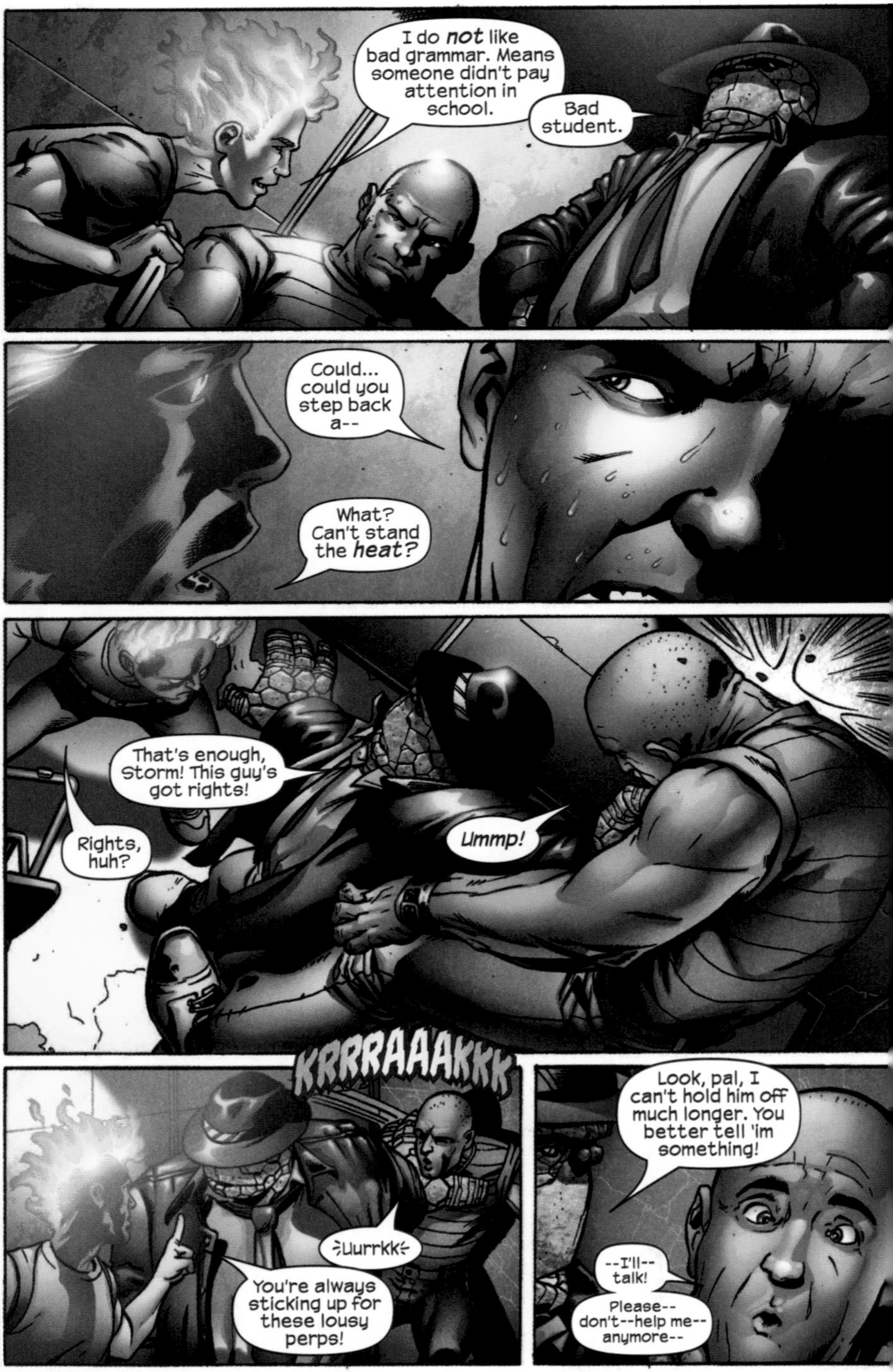
I do *not* like bad grammar. Means someone didn't pay attention in school.
Bad student.
Could... could you step back a--
What? Can't stand the *heat?*
That's enough, Storm! This guy's got rights!
Rights, huh?
Ummp!
KRRRAAAKKK
Uurrkk
You're always sticking up for these lousy perps!
Look, pal, I can't hold him off much longer. You better tell 'im something!
--I'll-- talk!
Please-- don't--help me-- anymore--

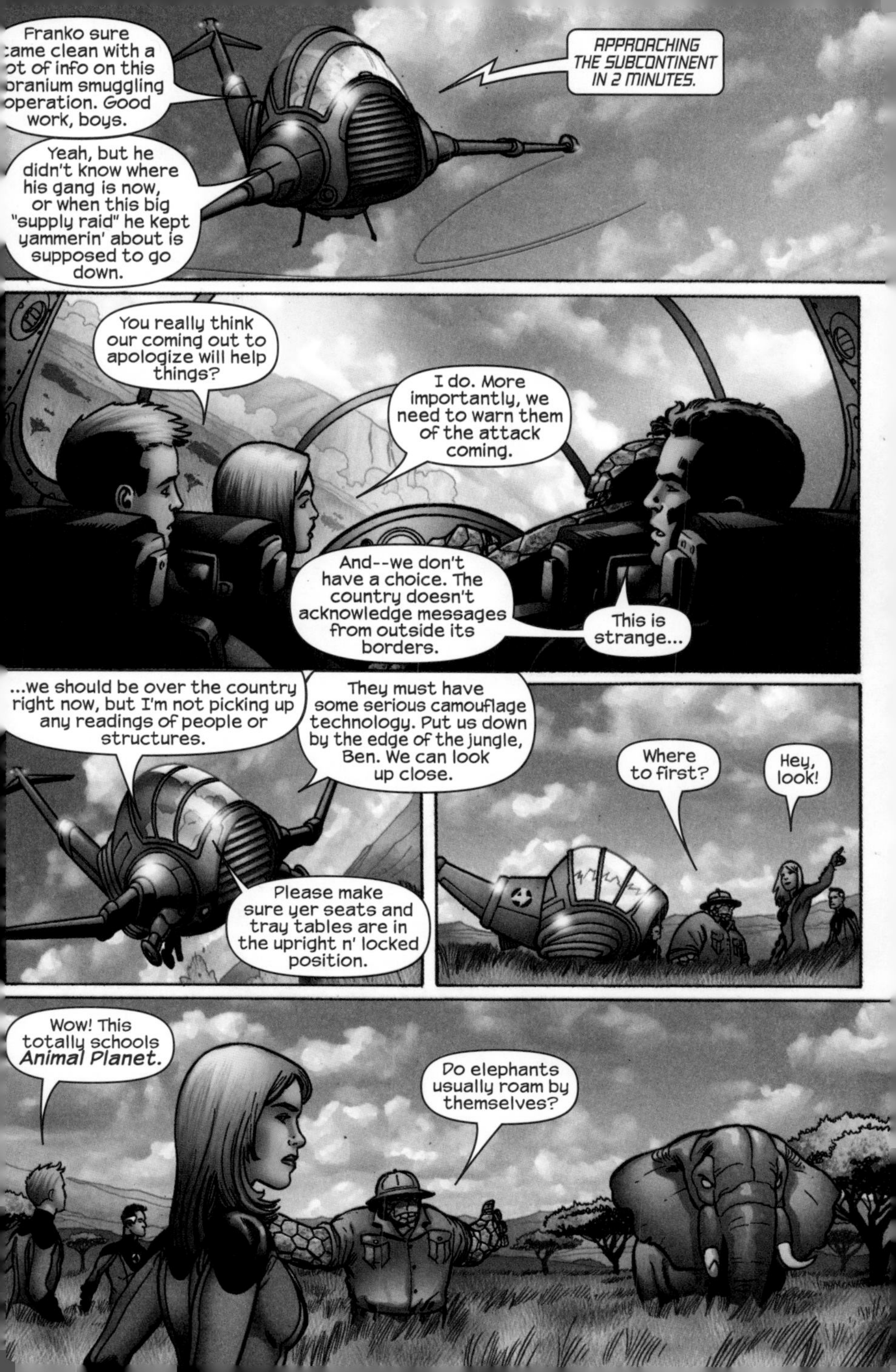

Franko sure came clean with a lot of info on this uranium smuggling operation. Good work, boys.
APPROACHING THE SUBCONTINENT IN 2 MINUTES.
Yeah, but he didn't know where his gang is now, or when this big "supply raid" he kept yammerin' about is supposed to go down.
You really think our coming out to apologize will help things?
I do. More importantly, we need to warn them of the attack coming.
And--we don't have a choice. The country doesn't acknowledge messages from outside its borders.
This is strange...
...we should be over the country right now, but I'm not picking up any readings of people or structures.
They must have some serious camouflage technology. Put us down by the edge of the jungle, Ben. We can look up close.
Please make sure yer seats and tray tables are in the upright n' locked position.
Where to first?
Hey, look!
Wow! This totally schools Animal Planet.
Do elephants usually roam by themselves?

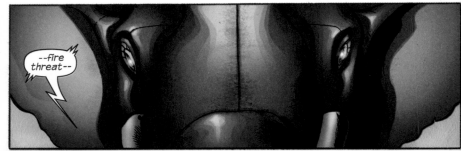

--fire threat--

--coat with non-combustible gel--

Ahgh! I'm always getting gooed!

Hey, that's no--

--elephant--whoa! All right, buster, you're askin' for it!

Arrrhhh!

ZZZAAPZZZAAP

Whew!

Let him go, Ele-bot!

Everyone, into the jungle!

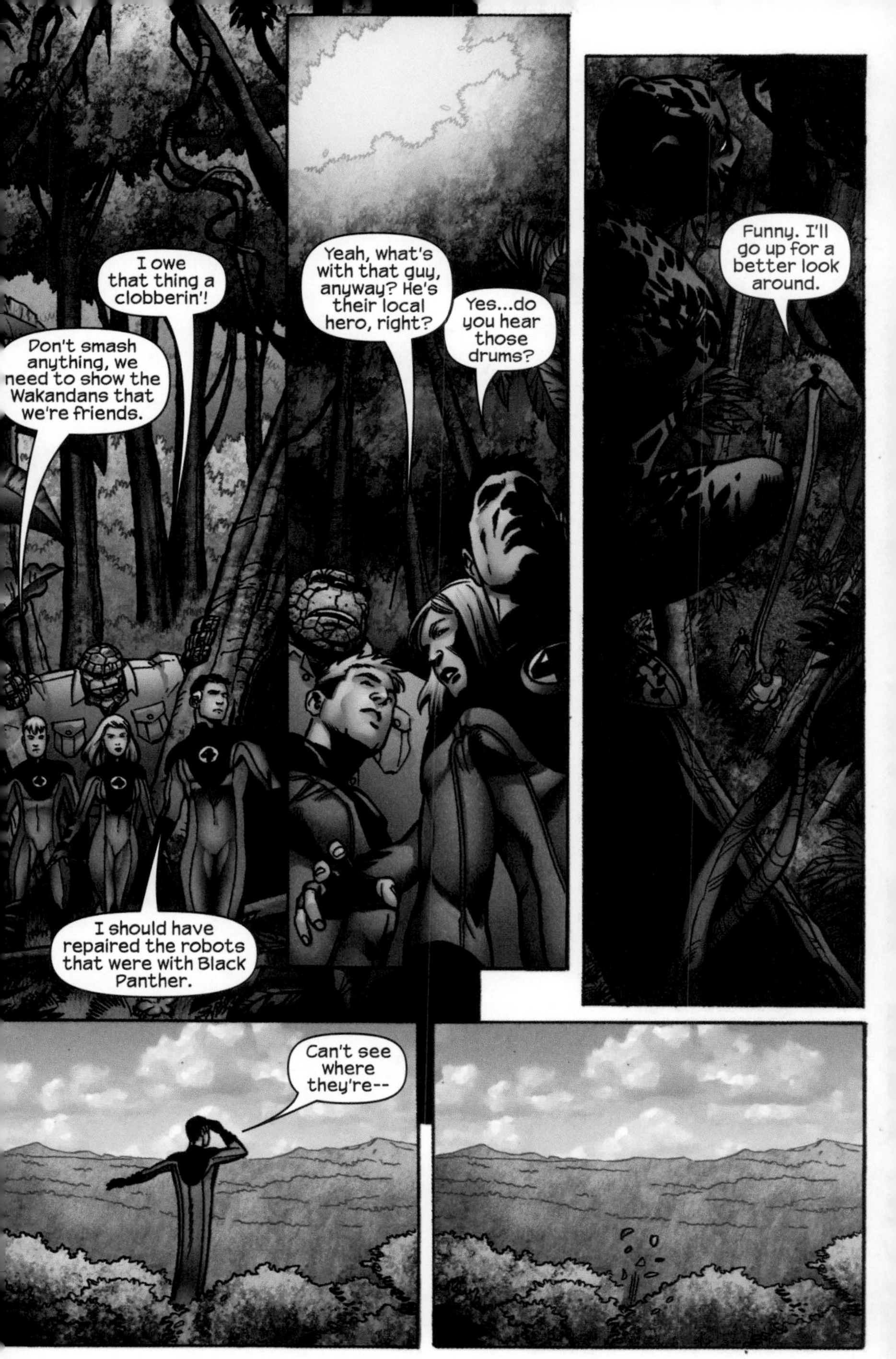

Don't smash anything, we need to show the Wakandans that we're friends.
I owe that thing a clobberin'!
I should have repaired the robots that were with Black Panther.
Yeah, what's with that guy, anyway? He's their local hero, right?
Yes...do you hear those drums?
Funny. I'll go up for a better look around.
Can't see where they're--

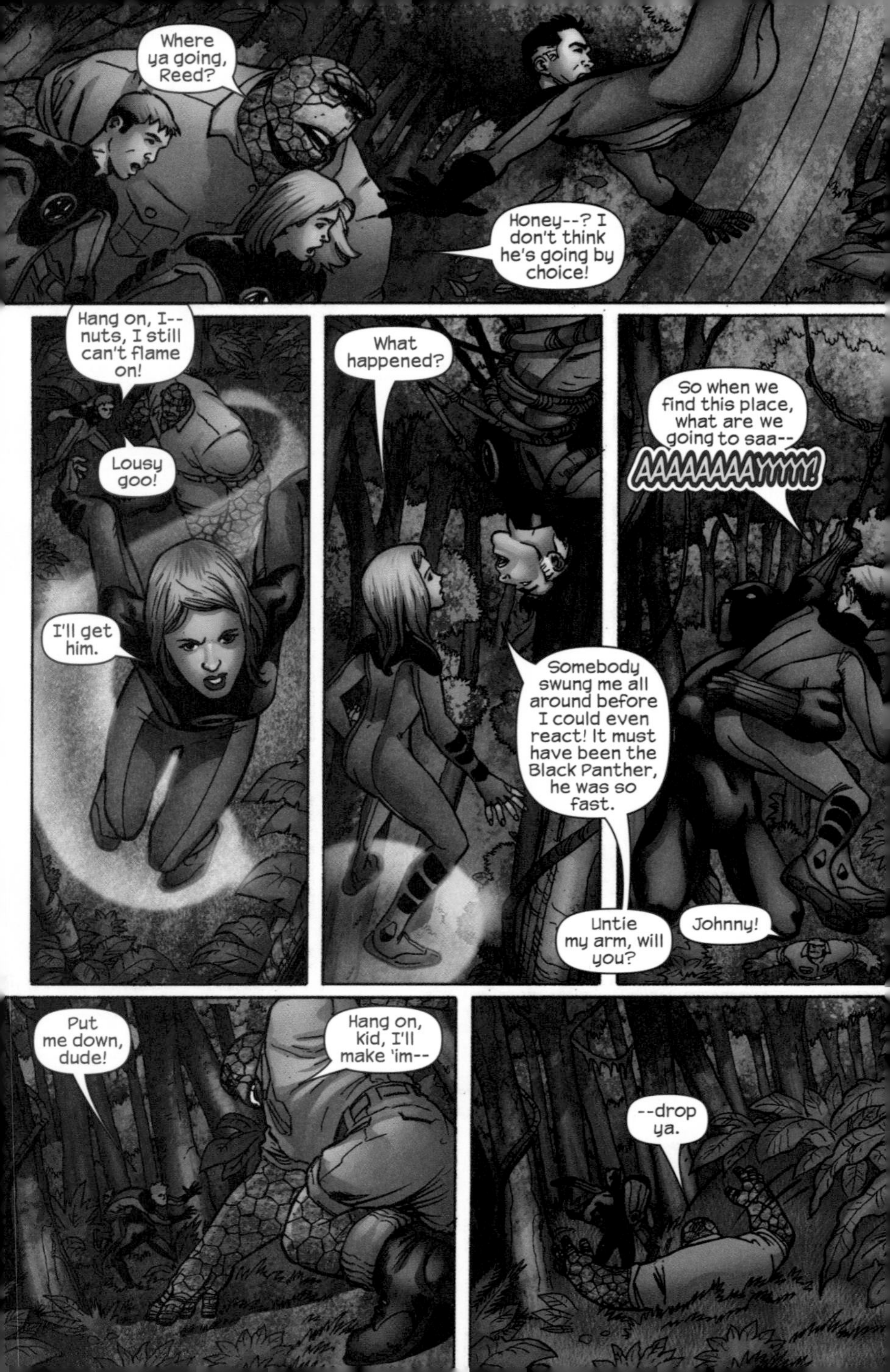
Where ya going, Reed?
Honey--? I don't think he's going by choice!
Hang on, I-- nuts, I still can't flame on!
Lousy goo!
I'll get him.
What happened?
Somebody swung me all around before I could even react! It must have been the Black Panther, he was so fast.
Untie my arm, will you?
So when we find this place, what are we going to saa--
AAAAAAAAYYYYY!
Johnny!
Put me down, dude!
Hang on, kid, I'll make 'im--
--drop ya.

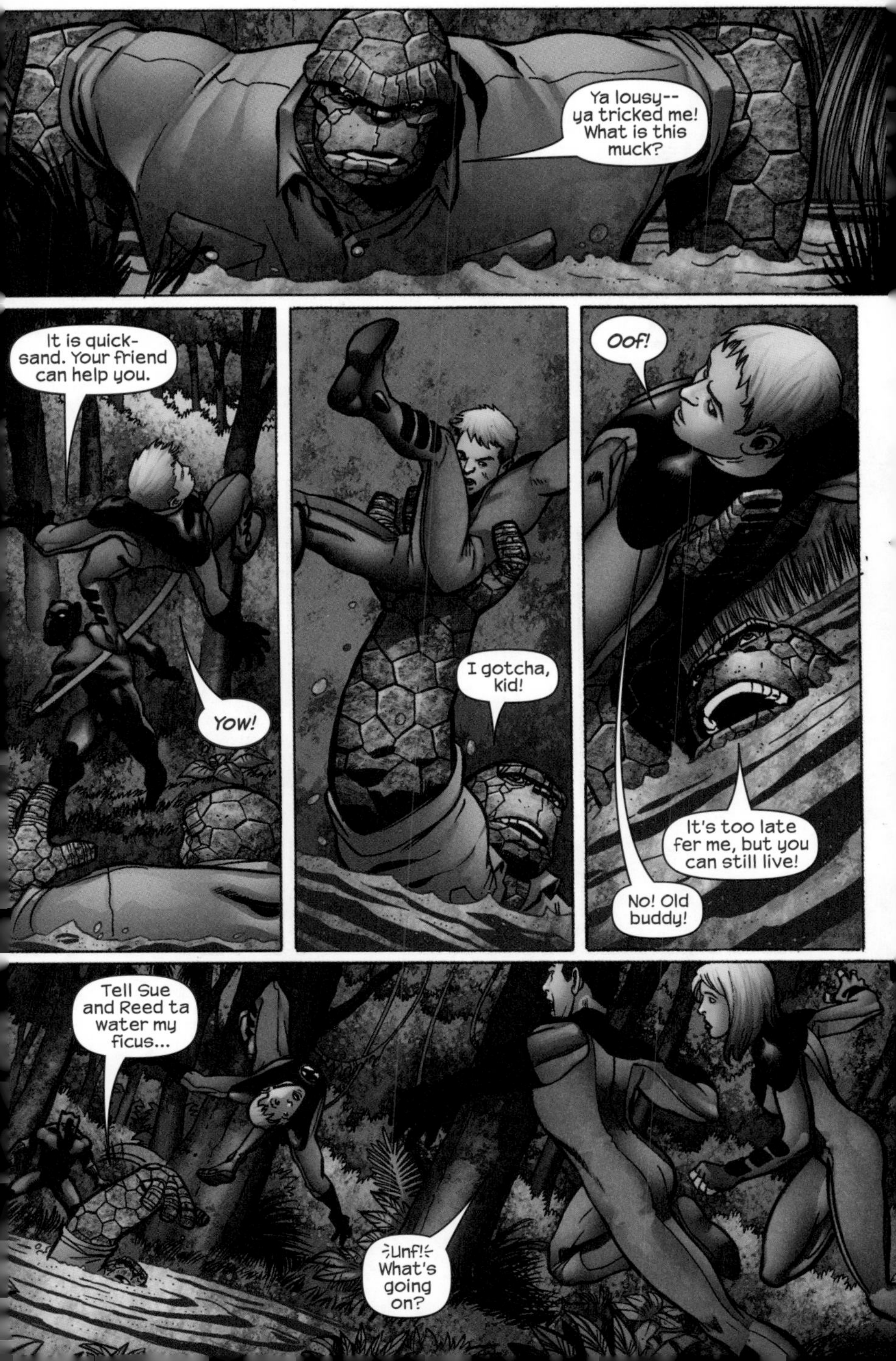
Ya lousy-- ya tricked me! What is this muck?
It is quick-sand. Your friend can help you.
YOW!
I gotcha, kid!
Oof!
It's too late fer me, but you can still live!
No! Old buddy!
Tell Sue and Reed ta water my ficus...
Unf! What's going on?

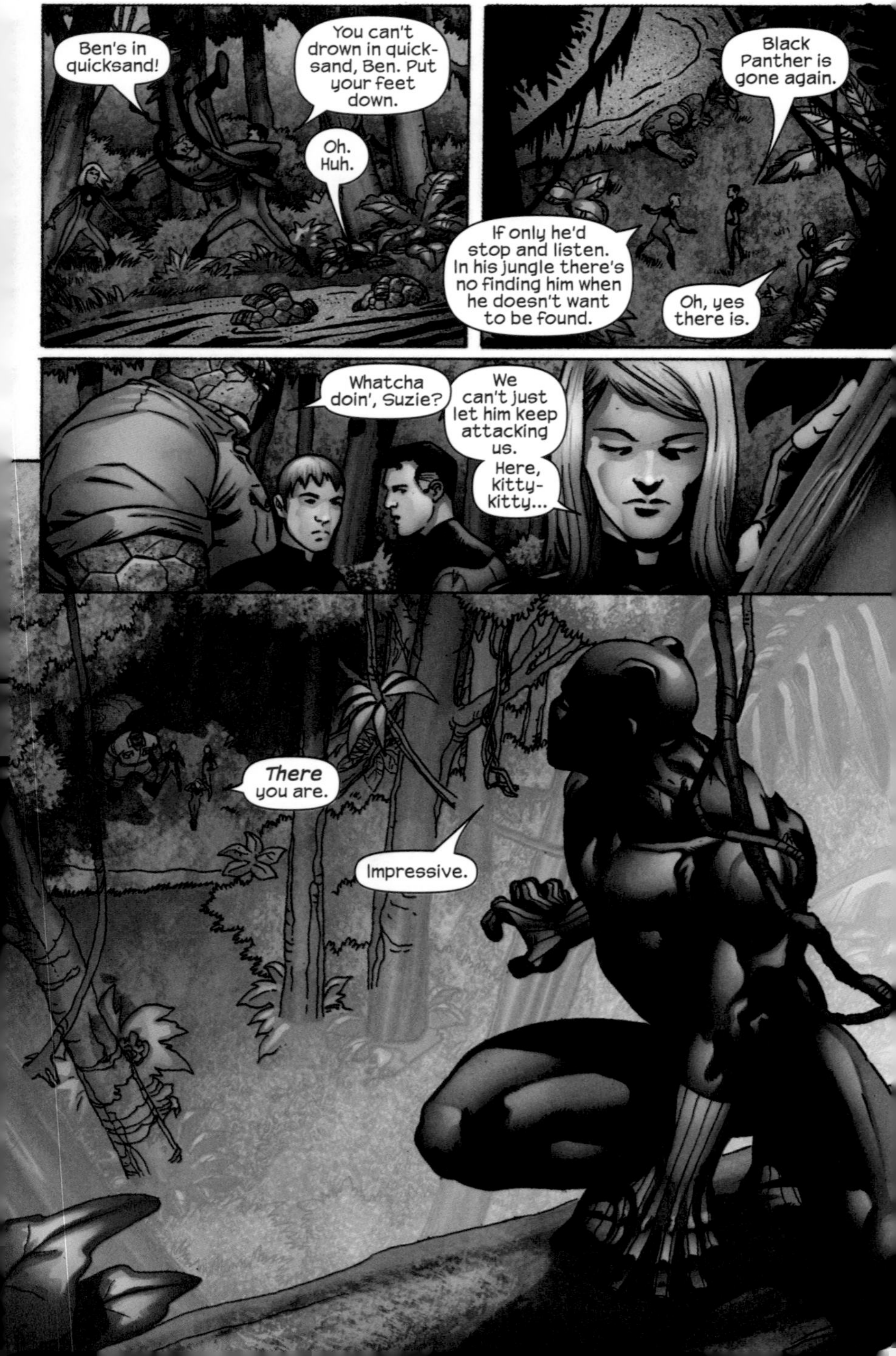
Ben's in quicksand!
You can't drown in quick-sand, Ben. Put your feet down.
Oh. Huh.
Black Panther is gone again.
If only he'd stop and listen. In his jungle there's no finding him when he doesn't want to be found.
Oh, yes there is.
Whatcha doin', Suzie?
We can't just let him keep attacking us.
Here, kitty-kitty...
There you are.
Impressive.

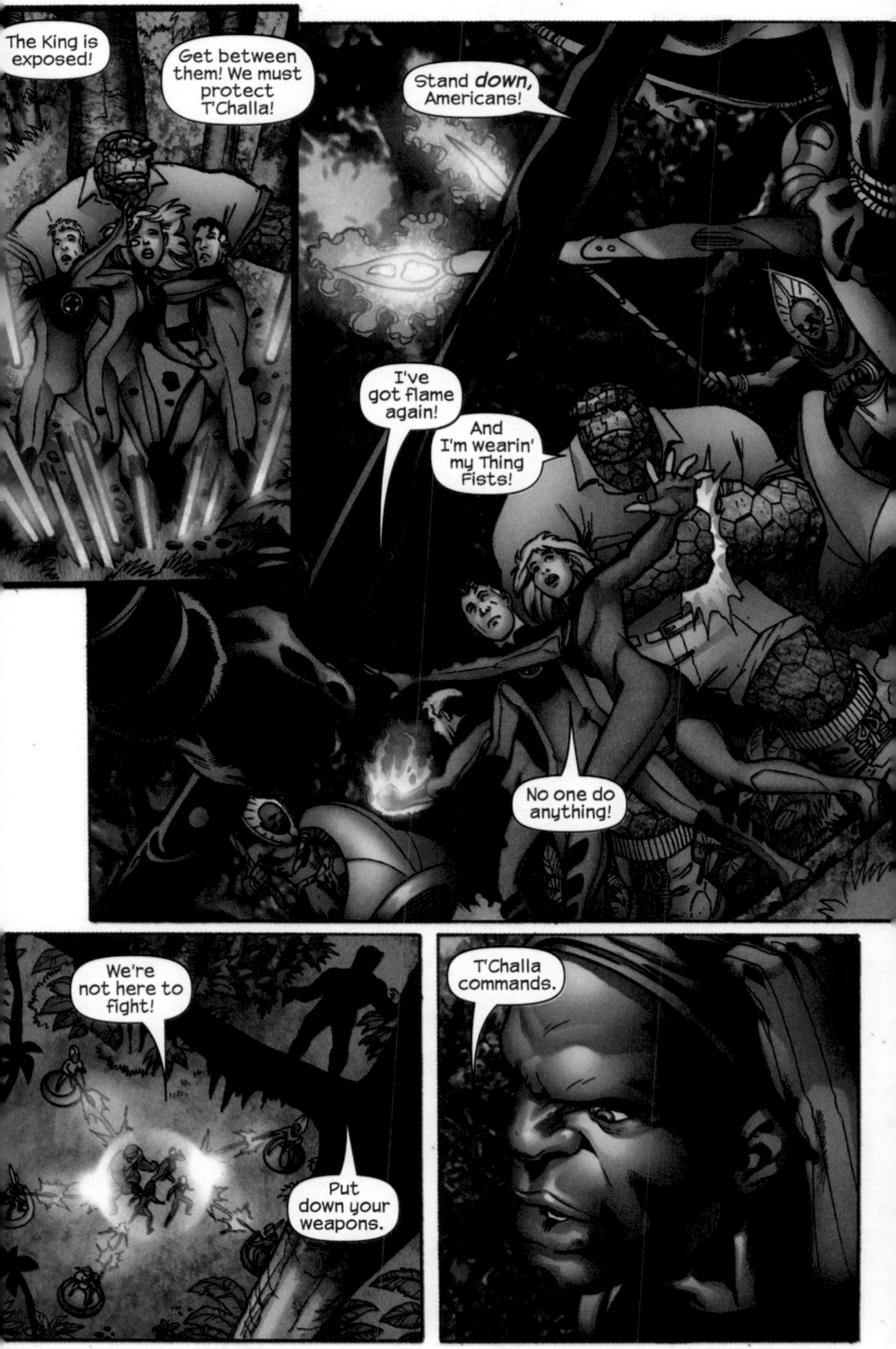

The King is exposed!
Get between them! We must protect T'Challa!
Stand *down,* Americans!
I've got flame again!
And I'm wearin' my Thing Fists!
No one do anything!
We're not here to fight!
Put down your weapons.
T'Challa commands.

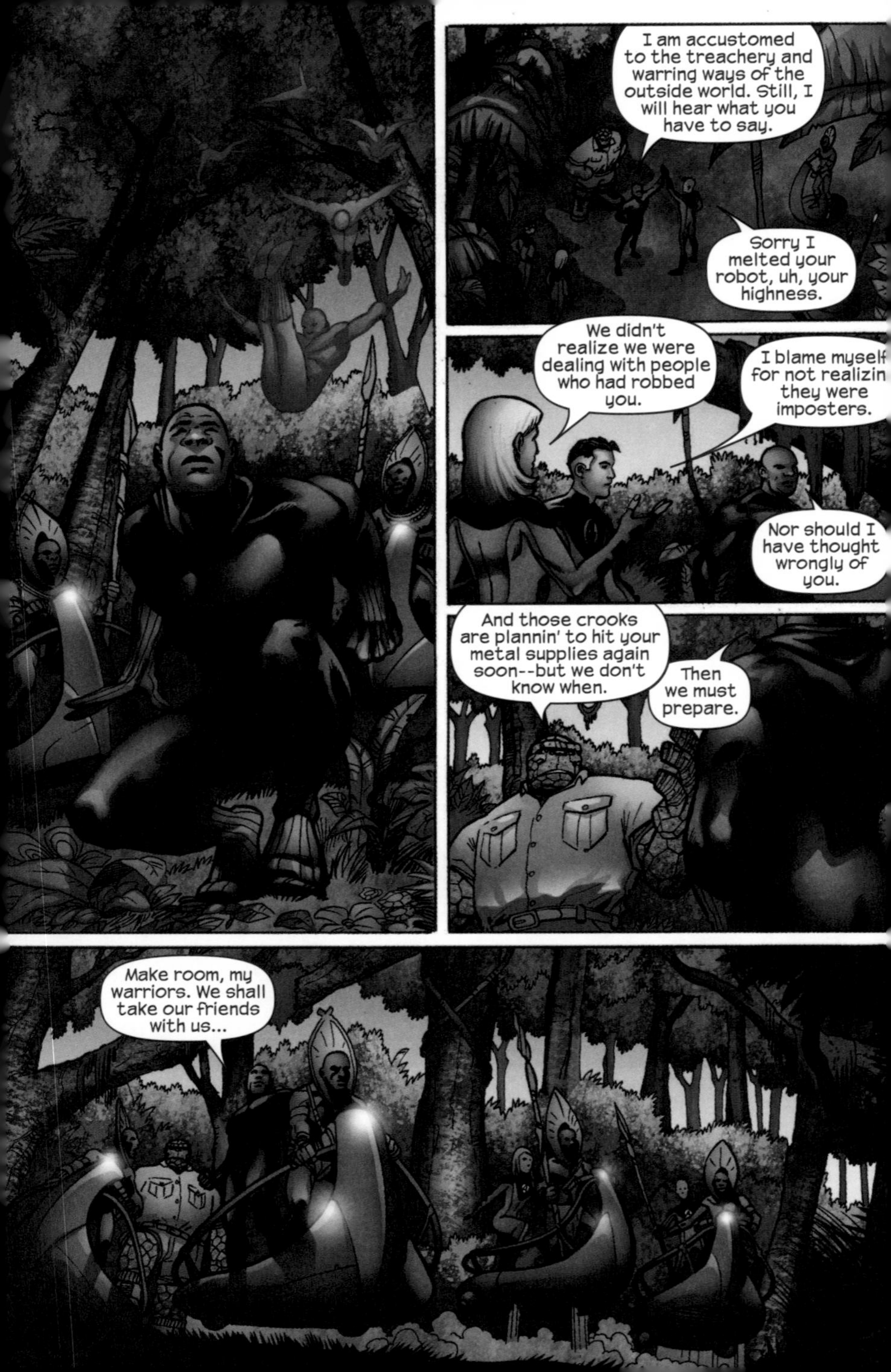
I am accustomed to the treachery and warring ways of the outside world. Still, I will hear what you have to say.
Sorry I melted your robot, uh, your highness.
We didn't realize we were dealing with people who had robbed you.
I blame myself for not realizin they were imposters.
Nor should I have thought wrongly of you.
And those crooks are plannin' to hit your metal supplies again soon--but we don't know when.
Then we must prepare.
Make room, my warriors. We shall take our friends with us...

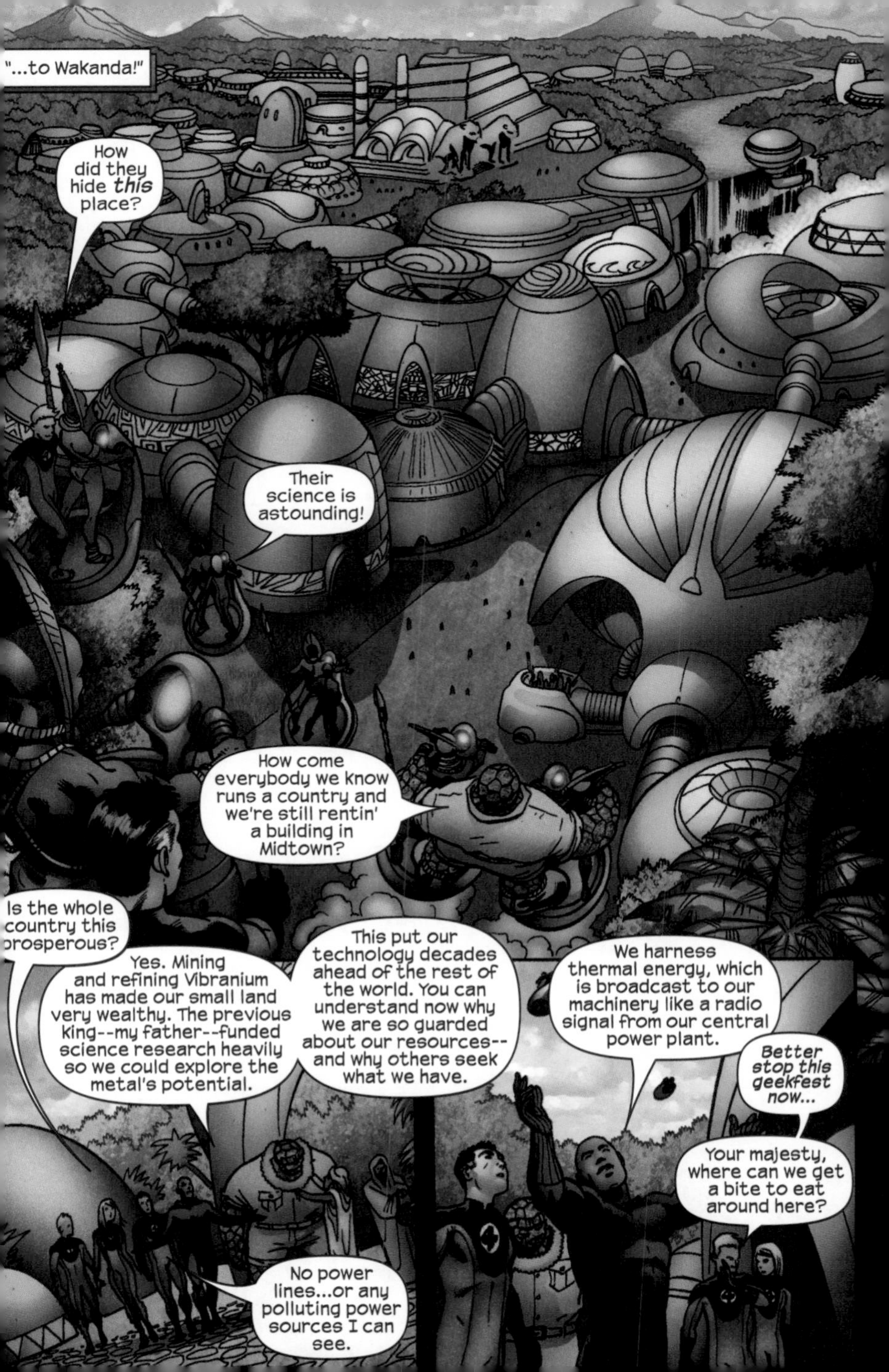
"...to Wakanda!"
How did they hide *this* place?
Their science is astounding!
How come everybody we know runs a country and we're still rentin' a building in Midtown?
Is the whole country this prosperous?
Yes. Mining and refining Vibranium has made our small land very wealthy. The previous king--my father--funded science research heavily so we could explore the metal's potential.
This put our technology decades ahead of the rest of the world. You can understand now why we are so guarded about our resources--and why others seek what we have.
No power lines...or any polluting power sources I can see.
We harness thermal energy, which is broadcast to our machinery like a radio signal from our central power plant.
Better stop this geekfest now...
Your majesty, where can we get a bite to eat around here?

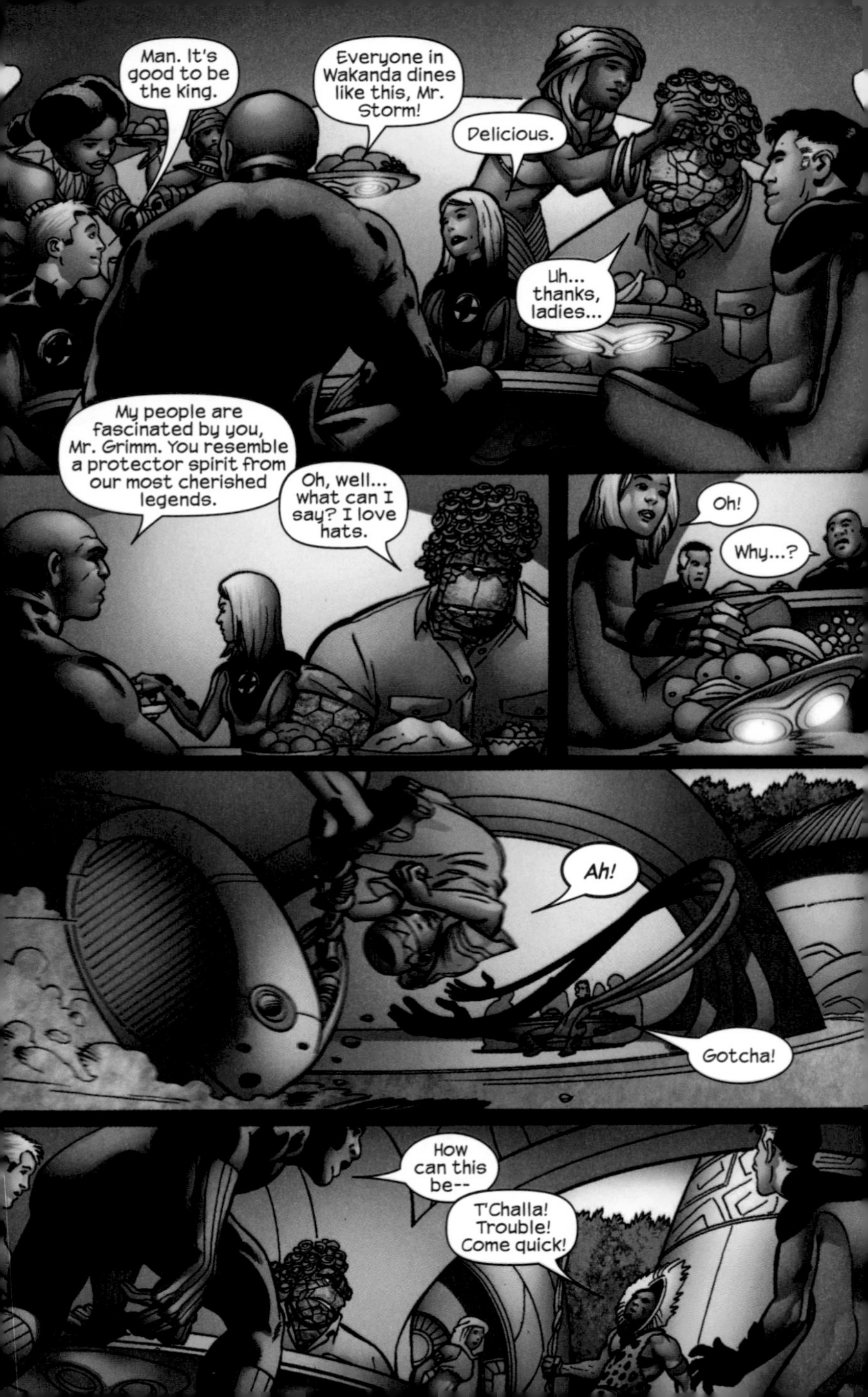
Man. It's good to be the king.
Everyone in Wakanda dines like this, Mr. Storm!
Delicious.
Uh... thanks, ladies...
My people are fascinated by you, Mr. Grimm. You resemble a protector spirit from our most cherished legends.
Oh, well... what can I say? I love hats.
Oh!
Why...?
Ah!
Gotcha!
How can this be--
T'Challa! Trouble! Come quick!

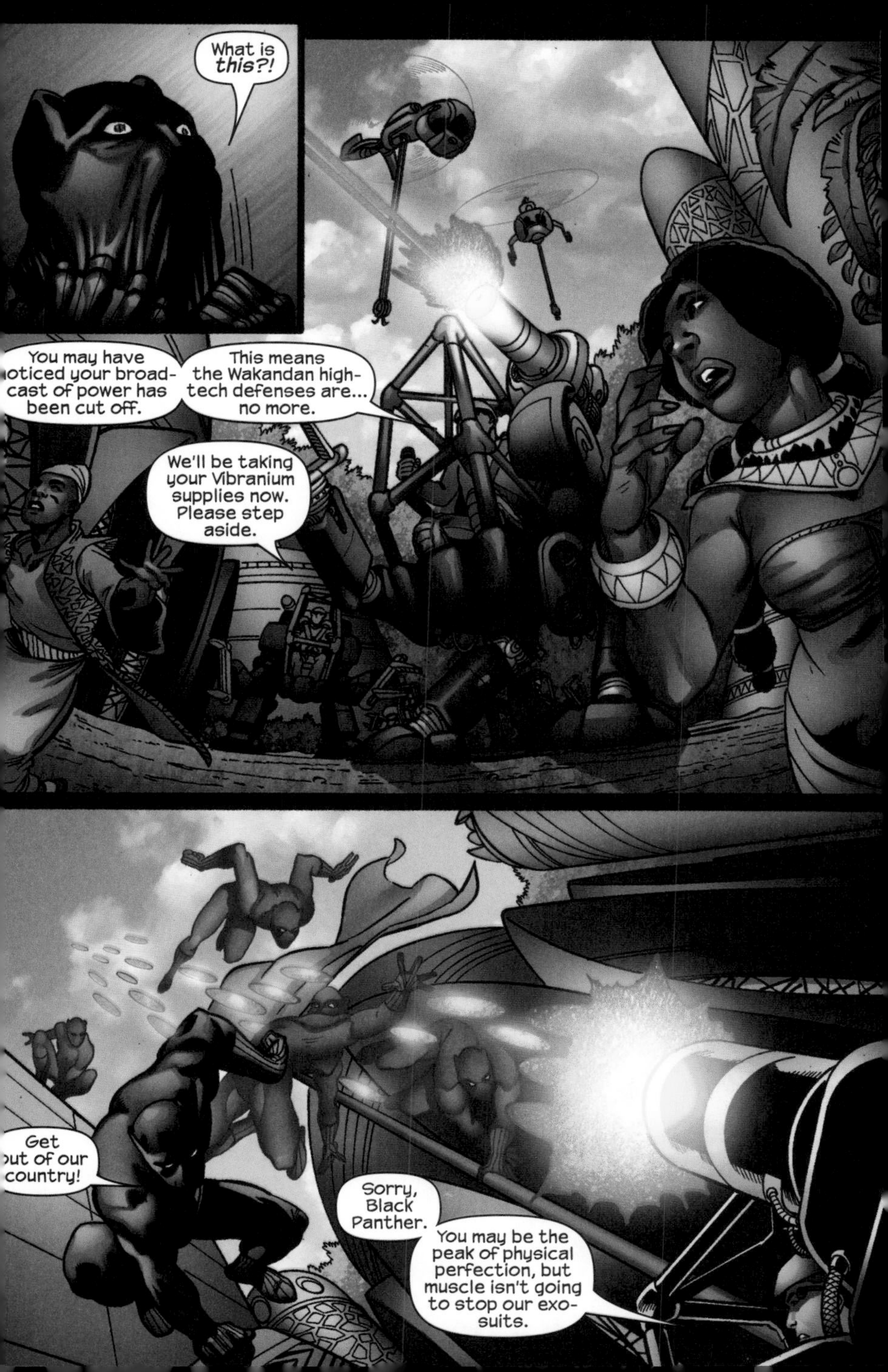
What is this?!
You may have noticed your broadcast of power has been cut off.
This means the Wakandan high-tech defenses are... no more.
We'll be taking your Vibranium supplies now. Please step aside.
Get out of our country!
Sorry, Black Panther.
You may be the peak of physical perfection, but muscle isn't going to stop our exo-suits.

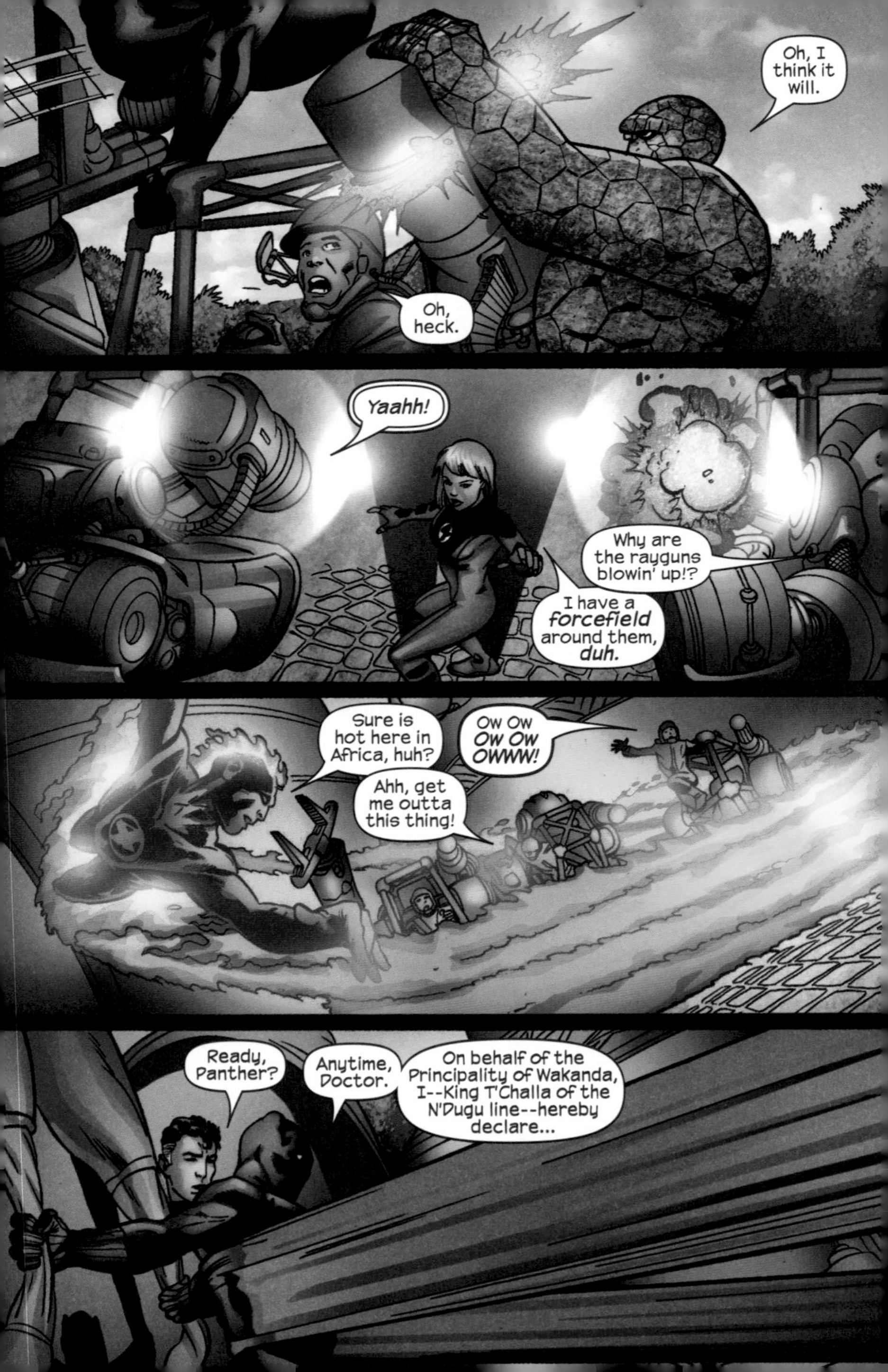

Oh, I think it will.
Oh, heck.
Yaahh!
Why are the rayguns blowin' up!?
I have a *forcefield* around them, *duh.*
Sure is hot here in Africa, huh?
Ow Ow *Ow Ow OWWW!*
Ahh, get me outta this thing!
Ready, Panther?
Anytime, Doctor.
On behalf of the Principality of Wakanda, I--King T'Challa of the N'Dugu line--hereby declare...

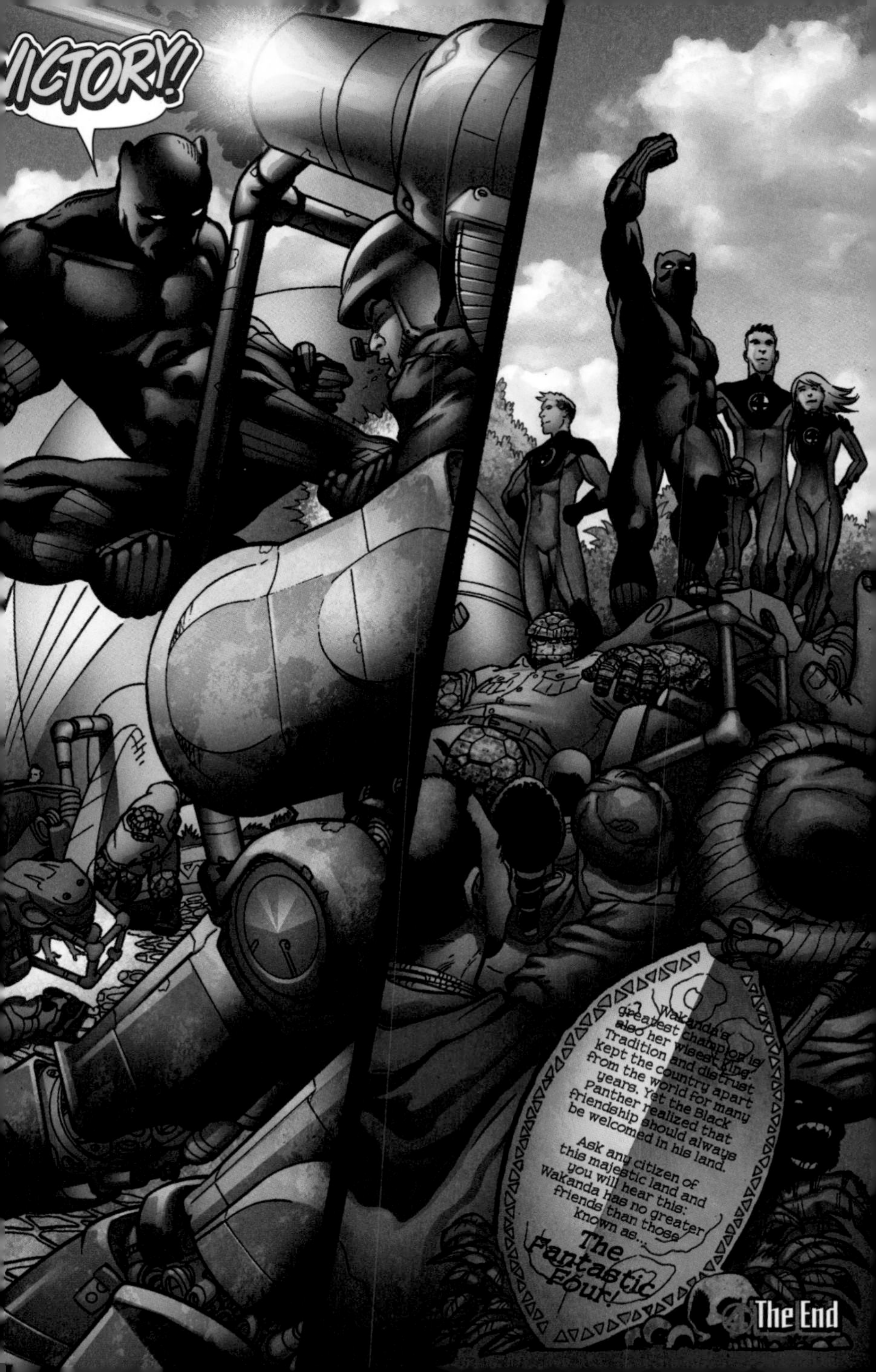
ICTORY!
Wakanda's greatest champion is also her wisest king. Tradition and distrust kept the country apart from the world for many years. Yet the Black Panther realized that friendship should always be welcomed in his land.
Ask any citizen of this majestic land and you will hear this: Wakanda has no greater friends than those known as...
The Fantastic Four!
The End

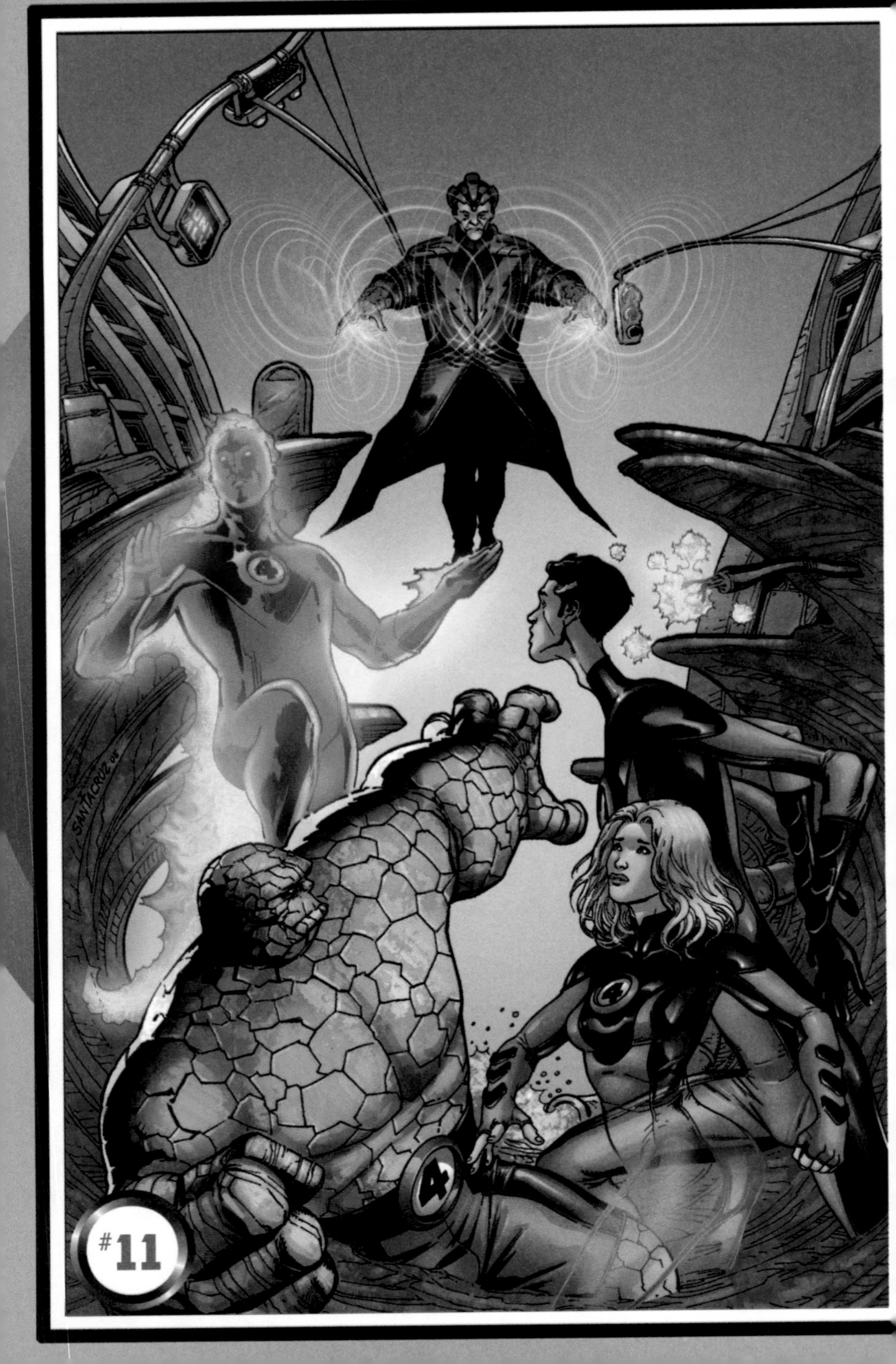
SANTACRUZ '05
#11

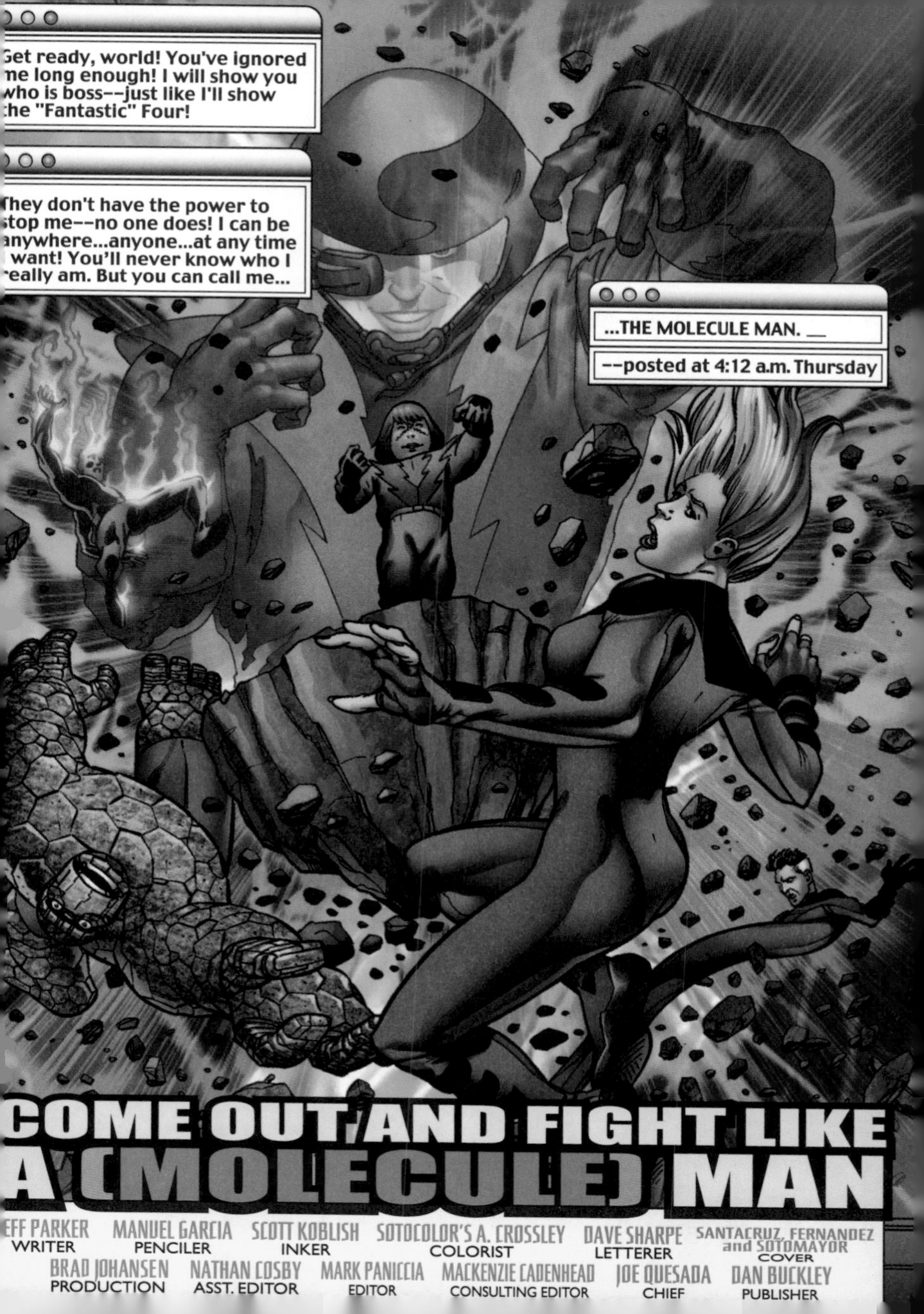
Get ready, world! You've ignored me long enough! I will show you who is boss--just like I'll show the "Fantastic" Four!
They don't have the power to stop me--no one does! I can be anywhere...anyone...at any time I want! You'll never know who I really am. But you can call me...
...THE MOLECULE MAN.
--posted at 4:12 a.m. Thursday
COME OUT AND FIGHT LIKE A (MOLECULE) MAN
JEFF PARKER WRITER
MANUEL GARCIA PENCILER
SCOTT KOBLISH INKER
SOTOCOLOR'S A. CROSSLEY COLORIST
DAVE SHARPE LETTERER
SANTACRUZ, FERNANDEZ and SOTOMAYOR COVER
BRAD JOHANSEN PRODUCTION
NATHAN COSBY ASST. EDITOR
MARK PANICCIA EDITOR
MACKENZIE CADENHEAD CONSULTING EDITOR
JOE QUESADA CHIEF
DAN BUCKLEY PUBLISHER

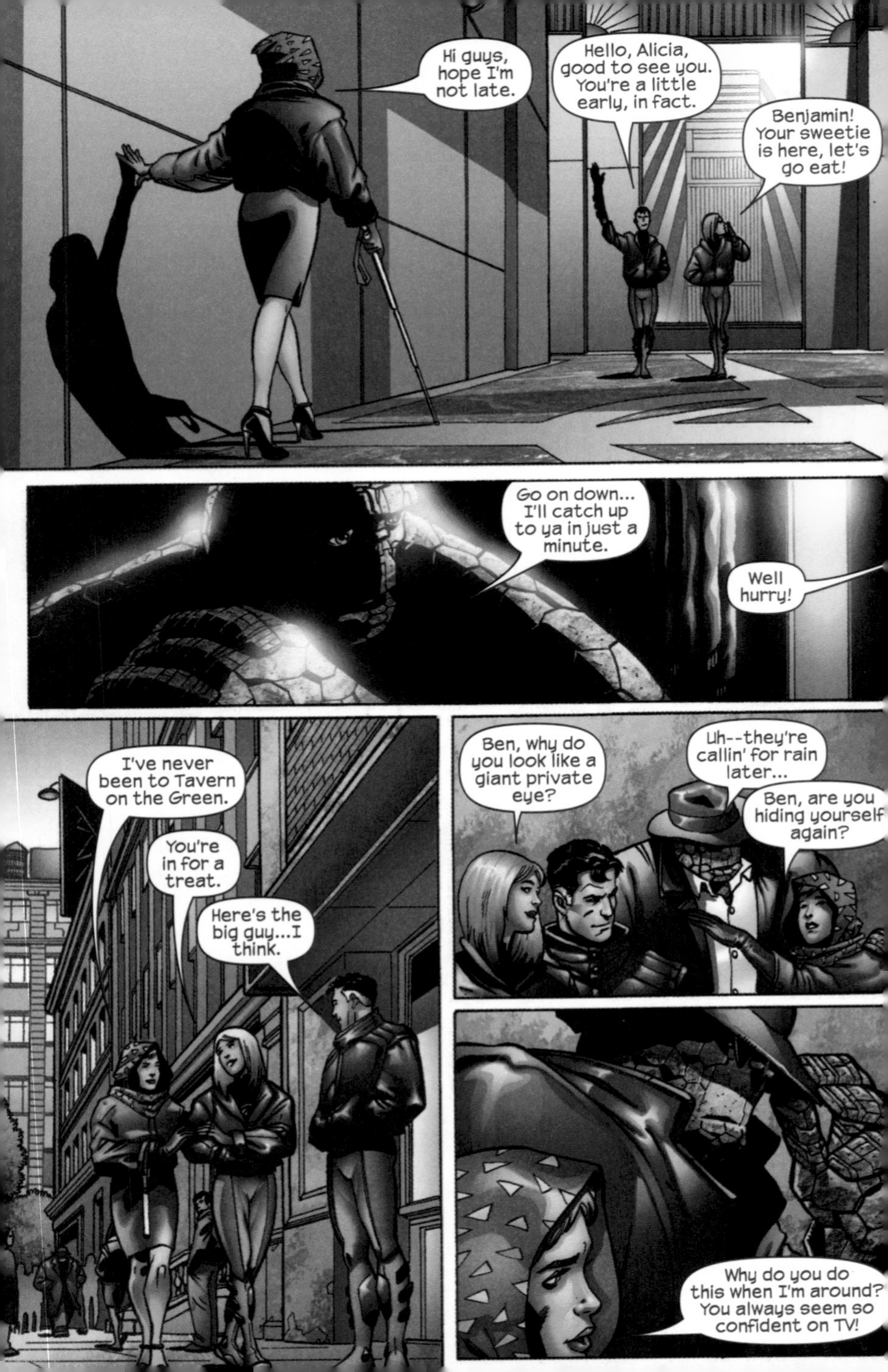
Hi guys, hope I'm not late.
Hello, Alicia, good to see you. You're a little early, in fact.
Benjamin! Your sweetie is here, let's go eat!
Go on down... I'll catch up to ya in just a minute.
Well hurry!
I've never been to Tavern on the Green.
You're in for a treat.
Here's the big guy...I think.
Ben, why do you look like a giant private eye?
Uh--they're callin' for rain later...
Ben, are you hiding yourself again?
Why do you do this when I'm around? You always seem so confident on TV!

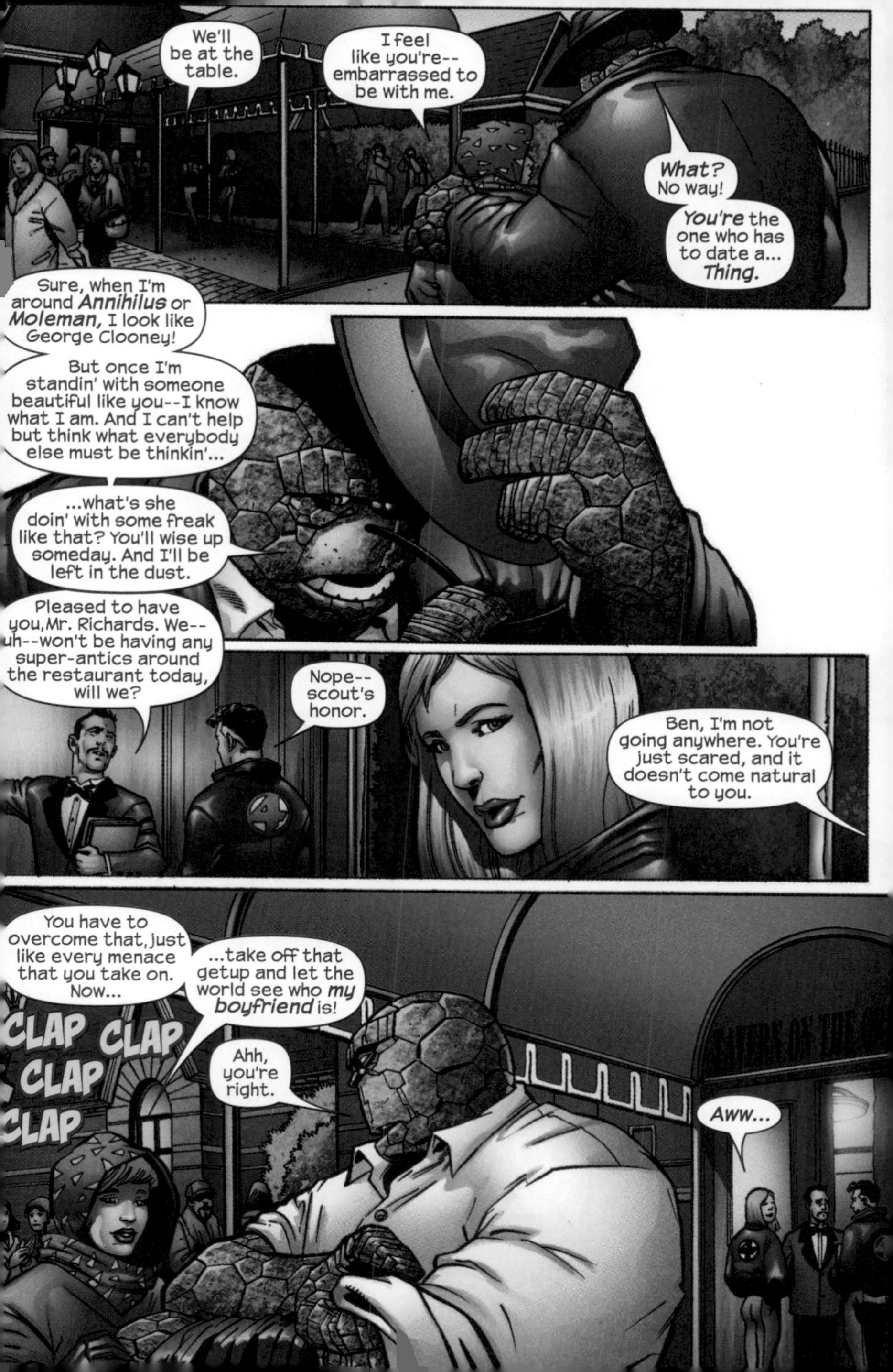
We'll be at the table.
I feel like you're-- embarrassed to be with me.
What? No way!
You're the one who has to date a... Thing.
Sure, when I'm around Annihilus or Moleman, I look like George Clooney!
But once I'm standin' with someone beautiful like you--I know what I am. And I can't help but think what everybody else must be thinkin'...
...what's she doin' with some freak like that? You'll wise up someday. And I'll be left in the dust.
Pleased to have you, Mr. Richards. We-- uh--won't be having any super-antics around the restaurant today, will we?
Nope-- scout's honor.
Ben, I'm not going anywhere. You're just scared, and it doesn't come natural to you.
You have to overcome that, just like every menace that you take on. Now...
...take off that getup and let the world see who my boyfriend is!
CLAP CLAP
CLAP
CLAP
Ahh, you're right.
Aww...

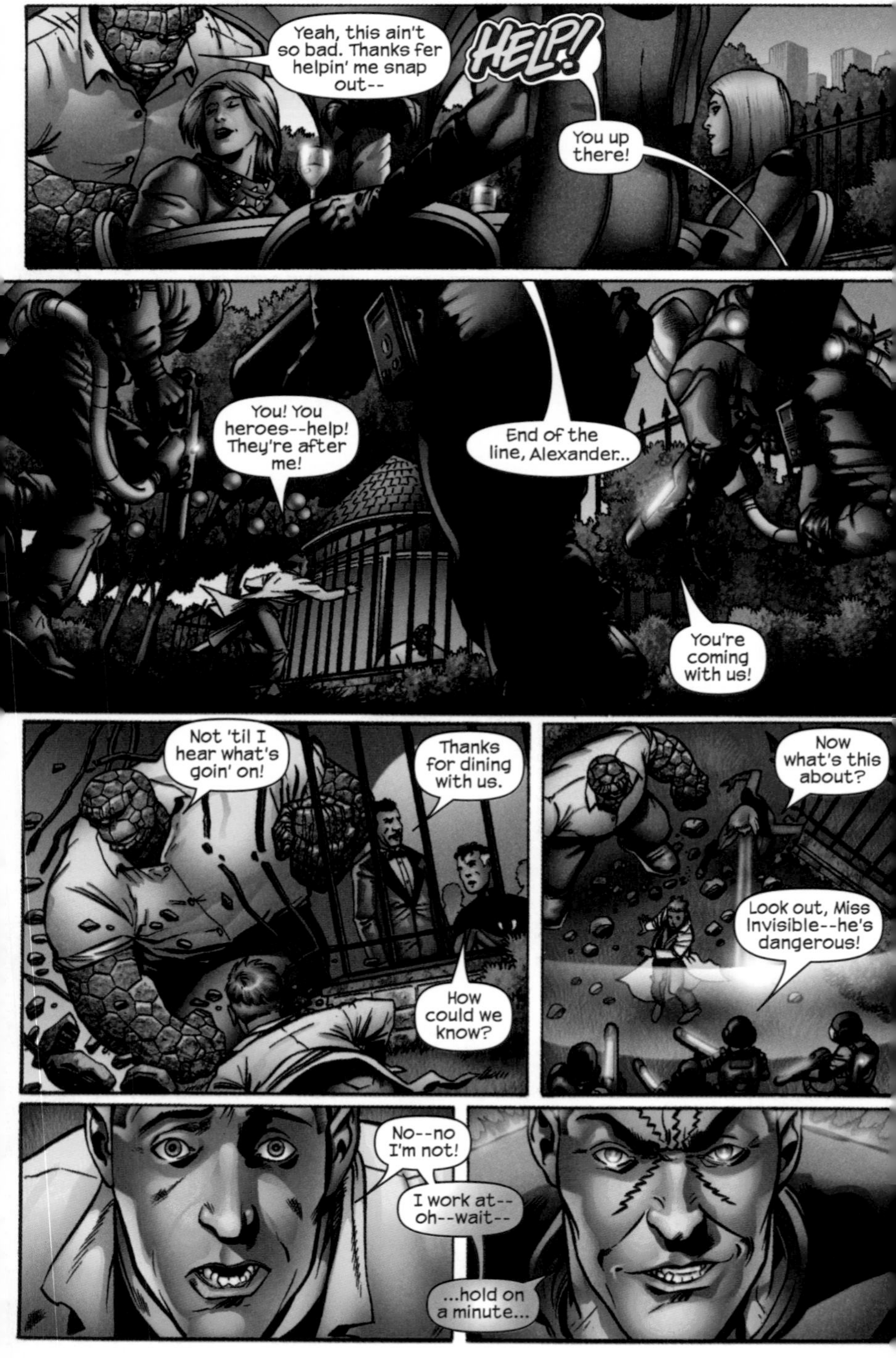

Yeah, this ain't so bad. Thanks fer helpin' me snap out--
HELP!
You up there!
You! You heroes--help! They're after me!
End of the line, Alexander...
You're coming with us!
Not 'til I hear what's goin' on!
Thanks for dining with us.
How could we know?
Now what's this about?
Look out, Miss Invisible--he's dangerous!
No--no I'm not!
I work at-- oh--wait--
...hold on a minute...

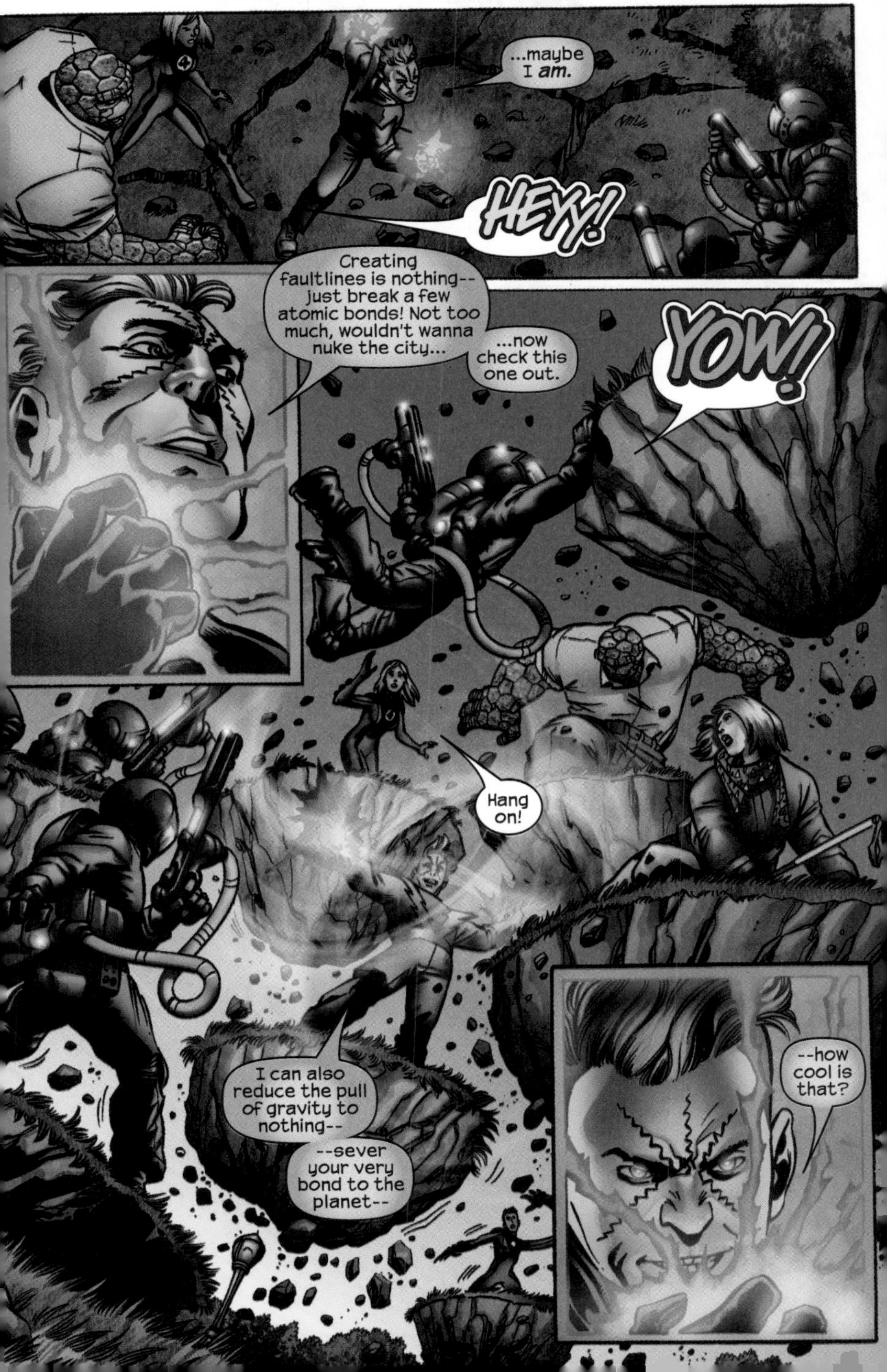
...maybe I am.
HEYY!
Creating faultlines is nothing-- just break a few atomic bonds! Not too much, wouldn't wanna nuke the city...
...now check this one out.
YOW!
Hang on!
I can also reduce the pull of gravity to nothing--
--sever your very bond to the planet--
--how cool is that?

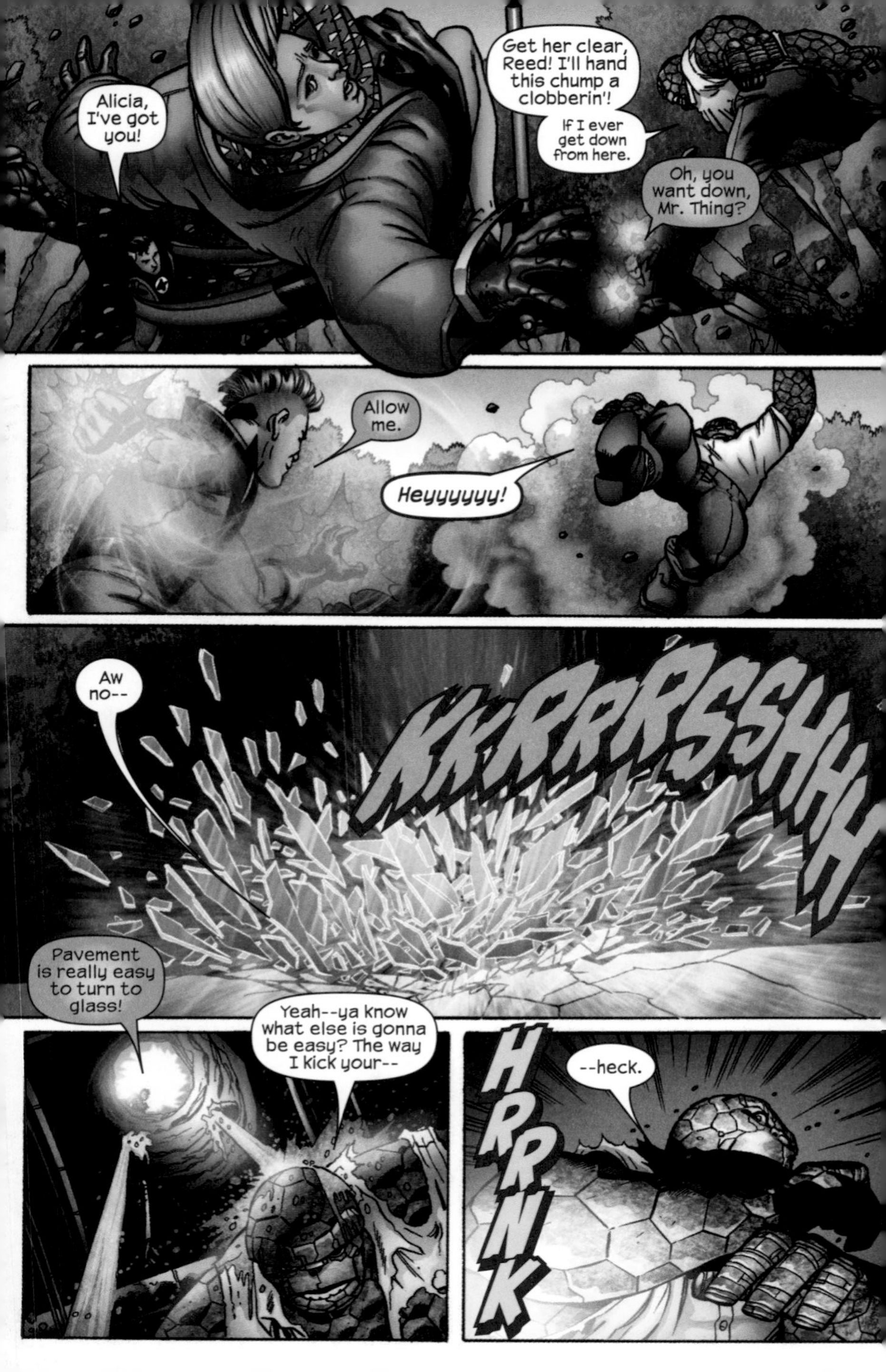
Alicia, I've got you!
Get her clear, Reed! I'll hand this chump a clobberin'!
If I ever get down from here.
Oh, you want down, Mr. Thing?
Allow me.
Heyyyyyy!
Aw no--
KKRRRRSSHH
Pavement is really easy to turn to glass!
Yeah--ya know what else is gonna be easy? The way I kick your--
HRRNK
--heck.

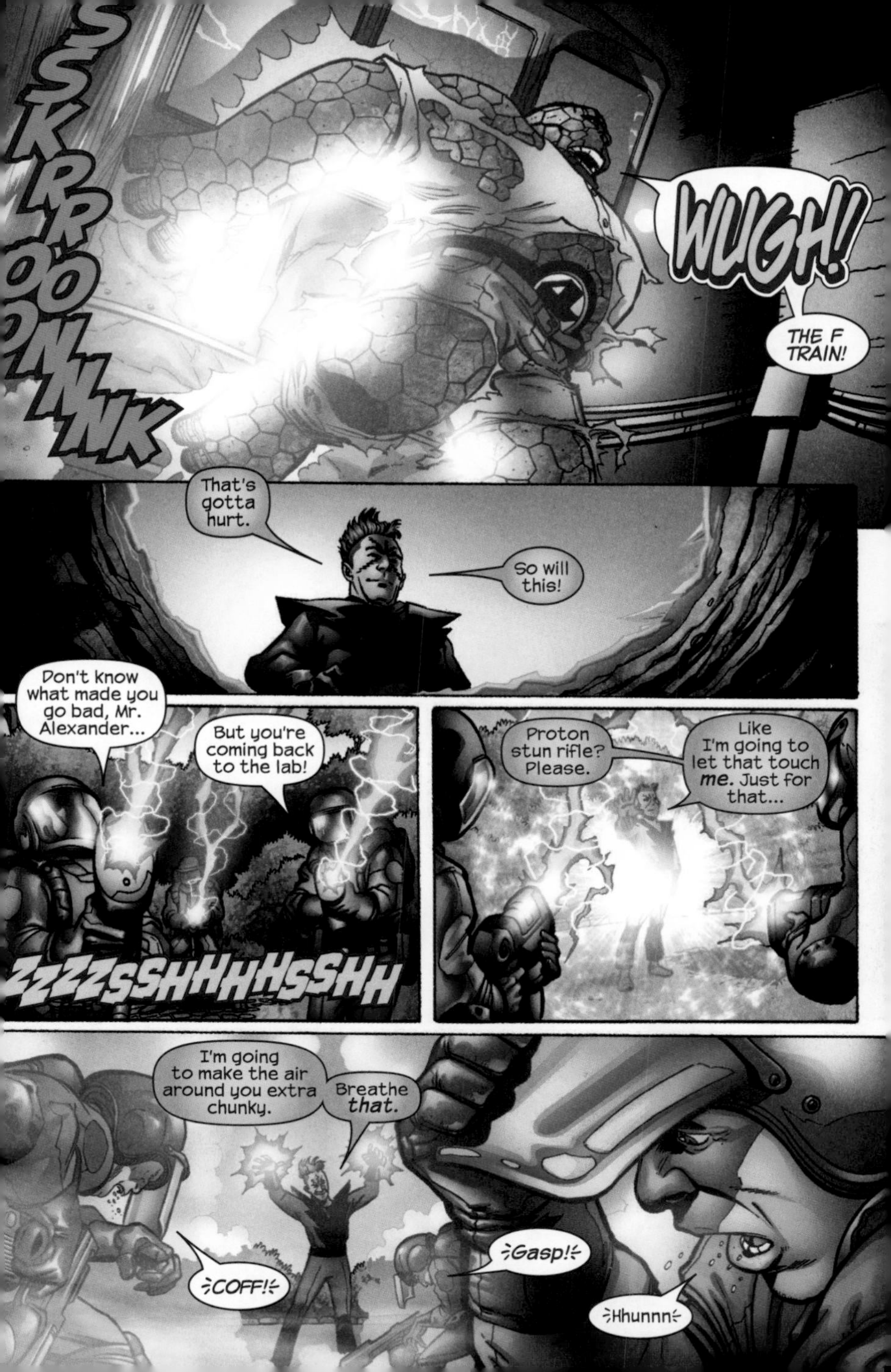

SSKRROONNNK
WUGH!
THE F TRAIN!
That's gotta hurt.
So will this!
Don't know what made you go bad, Mr. Alexander...
But you're coming back to the lab!
ZZZZSSHHHHSSHH
Proton stun rifle? Please.
Like I'm going to let that touch *me.* Just for that...
I'm going to make the air around you extra chunky.
Breathe *that.*
COFF!
Gasp!
Hhunnn

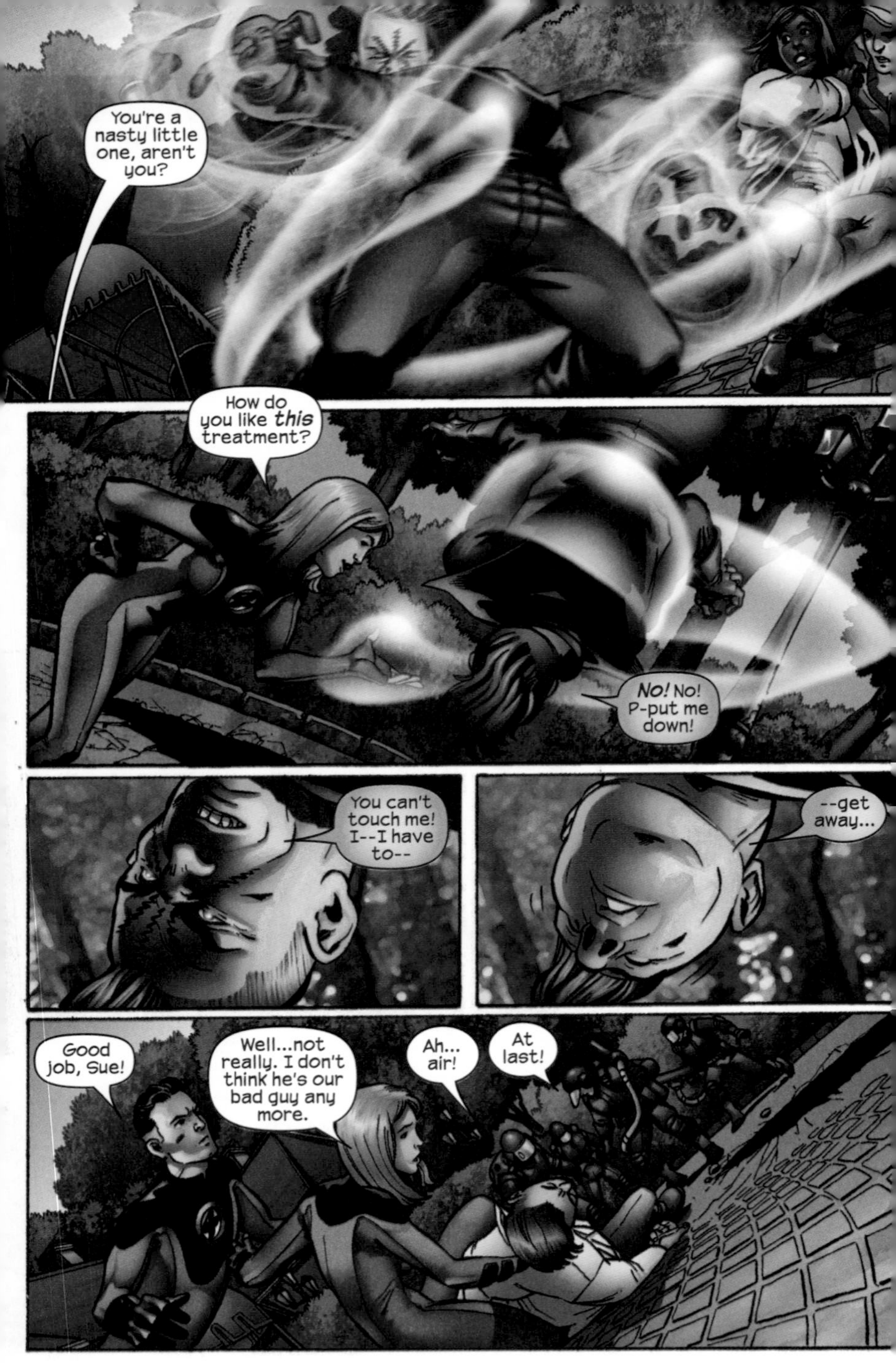

You're a nasty little one, aren't you?
How do you like *this* treatment?
No! No! P-put me down!
You can't touch me! I--I have to--
--get away...
Good job, Sue!
Well...not really. I don't think he's our bad guy any more.
Ah... air!
At last!

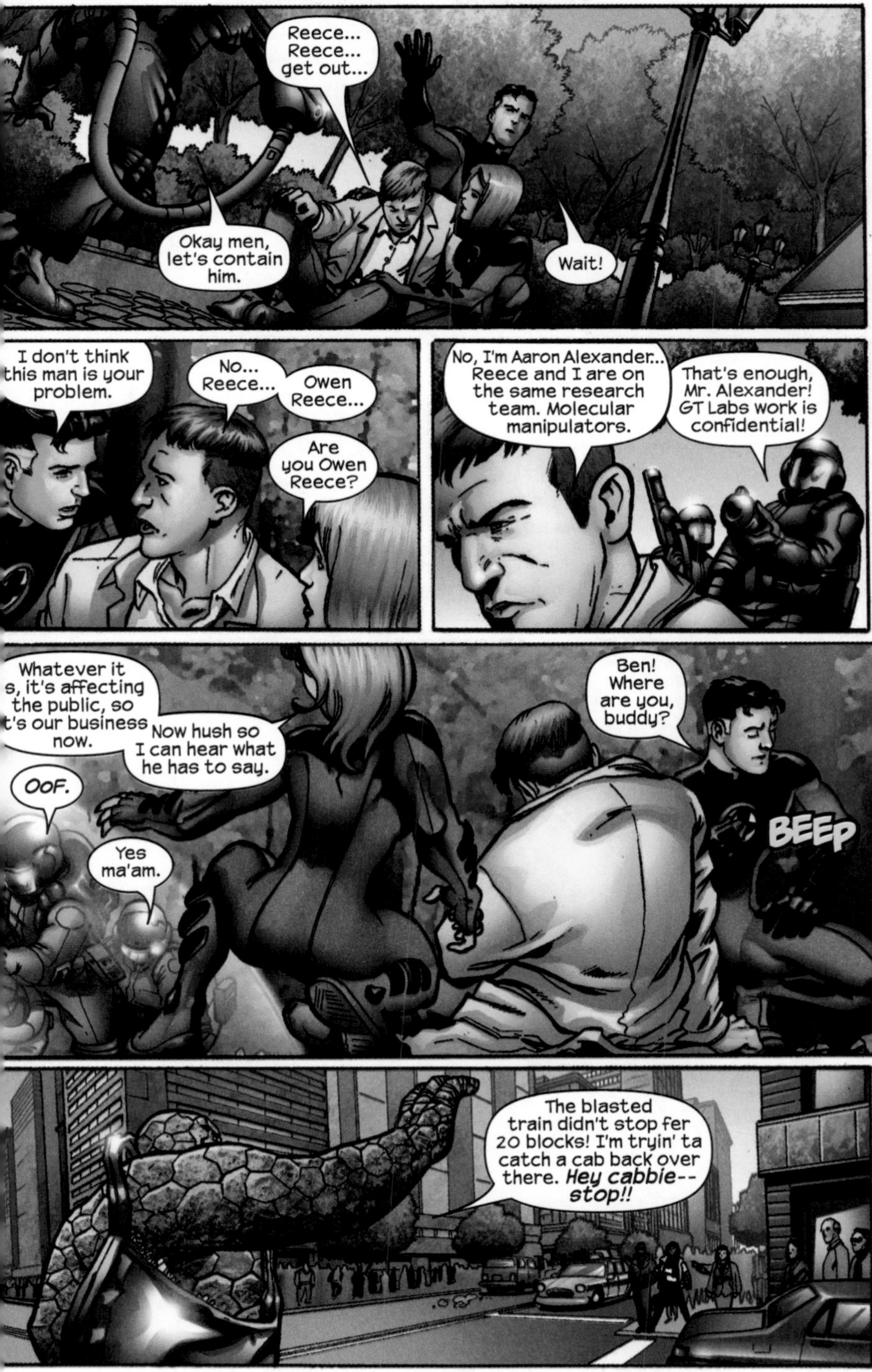
Reece... Reece... get out...
Okay men, let's contain him.
Wait!
I don't think this man is your problem.
No... Reece...
Owen Reece...
Are you Owen Reece?
No, I'm Aaron Alexander... Reece and I are on the same research team. Molecular manipulators.
That's enough, Mr. Alexander! GT Labs work is confidential!
Whatever it s, it's affecting the public, so t's our business now.
Now hush so I can hear what he has to say.
OOF.
Yes ma'am.
Ben! Where are you, buddy?
BEEP
The blasted train didn't stop fer 20 blocks! I'm tryin' ta catch a cab back over there. *Hey cabbie-- stop!!*

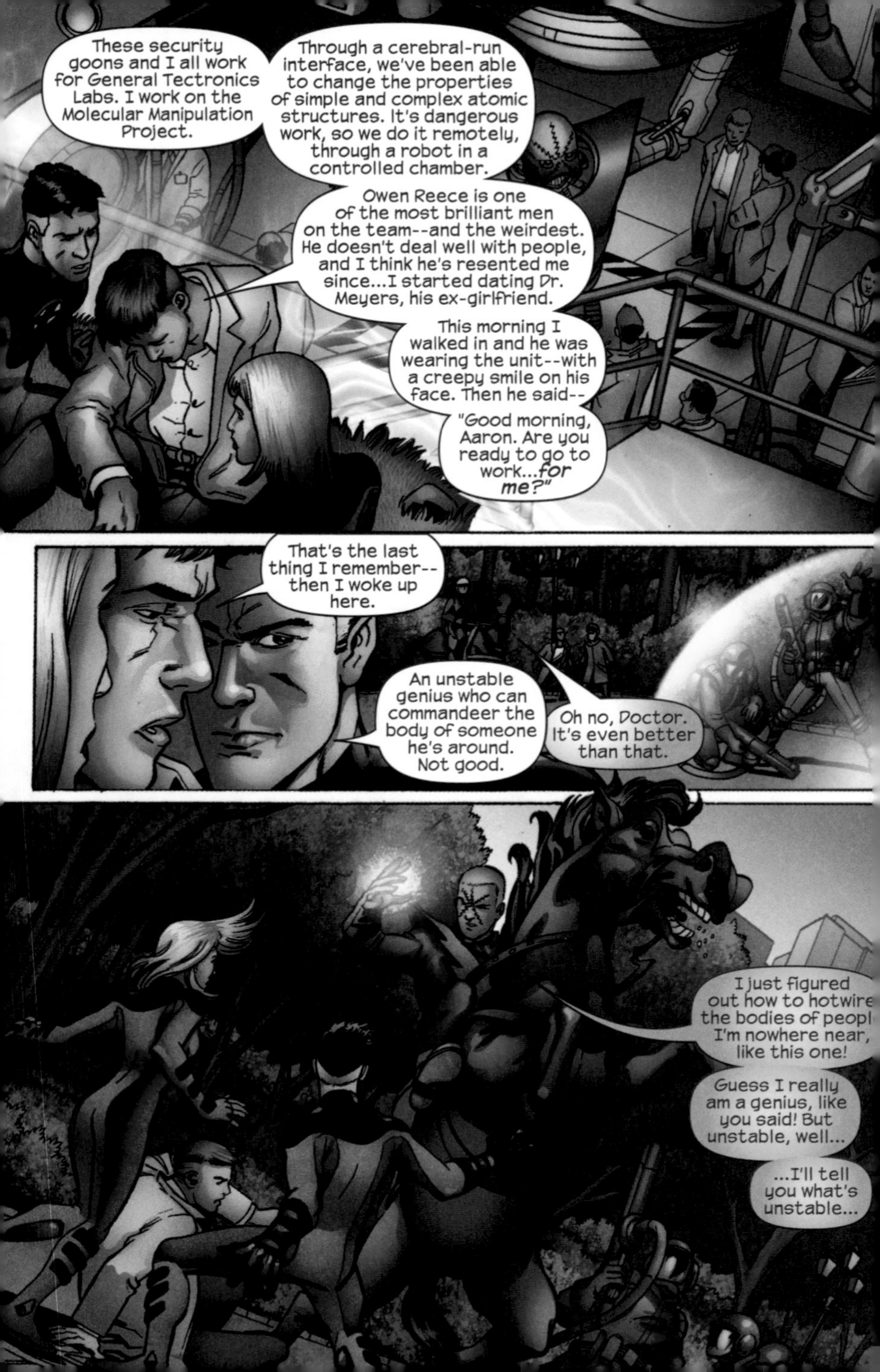
These security goons and I all work for General Tectronics Labs. I work on the Molecular Manipulation Project.
Through a cerebral-run interface, we've been able to change the properties of simple and complex atomic structures. It's dangerous work, so we do it remotely, through a robot in a controlled chamber.
Owen Reece is one of the most brilliant men on the team--and the weirdest. He doesn't deal well with people, and I think he's resented me since...I started dating Dr. Meyers, his ex-girlfriend.
This morning I walked in and he was wearing the unit--with a creepy smile on his face. Then he said--
"Good morning, Aaron. Are you ready to go to work...*for me?*"
That's the last thing I remember--then I woke up here.
An unstable genius who can commandeer the body of someone he's around. Not good.
Oh no, Doctor. It's even better than that.
I just figured out how to hotwire the bodies of peopl I'm nowhere near, like this one!
Guess I really am a genius, like you said! But unstable, well...
...I'll tell you what's unstable...

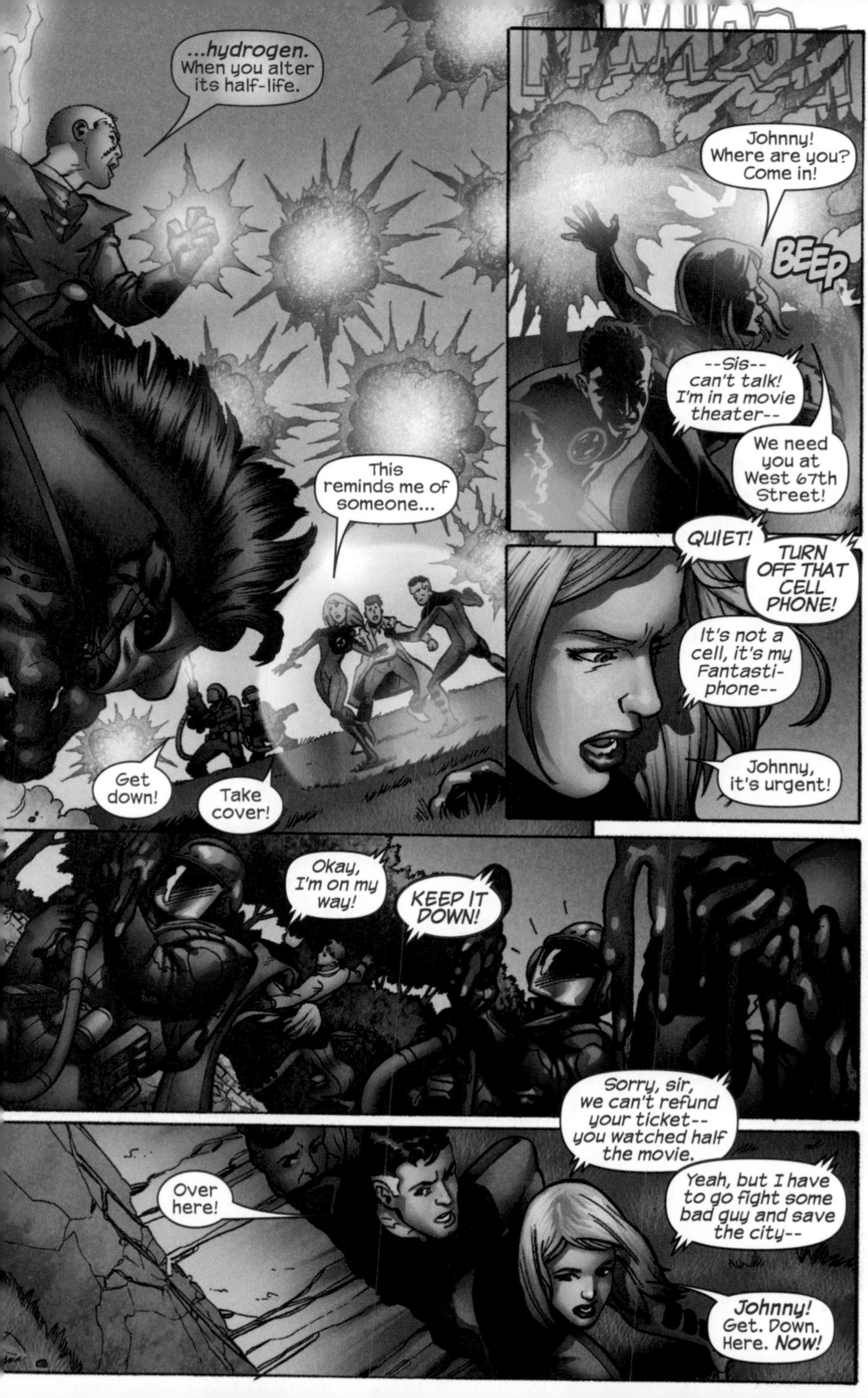
...hydrogen. When you alter its half-life.
This reminds me of someone...
Get down!
Take cover!
Johnny! Where are you? Come in!
BEEP
--Sis-- can't talk! I'm in a movie theater--
We need you at West 67th Street!
QUIET!
TURN OFF THAT CELL PHONE!
It's not a cell, it's my Fantasti-phone--
Johnny, it's urgent!
Okay, I'm on my way!
KEEP IT DOWN!
Sorry, sir, we can't refund your ticket--you watched half the movie.
Yeah, but I have to go fight some bad guy and save the city--
Over here!
Johnny! Get. Down. Here. NOW!

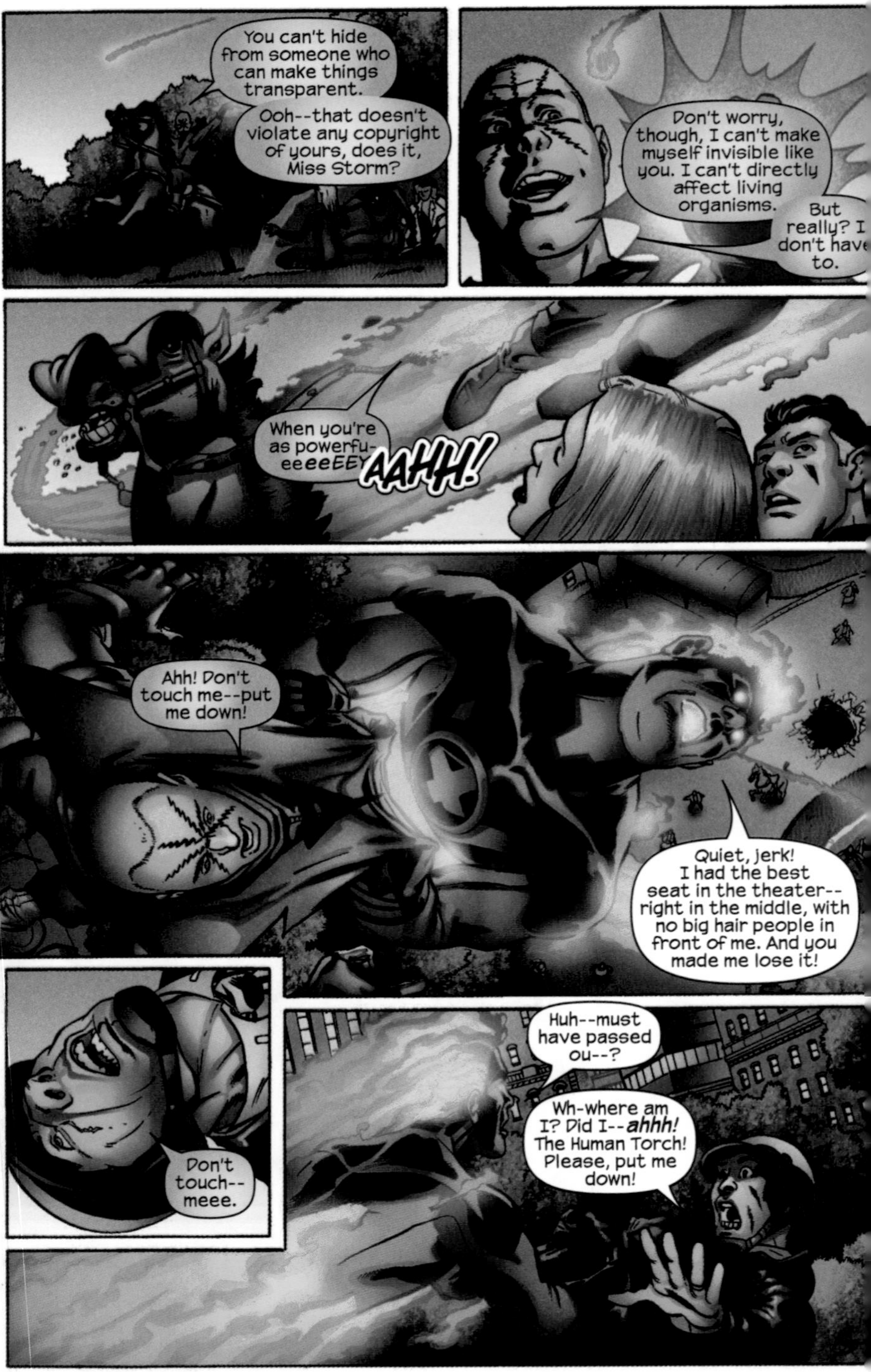
You can't hide from someone who can make things transparent.
Ooh--that doesn't violate any copyright of yours, does it, Miss Storm?
Don't worry, though, I can't make myself invisible like you. I can't directly affect living organisms.
But really? I don't have to.
When you're as powerfu-eeeeeEEY
AAHH!
Ahh! Don't touch me--put me down!
Quiet, jerk! I had the best seat in the theater--right in the middle, with no big hair people in front of me. And you made me lose it!
Don't touch--meee.
Huh--must have passed ou--?
Wh-where am I? Did I--ahhh! The Human Torch! Please, put me down!

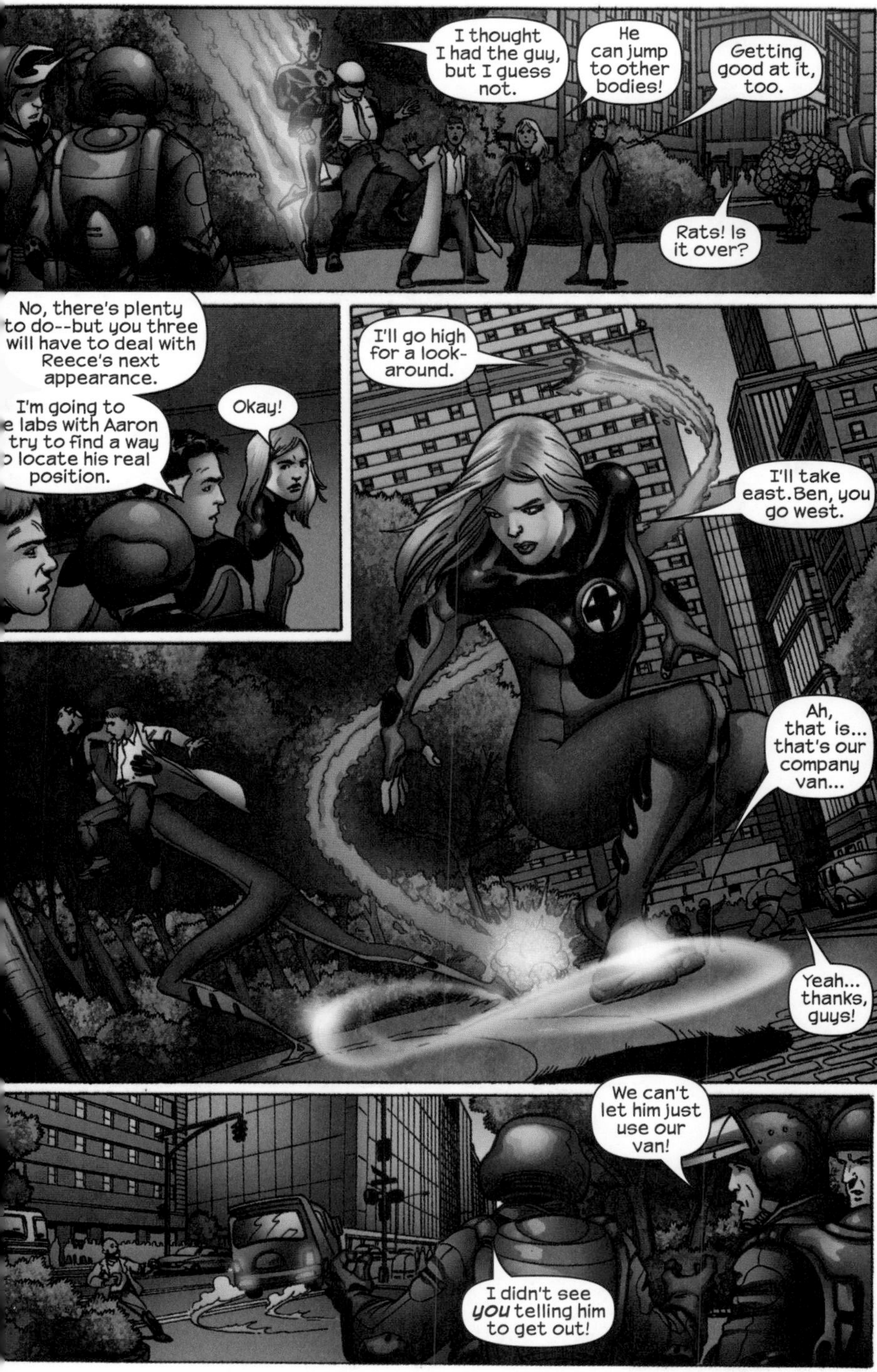

I thought I had the guy, but I guess not.
He can jump to other bodies!
Getting good at it, too.
Rats! Is it over?
No, there's plenty to do--but you three will have to deal with Reece's next appearance.
I'm going to e labs with Aaron try to find a way o locate his real position.
Okay!
I'll go high for a look-around.
I'll take east. Ben, you go west.
Ah, that is... that's our company van...
Yeah... thanks, guys!
We can't let him just use our van!
I didn't see *you* telling him to get out!

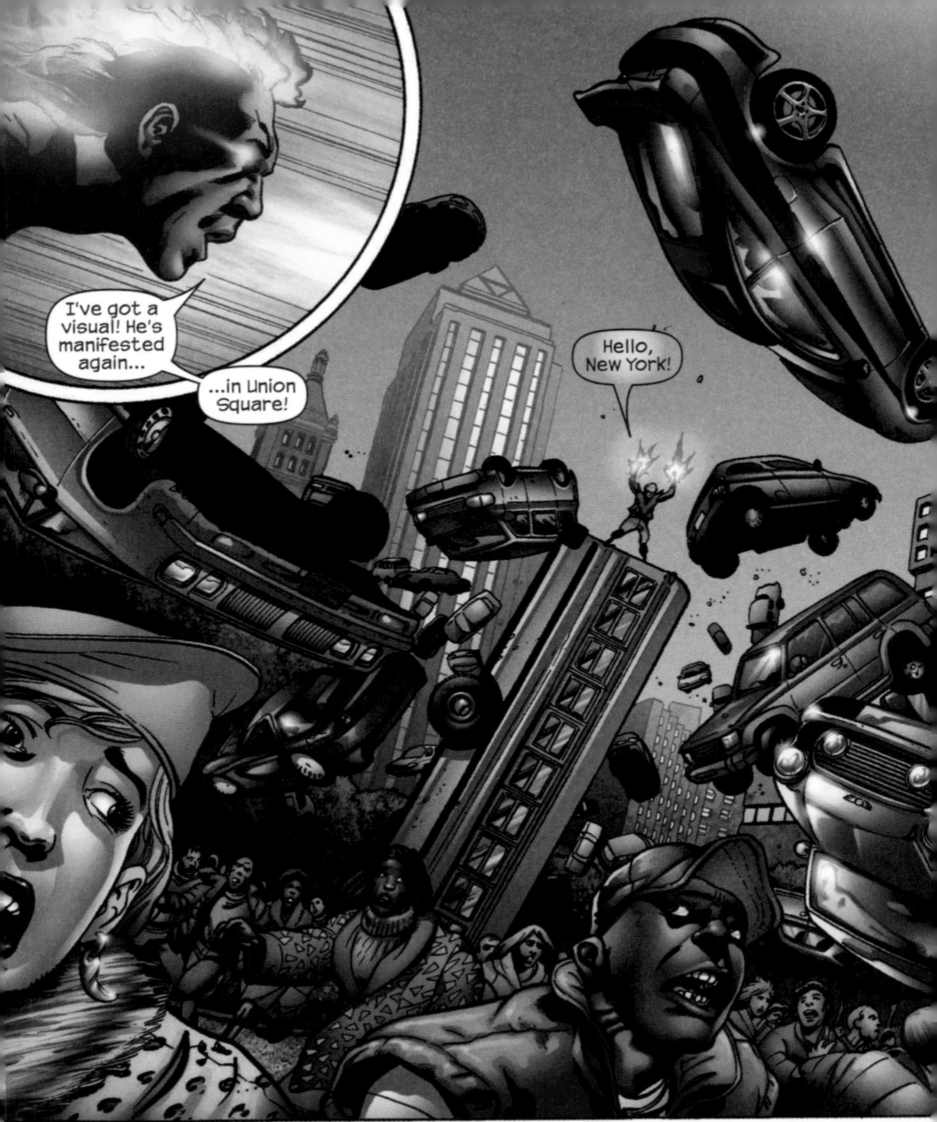
I've got a visual! He's manifested again...
...in Union Square!
Hello, New York!

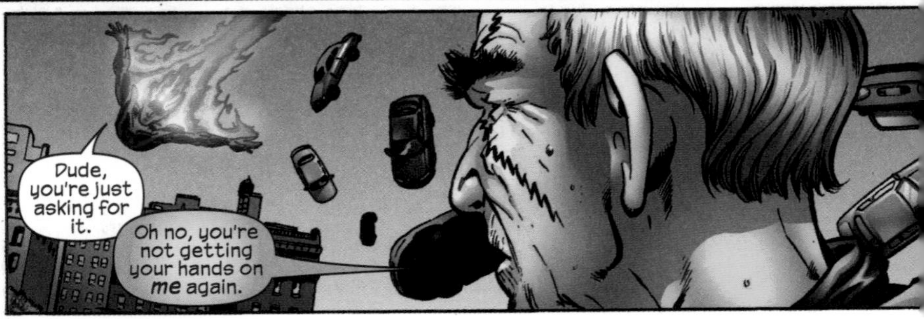
Dude, you're just asking for it.
Oh no, you're not getting your hands on *me* again.

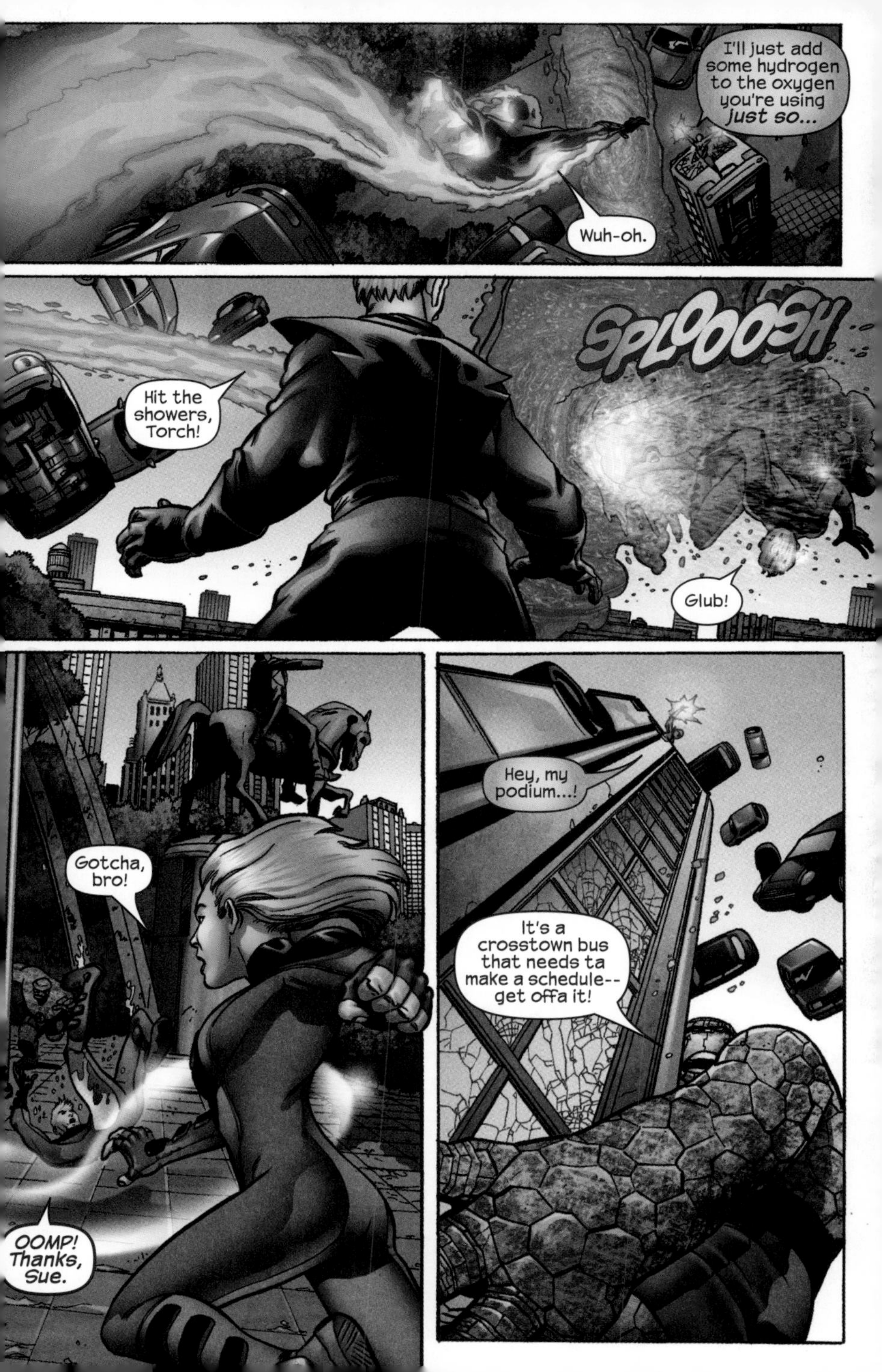
I'll just add some hydrogen to the oxygen you're using just so...
Wuh-oh.
SPLOOOSH
Hit the showers, Torch!
Glub!
Gotcha, bro!
OOMP! Thanks, Sue.
Hey, my podium...!
It's a crosstown bus that needs ta make a schedule-- get offa it!

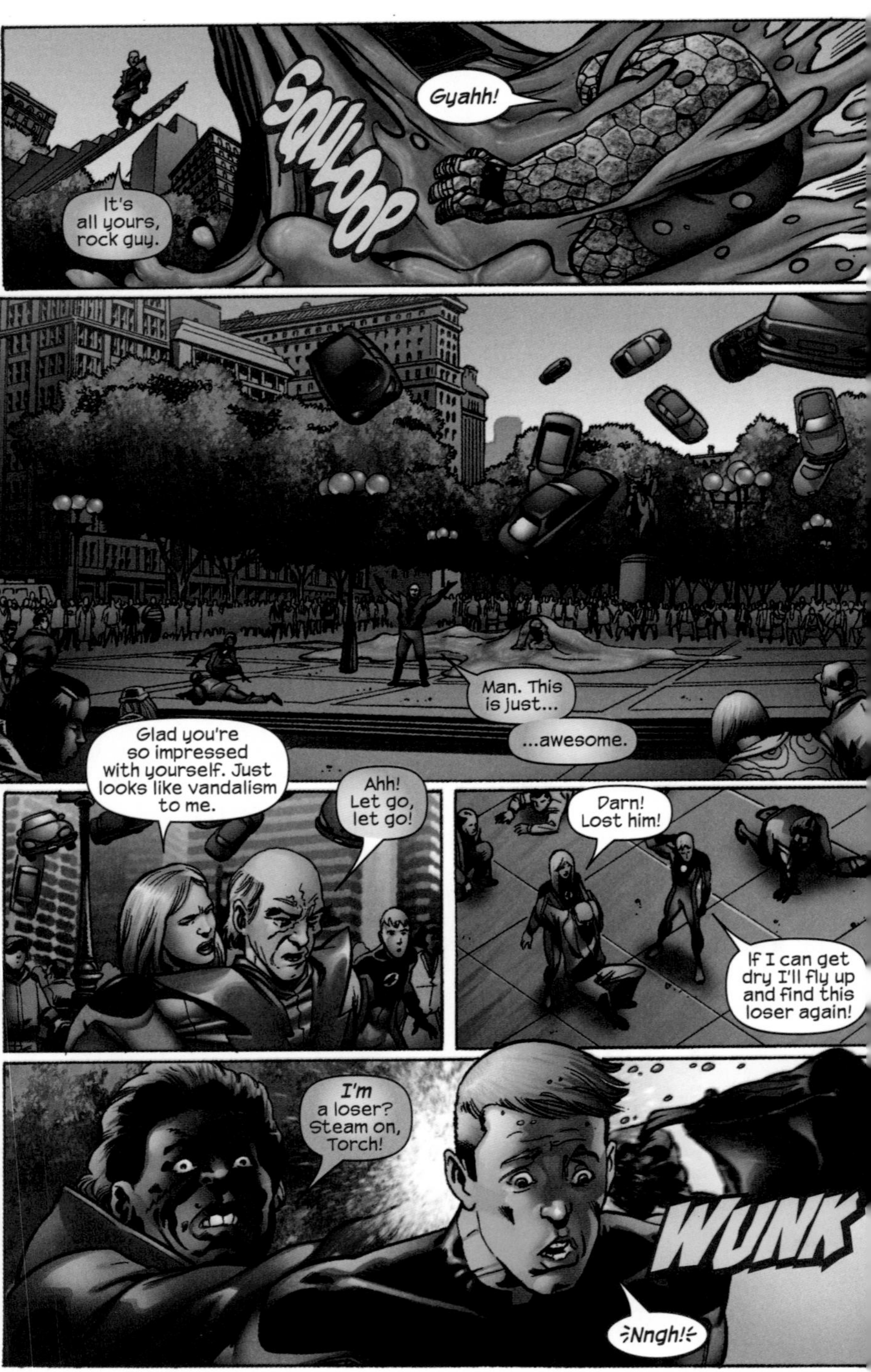
SQULOOP
Gyahh!
It's all yours, rock guy.
Man. This is just...
...awesome.
Glad you're so impressed with yourself. Just looks like vandalism to me.
Ahh! Let go, let go!
Darn! Lost him!
If I can get dry I'll fly up and find this loser again!
I'm a loser? Steam on, Torch!
WUNK
Nngh!

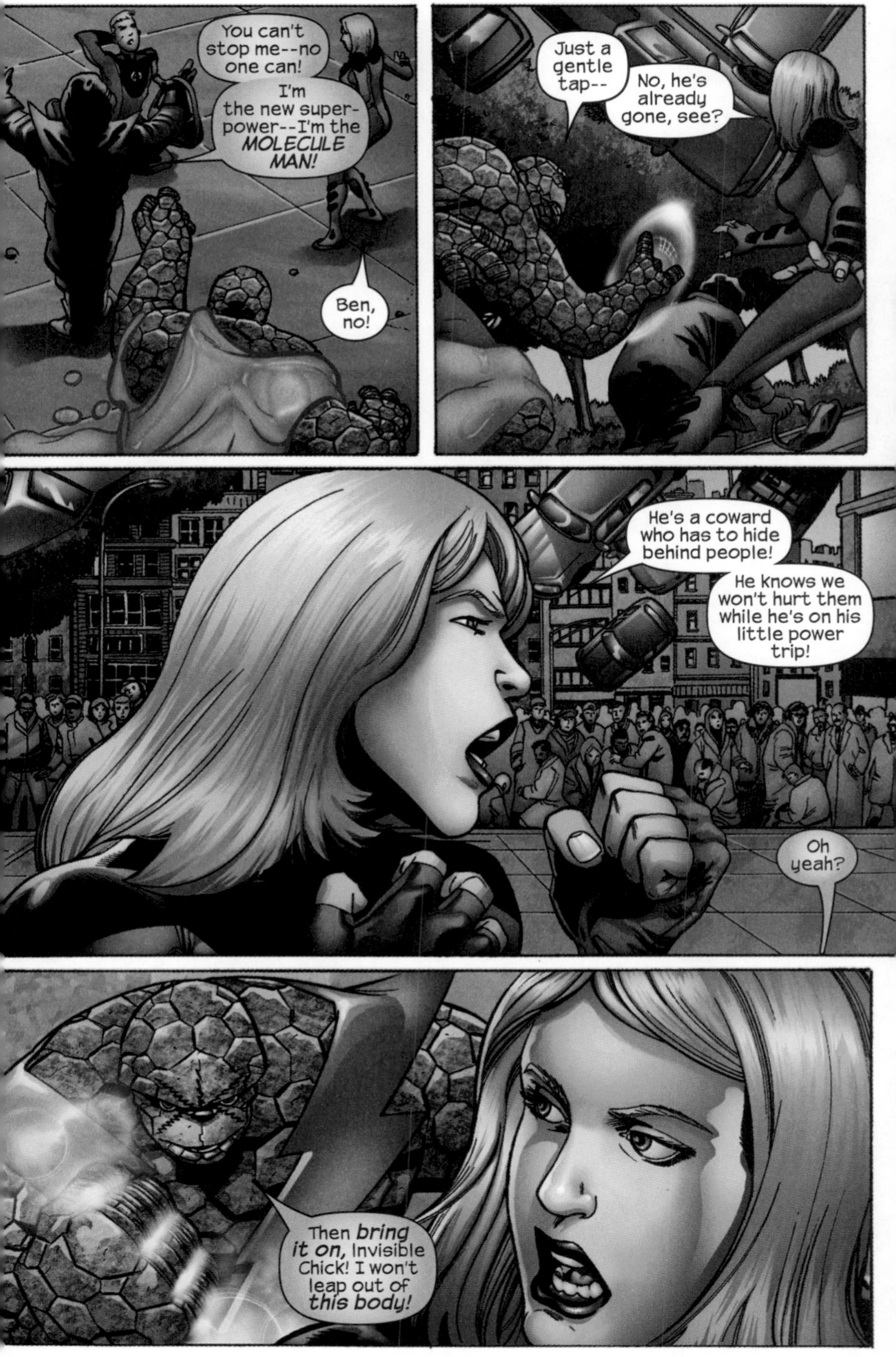
You can't stop me--no one can!
I'm the new super-power--I'm the *MOLECULE MAN!*
Ben, no!
Just a gentle tap--
No, he's already gone, see?
He's a coward who has to hide behind people!
He knows we won't hurt them while he's on his little power trip!
Oh yeah?
Then *bring it on,* Invisible Chick! I won't leap out of *this body!*

Okay... I *will!*

SLAM

Oof!

SKRONCCH

Did you think hiding in my friend would scare me off? Huh?

Agh!

See, Ben would *want* me cut loose-- that's the kind of thing a hero like him is prepared for.

Stop-- stop--

KKRKRKRKRKRR

That's what interacting in the real world is all about--taking *risks.*

Now come out here and--

Suzie! Easy! I think ya made yer point!

No, she hasn't! You don't know me!

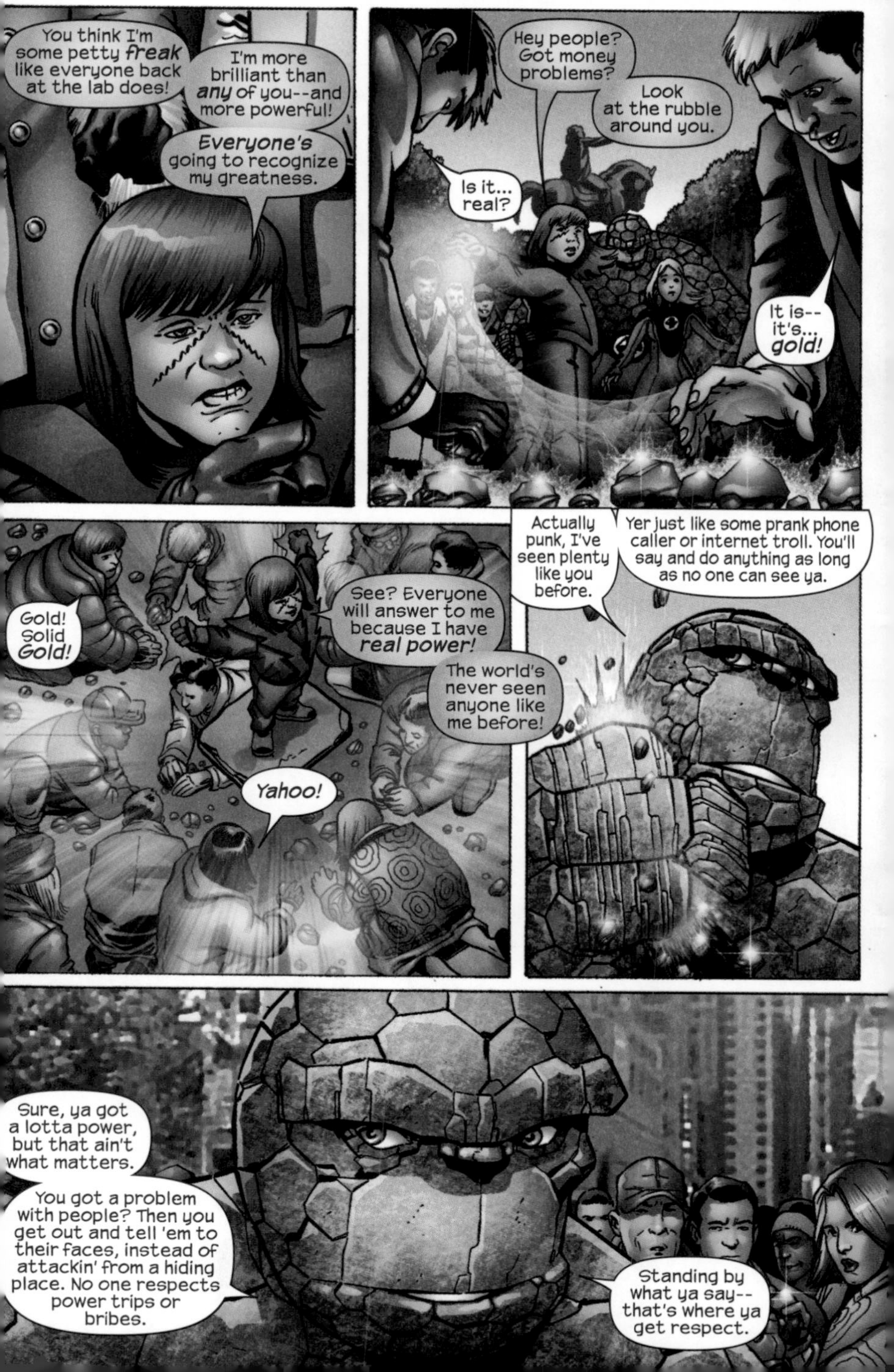

You think I'm some petty *freak* like everyone back at the lab does!
I'm more brilliant than *any* of you--and more powerful!
Everyone's going to recognize my greatness.
Hey people? Got money problems?
Look at the rubble around you.
Is it... real?
It is-- it's... *gold!*
Gold! Solid *Gold!*
See? Everyone will answer to me because I have *real power!*
The world's never seen anyone like me before!
Yahoo!
Actually punk, I've seen plenty like you before.
Yer just like some prank phone caller or internet troll. You'll say and do anything as long as no one can see ya.
Sure, ya got a lotta power, but that ain't what matters.
You got a problem with people? Then you get out and tell 'em to their faces, instead of attackin' from a hiding place. No one respects power trips or bribes.
Standing by what ya say--that's where ya get respect.

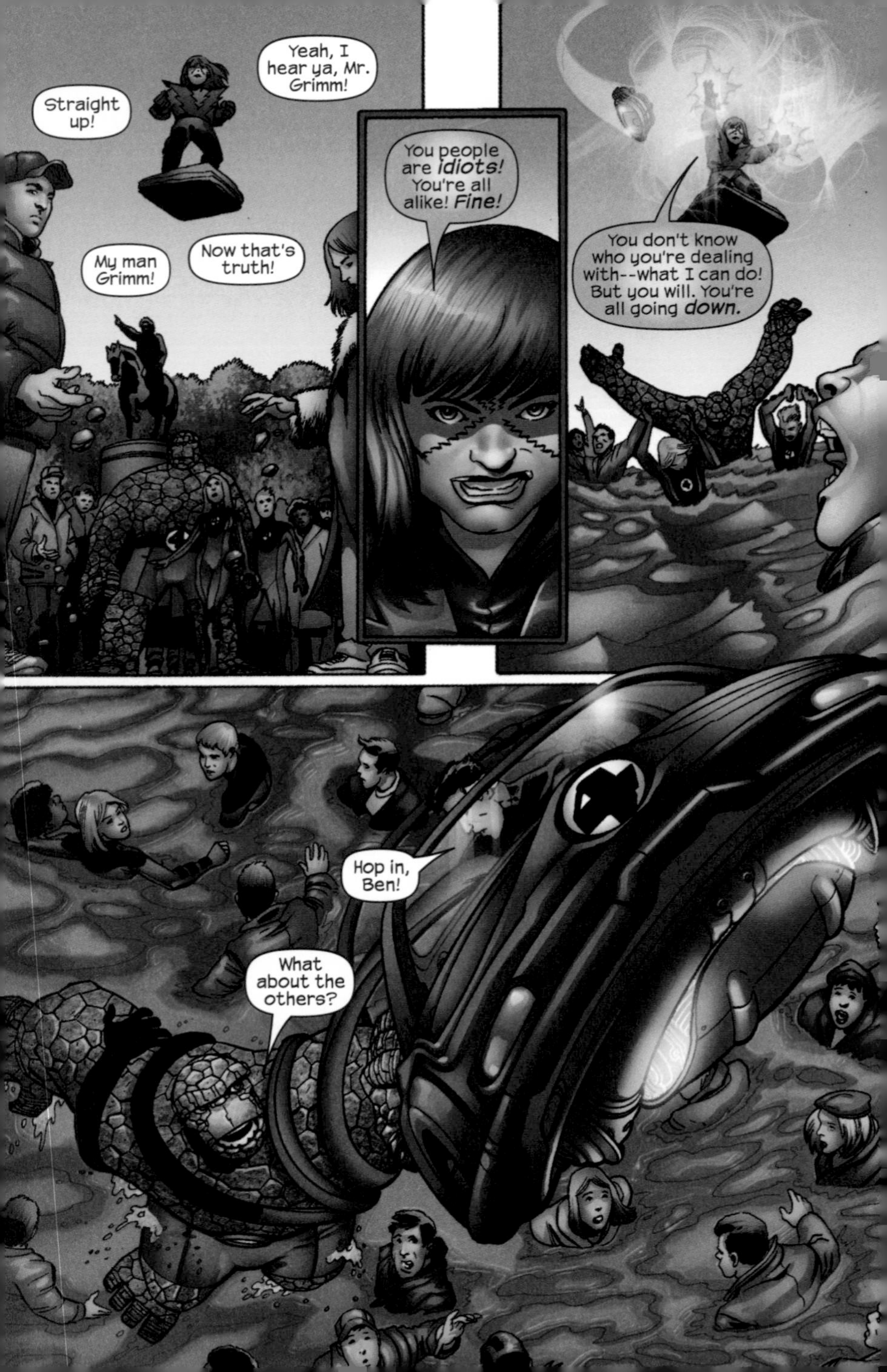
Straight up!
Yeah, I hear ya, Mr. Grimm!
My man Grimm!
Now that's truth!
You people are *idiots!* You're all alike! *Fine!*
You don't know who you're dealing with--what I can do! But you will. You're all going *down.*
Hop in, Ben!
What about the others?

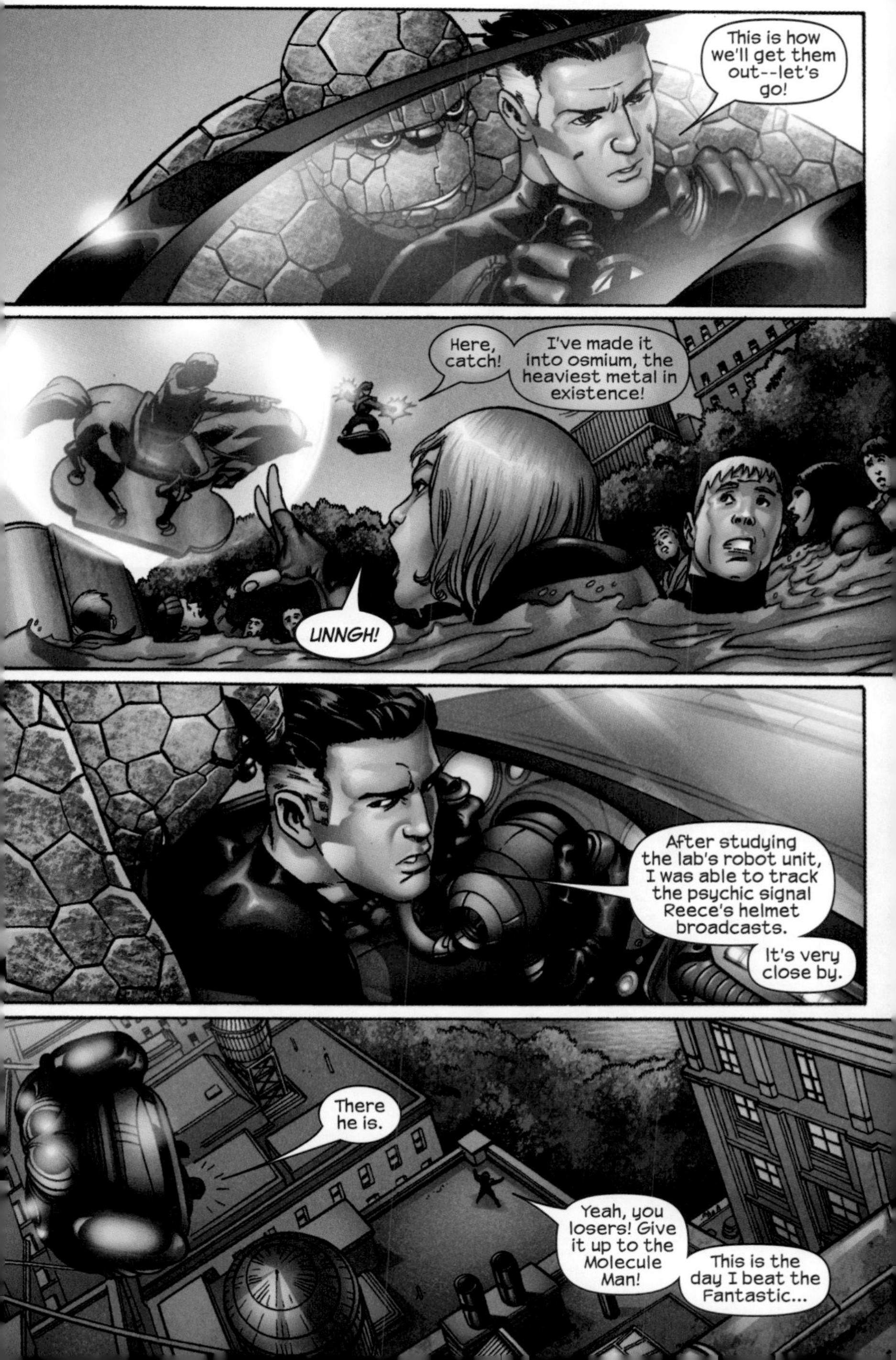
This is how we'll get them out--let's go!
Here, catch!
I've made it into osmium, the heaviest metal in existence!
UNNGH!
After studying the lab's robot unit, I was able to track the psychic signal Reece's helmet broadcasts.
It's very close by.
There he is.
Yeah, you losers! Give it up to the Molecule Man!
This is the day I beat the Fantastic...

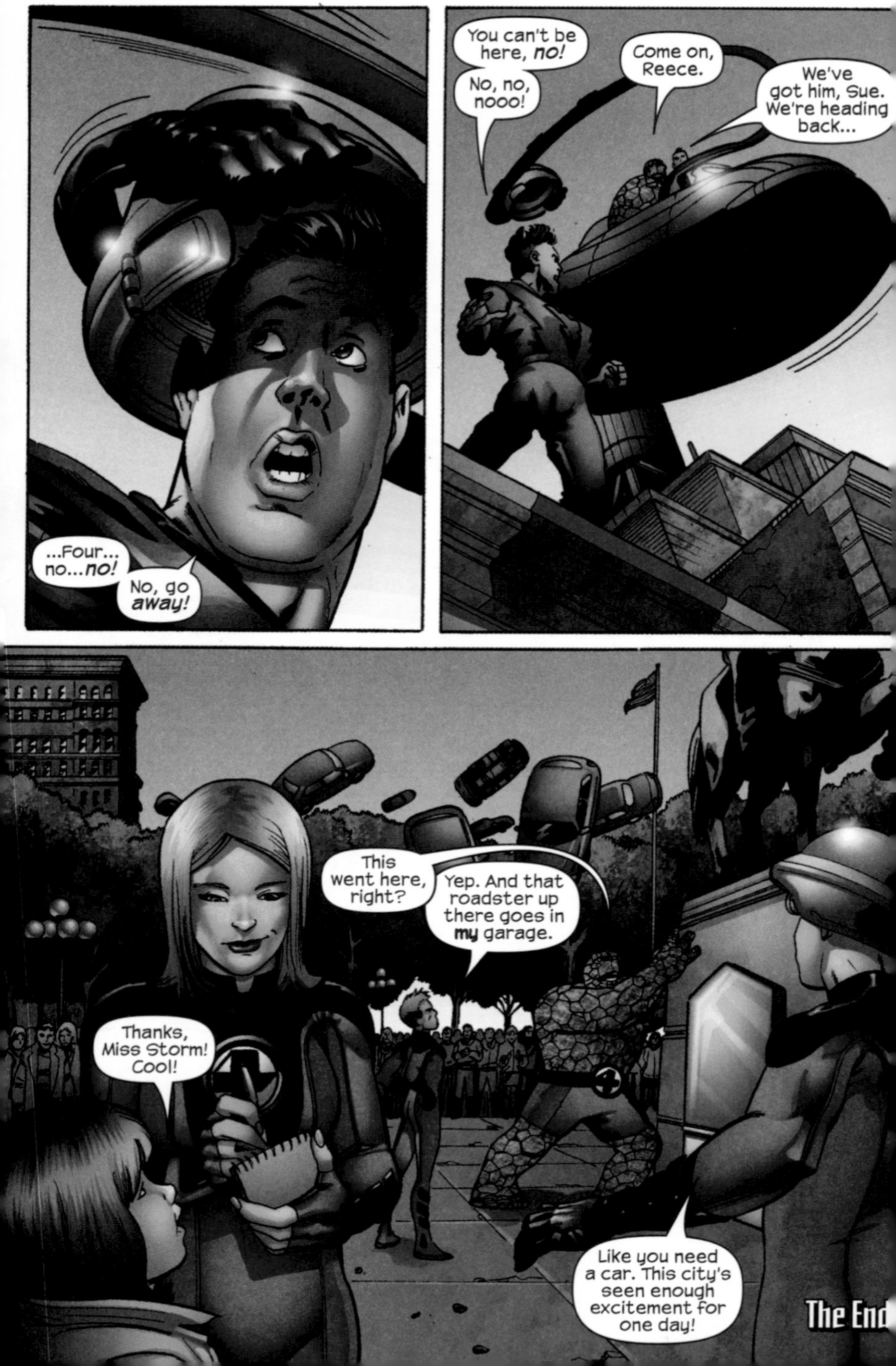

...Four... no...*no!*
No, go *away!*
You can't be here, *no!*
No, no, nooo!
Come on, Reece.
We've got him, Sue. We're heading back...
This went here, right?
Yep. And that roadster up there goes in **my** garage.
Thanks, Miss Storm! Cool!
Like you need a car. This city's seen enough excitement for one day!
The End

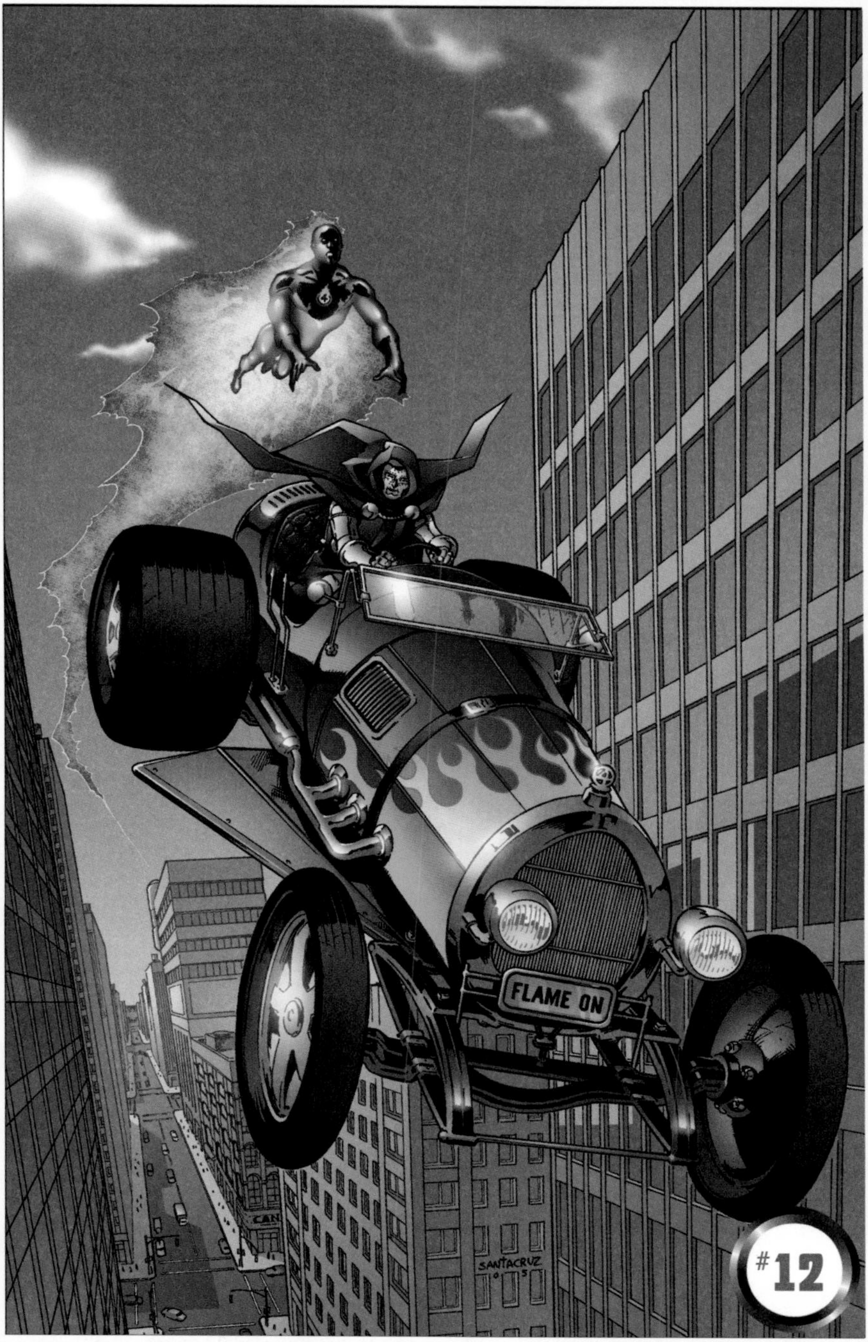
FLAME ON
SANTACRUZ
#12

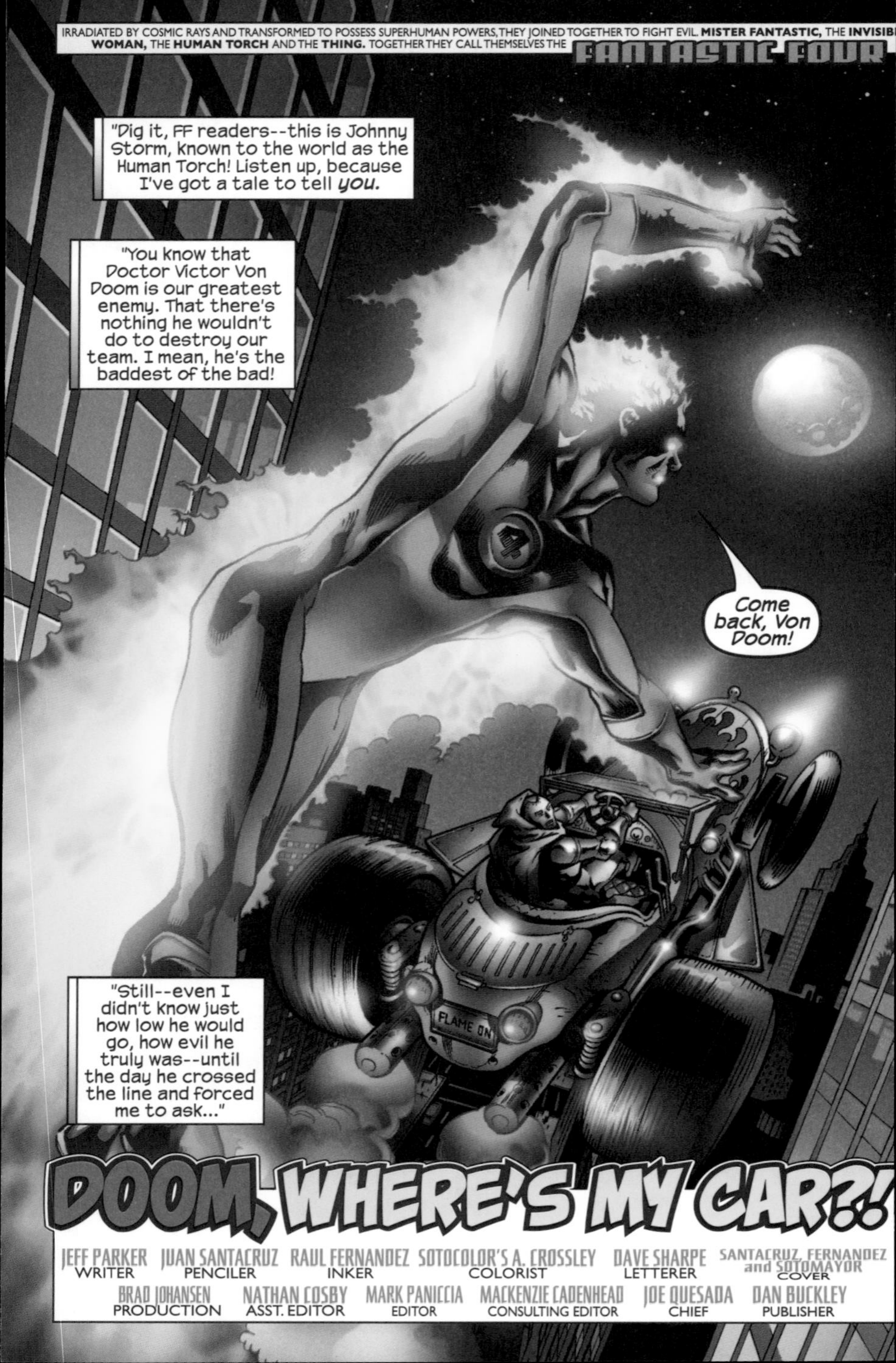

IRRADIATED BY COSMIC RAYS AND TRANSFORMED TO POSSESS SUPERHUMAN POWERS, THEY JOINED TOGETHER TO FIGHT EVIL. MISTER FANTASTIC, THE INVISIB
WOMAN, THE HUMAN TORCH AND THE THING. TOGETHER THEY CALL THEMSELVES THE
FANTASTIC FOUR
"Dig it, FF readers--this is Johnny Storm, known to the world as the Human Torch! Listen up, because I've got a tale to tell *you.*
"You know that Doctor Victor Von Doom is our greatest enemy. That there's nothing he wouldn't do to destroy our team. I mean, he's the baddest of the bad!
Come back, Von Doom!
FLAME ON
"Still--even I didn't know just how low he would go, how evil he truly was--until the day he crossed the line and forced me to ask..."
DOOM, WHERE'S MY CAR?!
JEFF PARKER WRITER
JUAN SANTACRUZ PENCILER
RAUL FERNANDEZ INKER
SOTOCOLOR'S A. CROSSLEY COLORIST
DAVE SHARPE LETTERER
SANTACRUZ, FERNANDEZ and SOTOMAYOR COVER
BRAD JOHANSEN PRODUCTION
NATHAN COSBY ASST. EDITOR
MARK PANICCIA EDITOR
MACKENZIE CADENHEAD CONSULTING EDITOR
JOE QUESADA CHIEF
DAN BUCKLEY PUBLISHER

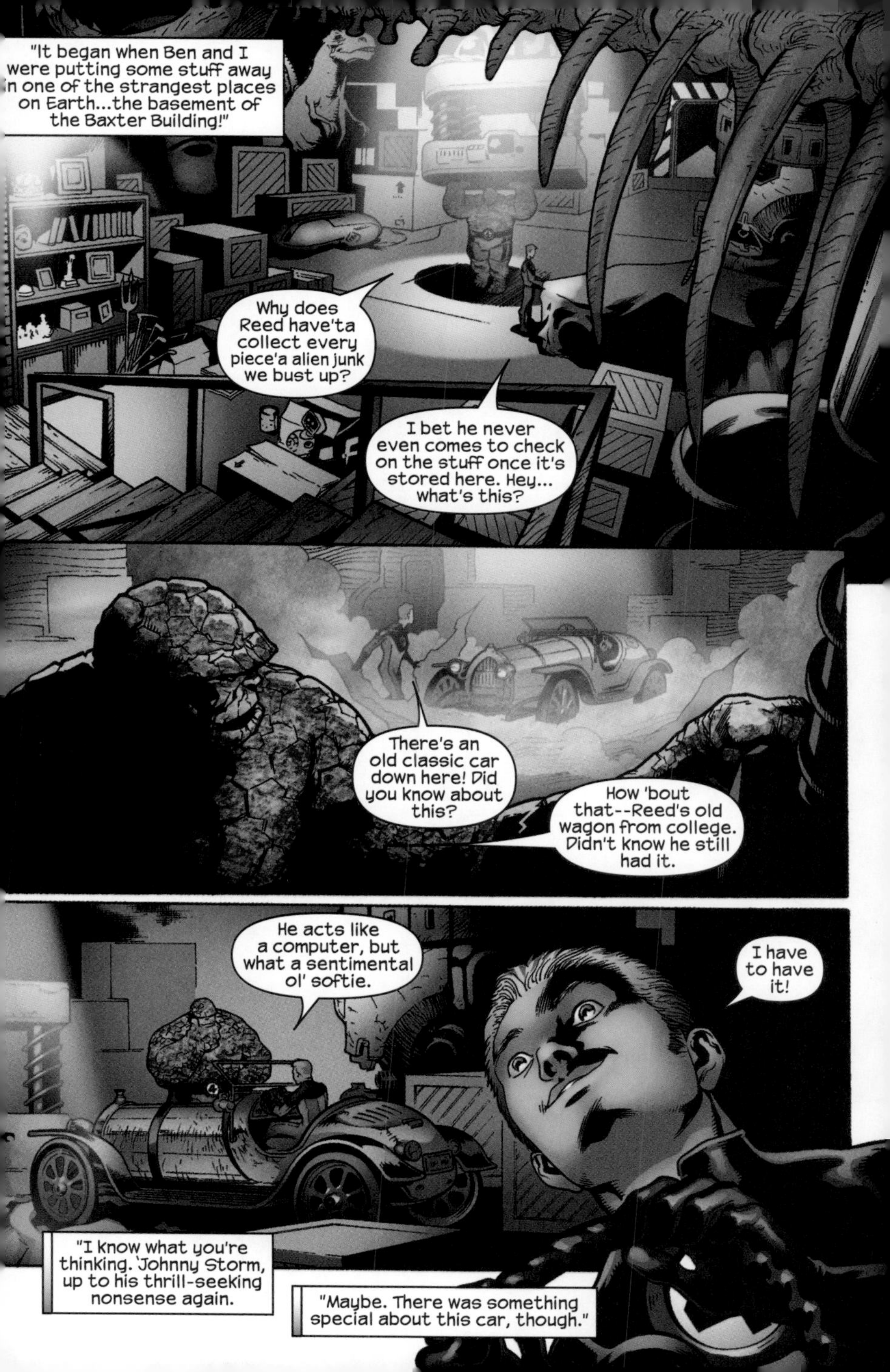
"It began when Ben and I were putting some stuff away in one of the strangest places on Earth...the basement of the Baxter Building!"
Why does Reed have'ta collect every piece'a alien junk we bust up?
I bet he never even comes to check on the stuff once it's stored here. Hey... what's this?
There's an old classic car down here! Did you know about this?
How 'bout that--Reed's old wagon from college. Didn't know he still had it.
He acts like a computer, but what a sentimental ol' softie.
I have to have it!
"I know what you're thinking. 'Johnny Storm, up to his thrill-seeking nonsense again.
"Maybe. There was something special about this car, though."

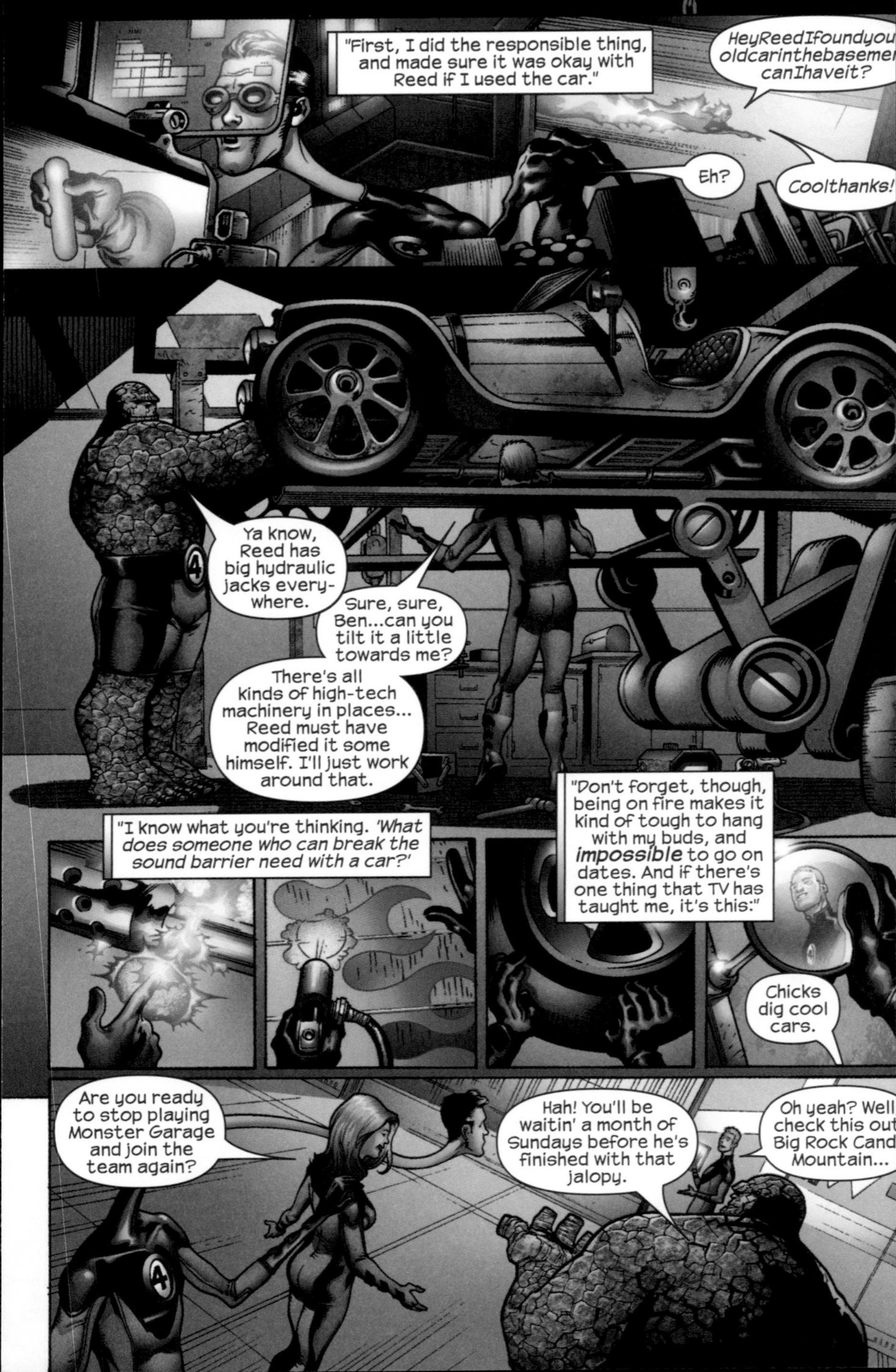
"First, I did the responsible thing, and made sure it was okay with Reed if I used the car."
HeyReedIfoundyou oldcarinthebasemen canIhaveit?
Eh?
Coolthanks!
Ya know, Reed has big hydraulic jacks every-where.
Sure, sure, Ben...can you tilt it a little towards me?
There's all kinds of high-tech machinery in places... Reed must have modified it some himself. I'll just work around that.
"I know what you're thinking. 'What does someone who can break the sound barrier need with a car?'
"Don't forget, though, being on fire makes it kind of tough to hang with my buds, and impossible to go on dates. And if there's one thing that TV has taught me, it's this:"
Chicks dig cool cars.
Are you ready to stop playing Monster Garage and join the team again?
Hah! You'll be waitin' a month of Sundays before he's finished with that jalopy.
Oh yeah? Well check this out Big Rock Cand Mountain...

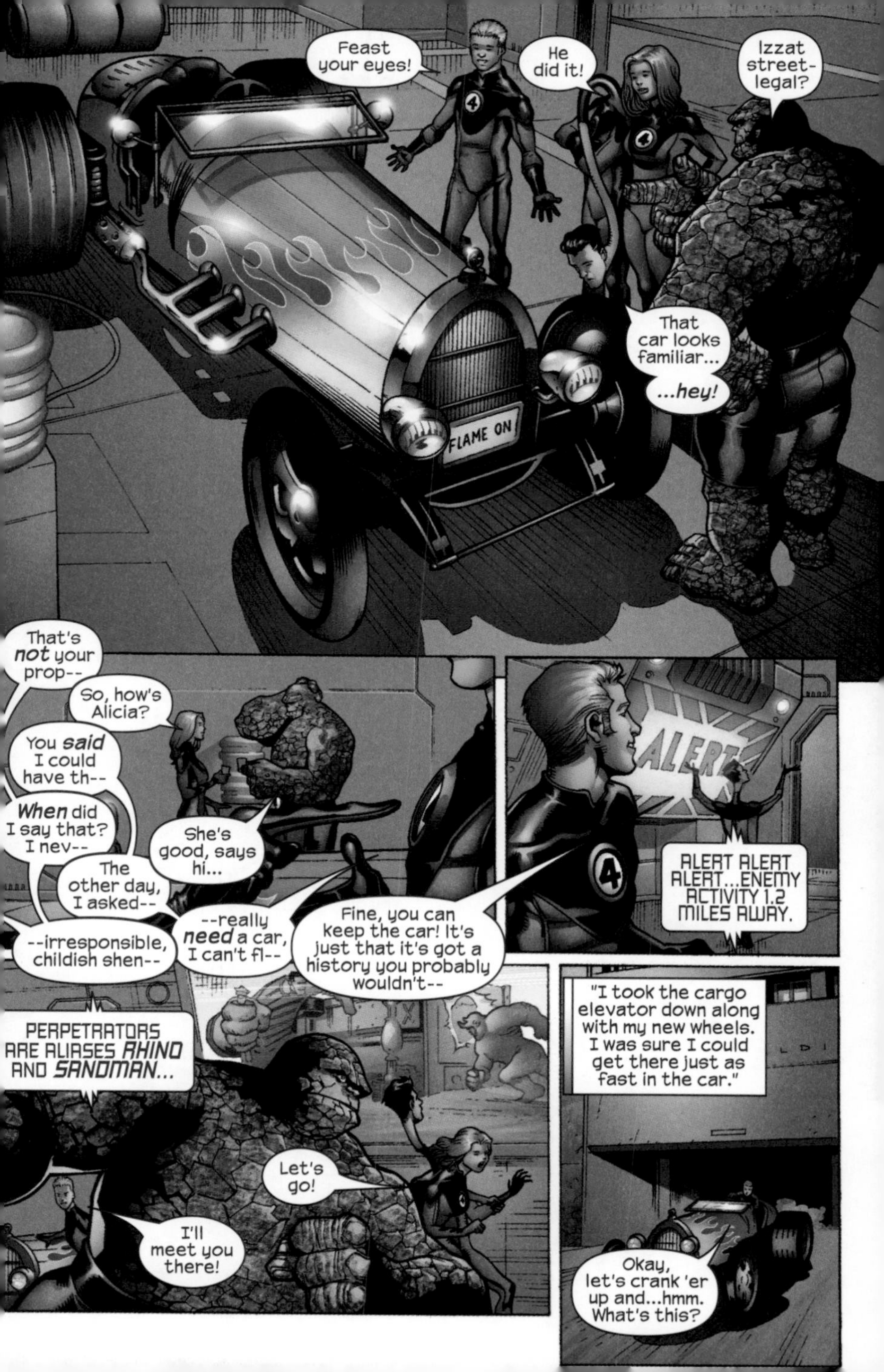

Feast your eyes!
He did it!
Izzat street-legal?
That car looks familiar...
...hey!
FLAME ON
That's not your prop--
So, how's Alicia?
You said I could have th--
When did I say that? I nev--
She's good, says hi...
The other day, I asked--
--irresponsible, childish shen--
--really need a car, I can't fl--
Fine, you can keep the car! It's just that it's got a history you probably wouldn't--
ALERT
ALERT ALERT ALERT...ENEMY ACTIVITY 1.2 MILES AWAY.
PERPETRATORS ARE ALIASES RHINO AND SANDMAN...
Let's go!
I'll meet you there!
"I took the cargo elevator down along with my new wheels. I was sure I could get there just as fast in the car."
Okay, let's crank 'er up and...hmm. What's this?

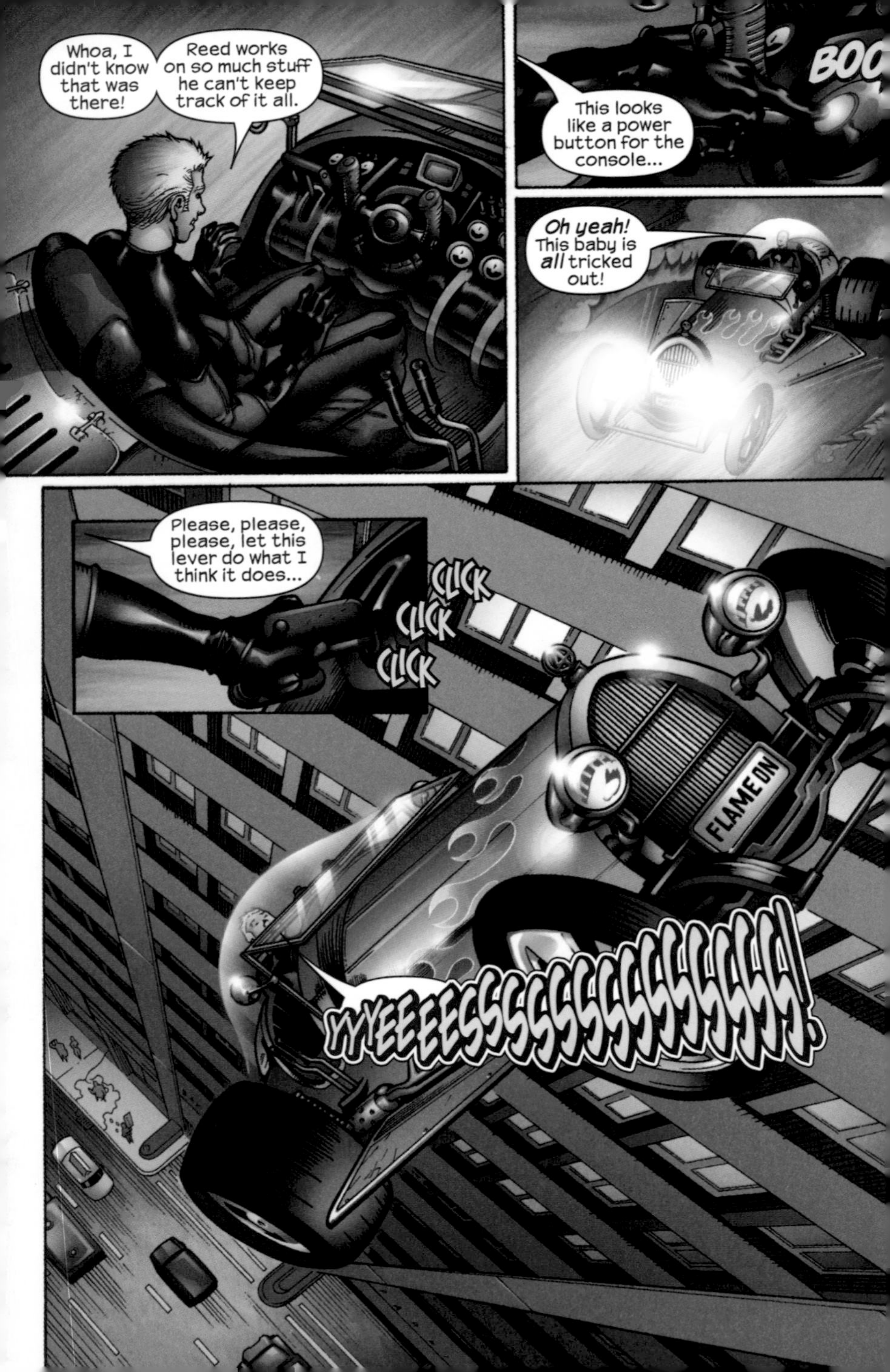

Whoa, I didn't know that was there!
Reed works on so much stuff he can't keep track of it all.
This looks like a power button for the console...
BOO
Oh yeah! This baby is all tricked out!
Please, please, please, let this lever do what I think it does...
CLICK
CLICK
CLICK
FLAME ON
YYYEEEESSSSSSSSSSSSSSSSS!

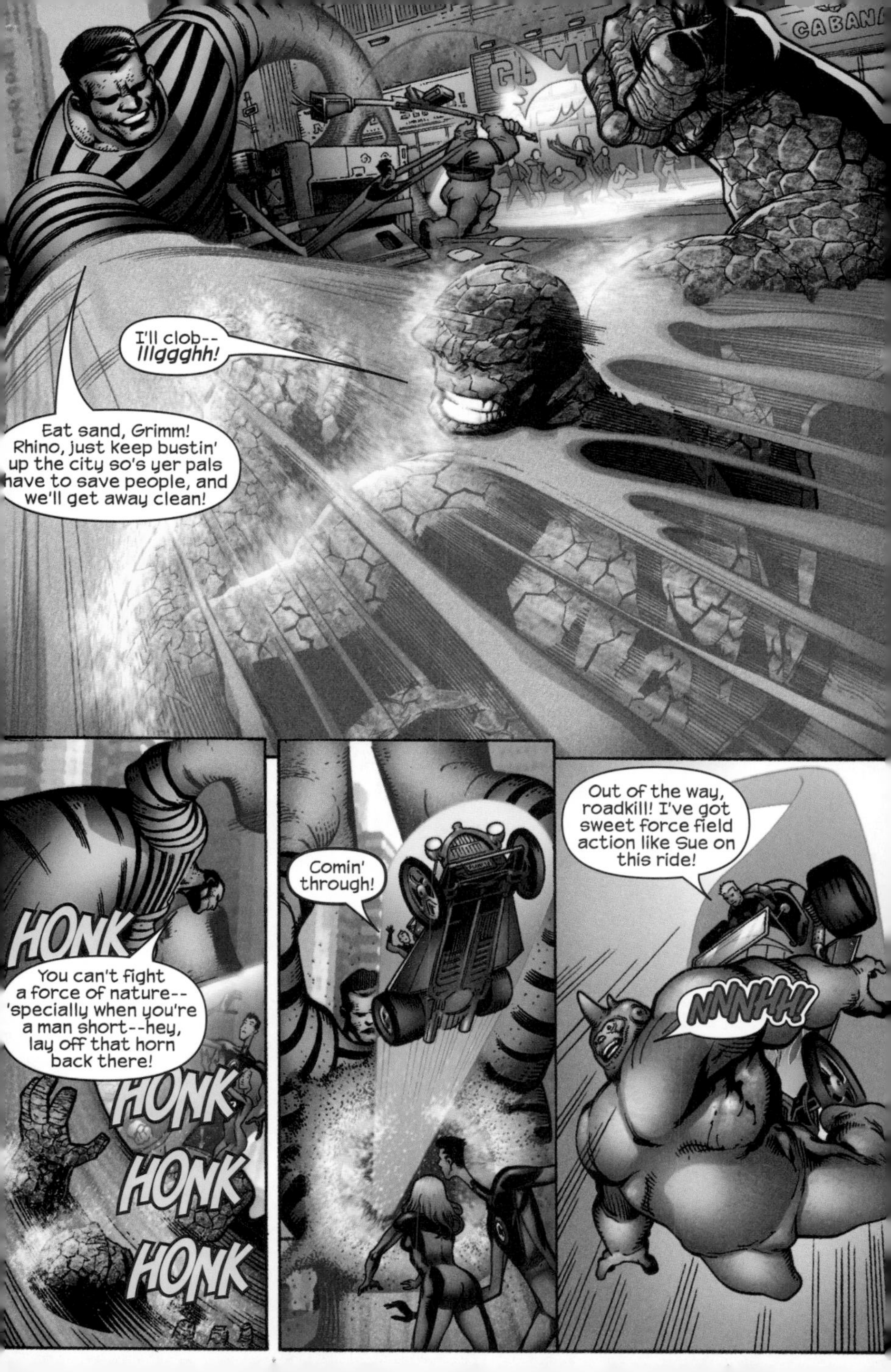
CABANA
I'll clob-- lllggghh!
Eat sand, Grimm! Rhino, just keep bustin' up the city so's yer pals have to save people, and we'll get away clean!
HONK
You can't fight a force of nature--'specially when you're a man short--hey, lay off that horn back there!
HONK
HONK
HONK
Comin' through!
Out of the way, roadkill! I've got sweet force field action like Sue on this ride!
NNNHH!

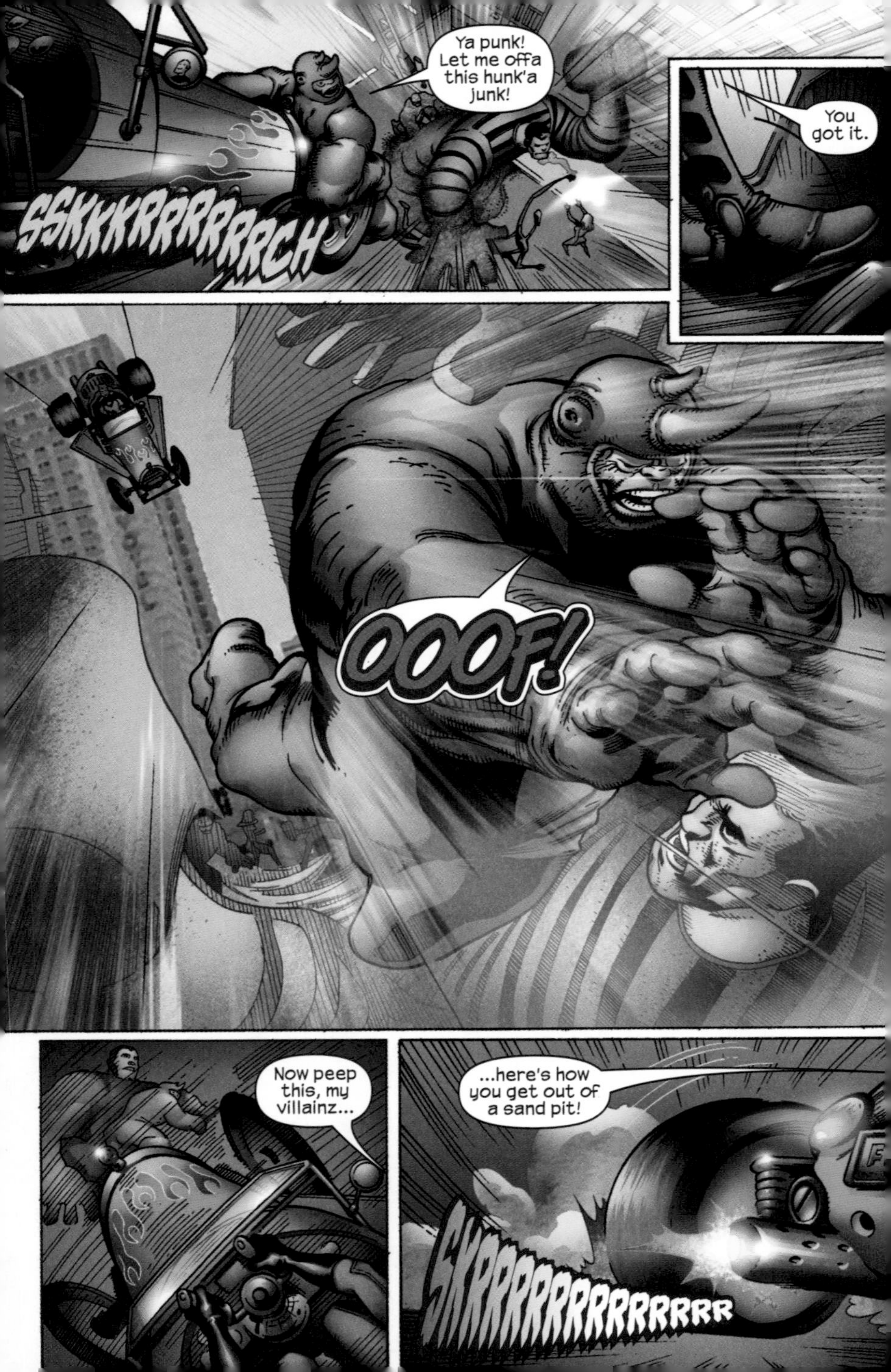

Ya punk! Let me offa this hunk'a junk!
SSKKKRRRRRRRCH
You got it.
OOOF!
Now peep this, my villainz...
...here's how you get out of a sand pit!
SKRRRRRRRRRRRRRR

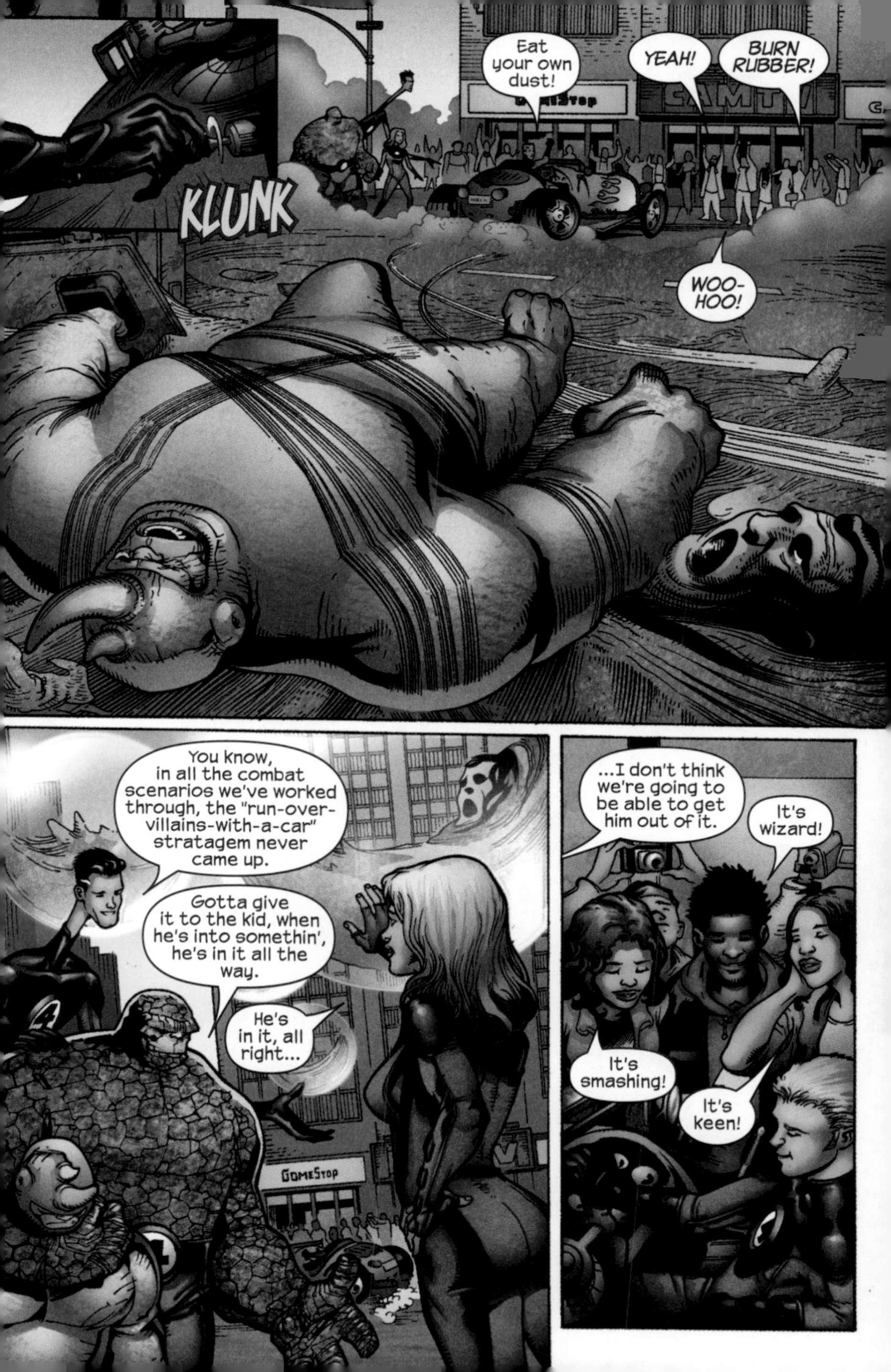
KLUNK
Eat your own dust!
YEAH!
BURN RUBBER!
WOO-HOO!
You know, in all the combat scenarios we've worked through, the "run-over-villains-with-a-car" stratagem never came up.
Gotta give it to the kid, when he's into somethin', he's in it all the way.
He's in it, all right...
...I don't think we're going to be able to get him out of it.
It's wizard!
It's smashing!
It's keen!

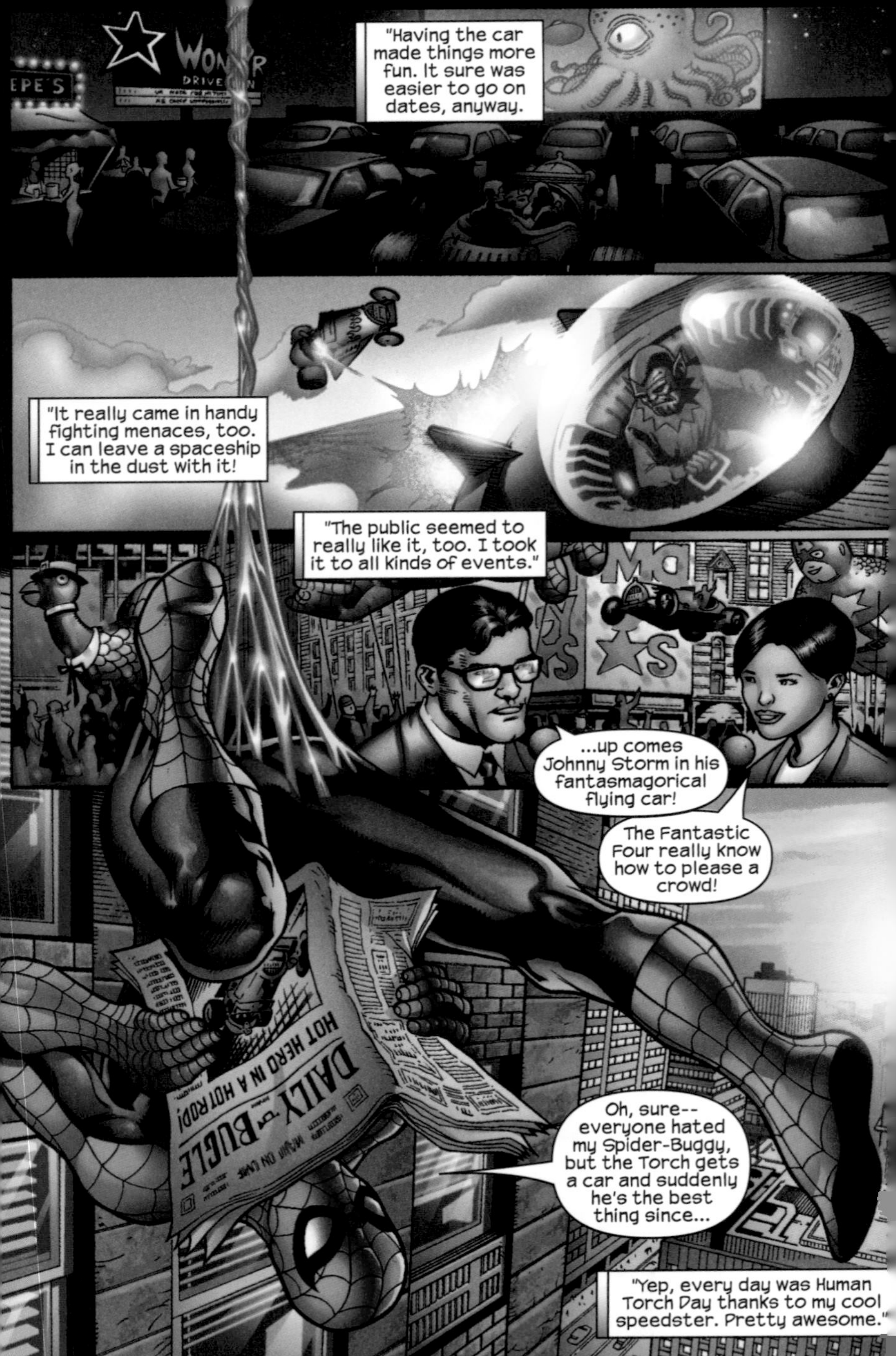
"Having the car made things more fun. It sure was easier to go on dates, anyway.
"It really came in handy fighting menaces, too. I can leave a spaceship in the dust with it!
"The public seemed to really like it, too. I took it to all kinds of events."
...up comes Johnny Storm in his fantasmagorical flying car!
The Fantastic Four really know how to please a crowd!
DAILY BUGLE
HOT HERO IN A HOTROD!
Oh, sure-- everyone hated my Spider-Buggy, but the Torch gets a car and suddenly he's the best thing since...
"Yep, every day was Human Torch Day thanks to my cool speedster. Pretty awesome."

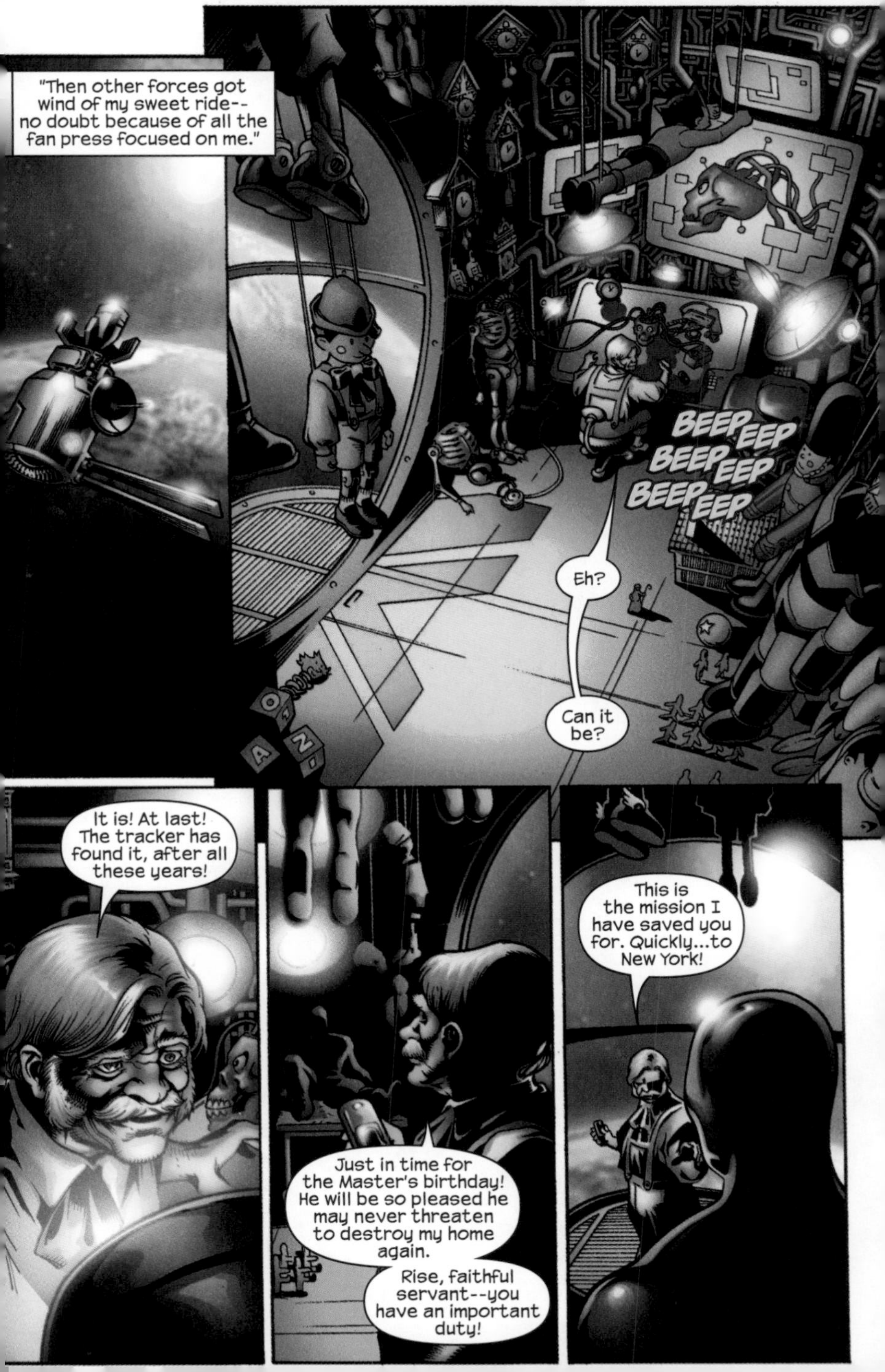
"Then other forces got wind of my sweet ride--no doubt because of all the fan press focused on me."
BEEP EEP
BEEP EEP
BEEP EEP
Eh?
Can it be?
It is! At last! The tracker has found it, after all these years!
Just in time for the Master's birthday! He will be so pleased he may never threaten to destroy my home again.
Rise, faithful servant--you have an important duty!
This is the mission I have saved you for. Quickly...to New York!

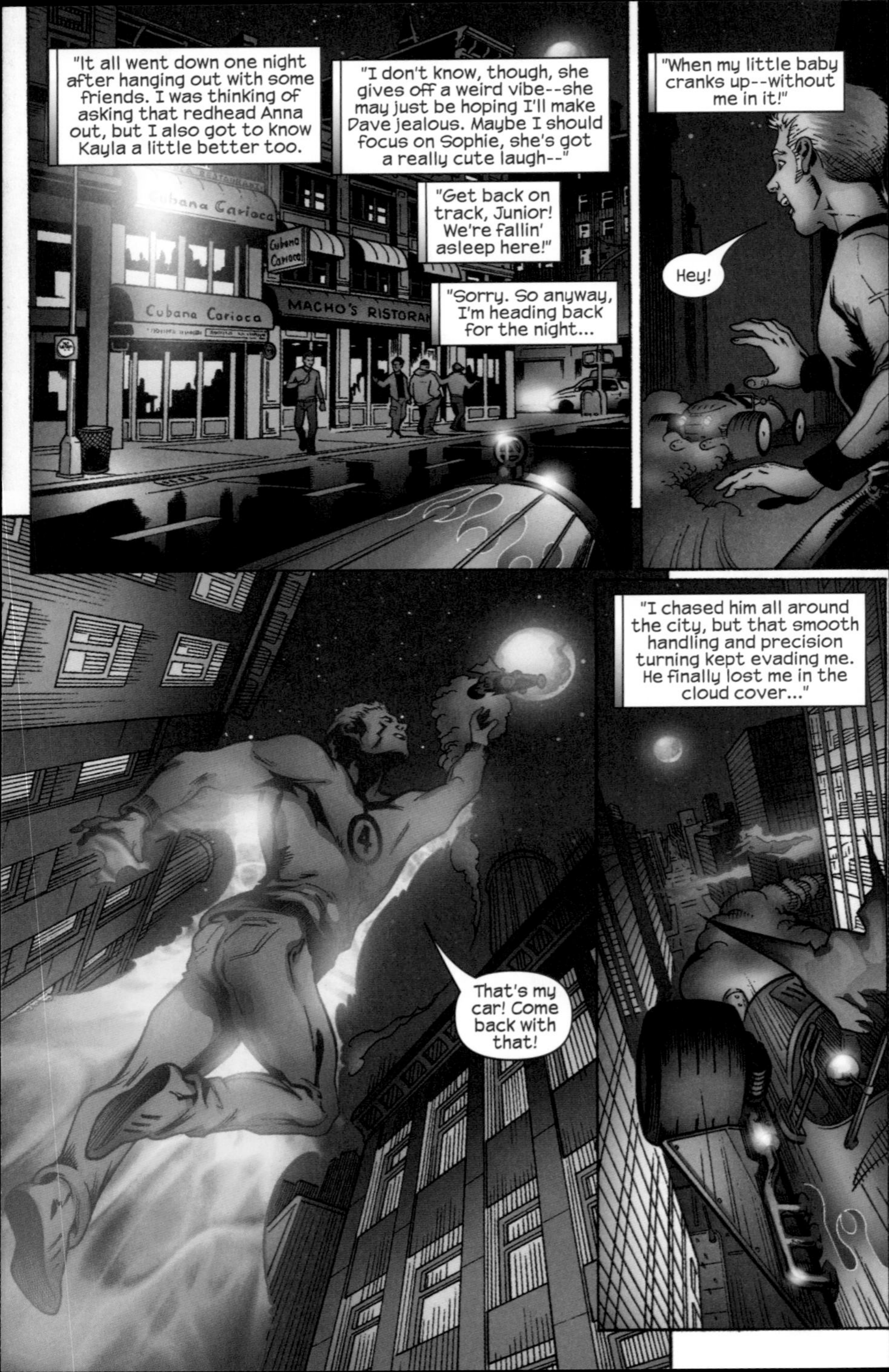
"It all went down one night after hanging out with some friends. I was thinking of asking that redhead Anna out, but I also got to know Kayla a little better too.
"I don't know, though, she gives off a weird vibe--she may just be hoping I'll make Dave jealous. Maybe I should focus on Sophie, she's got a really cute laugh--"
"Get back on track, Junior! We're fallin' asleep here!"
"Sorry. So anyway, I'm heading back for the night...
Cubana Carioca
Cubana Carioca
Cubana Carioca
MACHO'S RISTORAN
"When my little baby cranks up--without me in it!"
Hey!
That's my car! Come back with that!
"I chased him all around the city, but that smooth handling and precision turning kept evading me. He finally lost me in the cloud cover..."

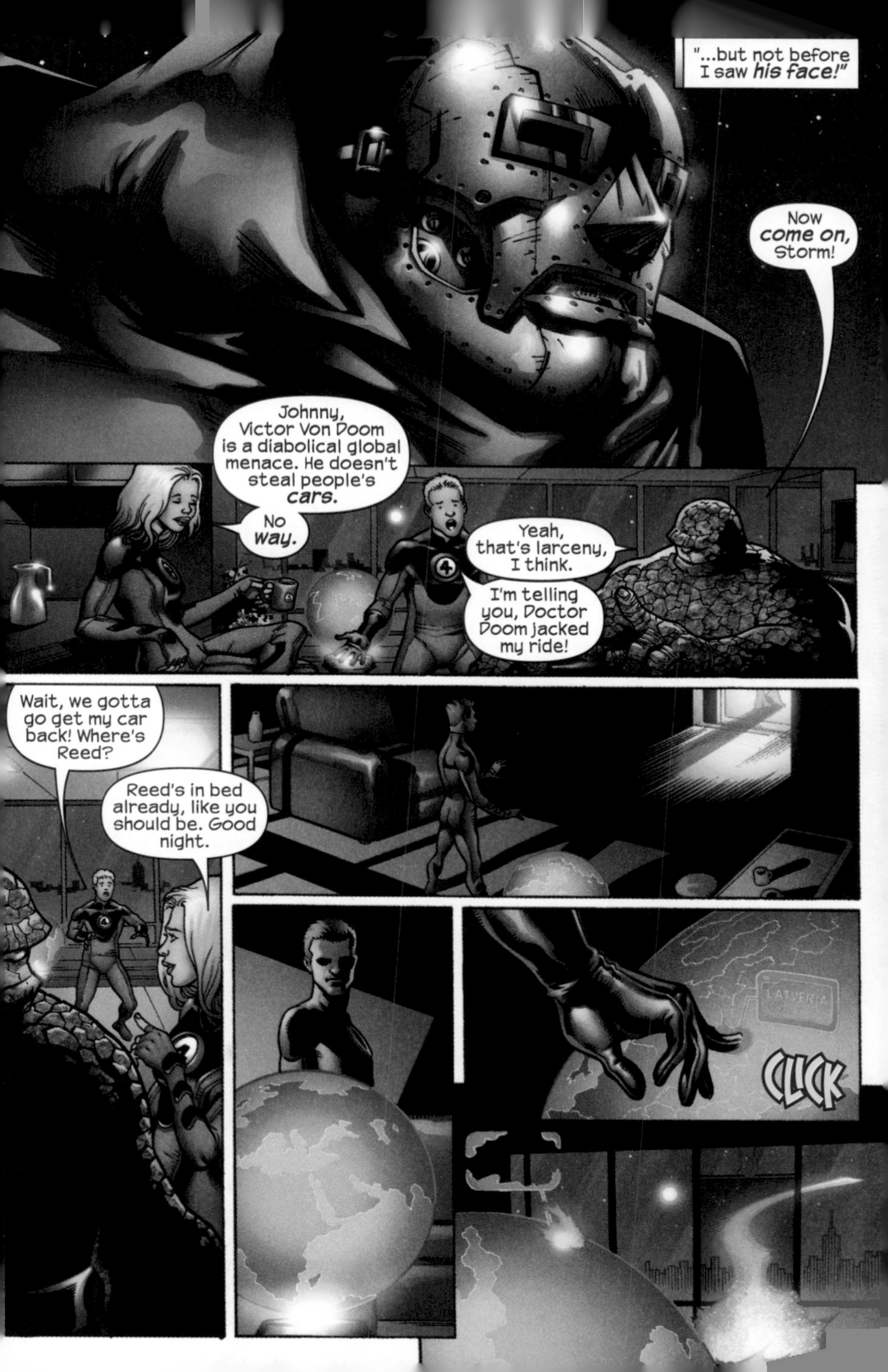
"...but not before I saw his face!"
Now come on, Storm!
Johnny, Victor Von Doom is a diabolical global menace. He doesn't steal people's cars.
No way.
Yeah, that's larceny, I think.
I'm telling you, Doctor Doom jacked my ride!
Wait, we gotta go get my car back! Where's Reed?
Reed's in bed already, like you should be. Good night.
LATVERIA
CLICK

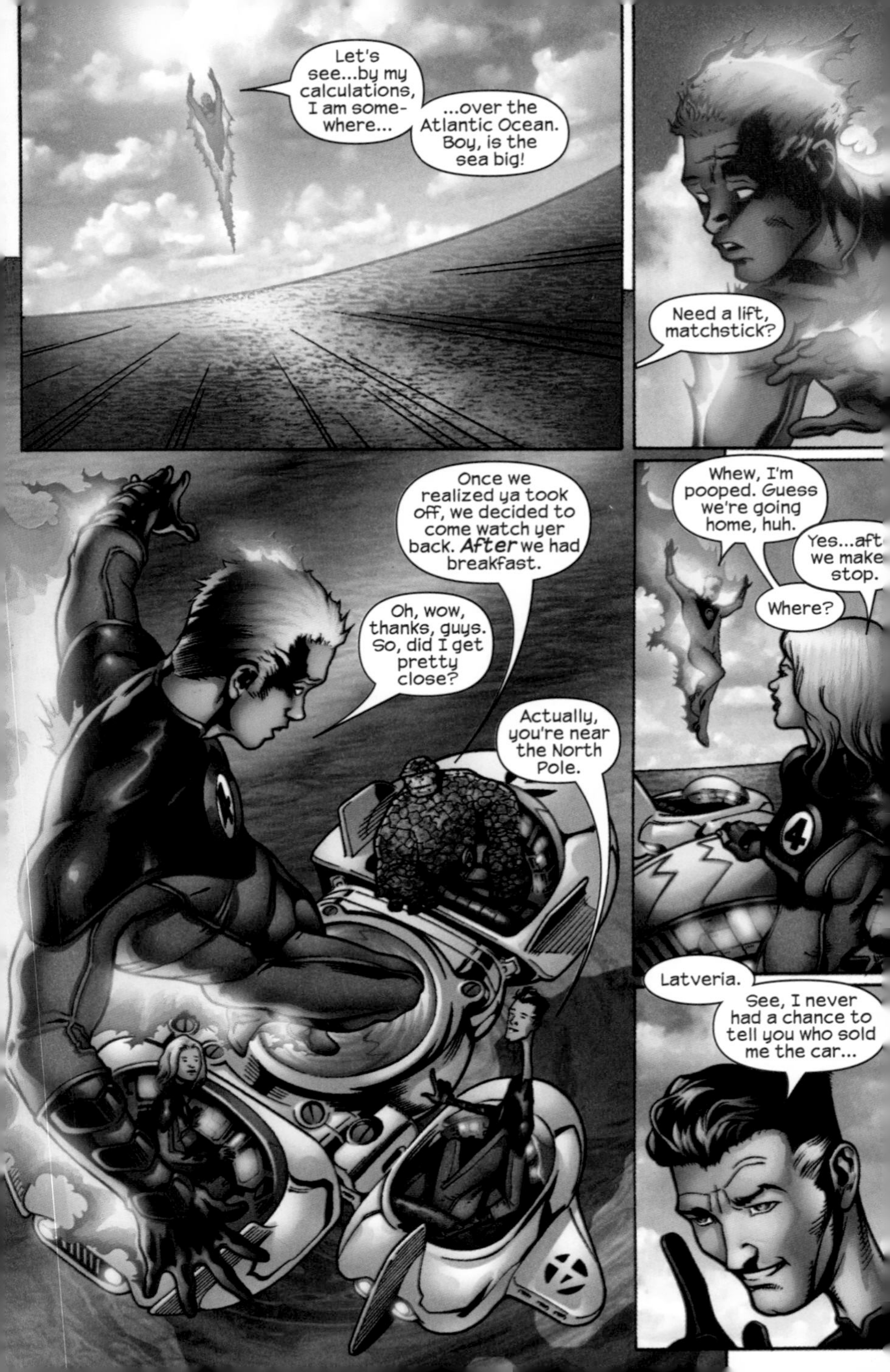
Let's see...by my calculations, I am some-where...
...over the Atlantic Ocean. Boy, is the sea big!
Need a lift, matchstick?
Once we realized ya took off, we decided to come watch yer back. *After* we had breakfast.
Oh, wow, thanks, guys. So, did I get pretty close?
Actually, you're near the North Pole.
Whew, I'm pooped. Guess we're going home, huh.
Yes...aft we make stop.
Where?
Latveria.
See, I never had a chance to tell you who sold me the car...

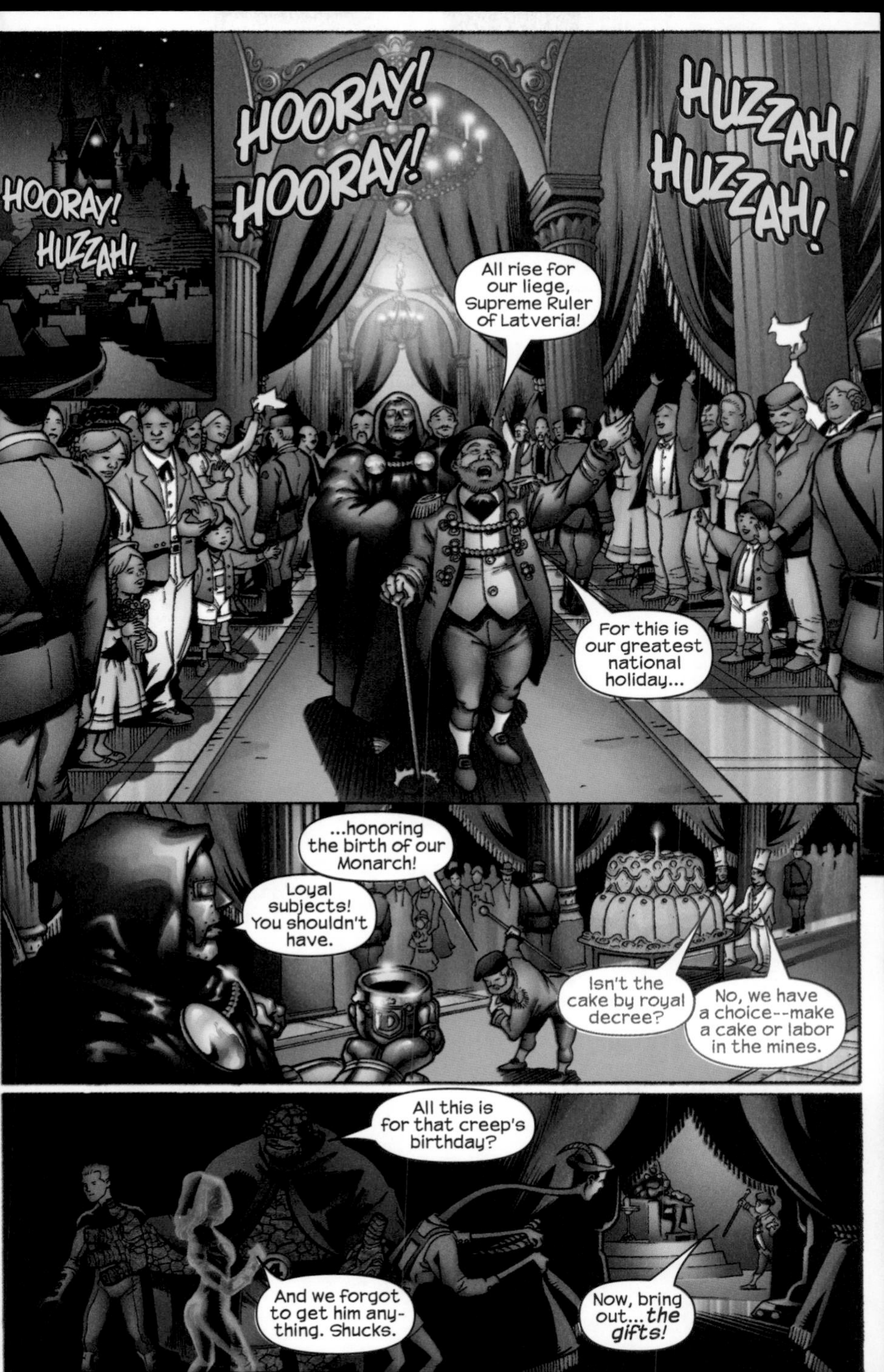
HOORAY! HUZZAH!
HOORAY! HOORAY!
HUZZAH! HUZZAH!
All rise for our liege, Supreme Ruler of Latveria!
For this is our greatest national holiday...
...honoring the birth of our Monarch!
Loyal subjects! You shouldn't have.
Isn't the cake by royal decree?
No, we have a choice--make a cake or labor in the mines.
All this is for that creep's birthday?
And we forgot to get him any-thing. Shucks.
Now, bring out... *the gifts!*

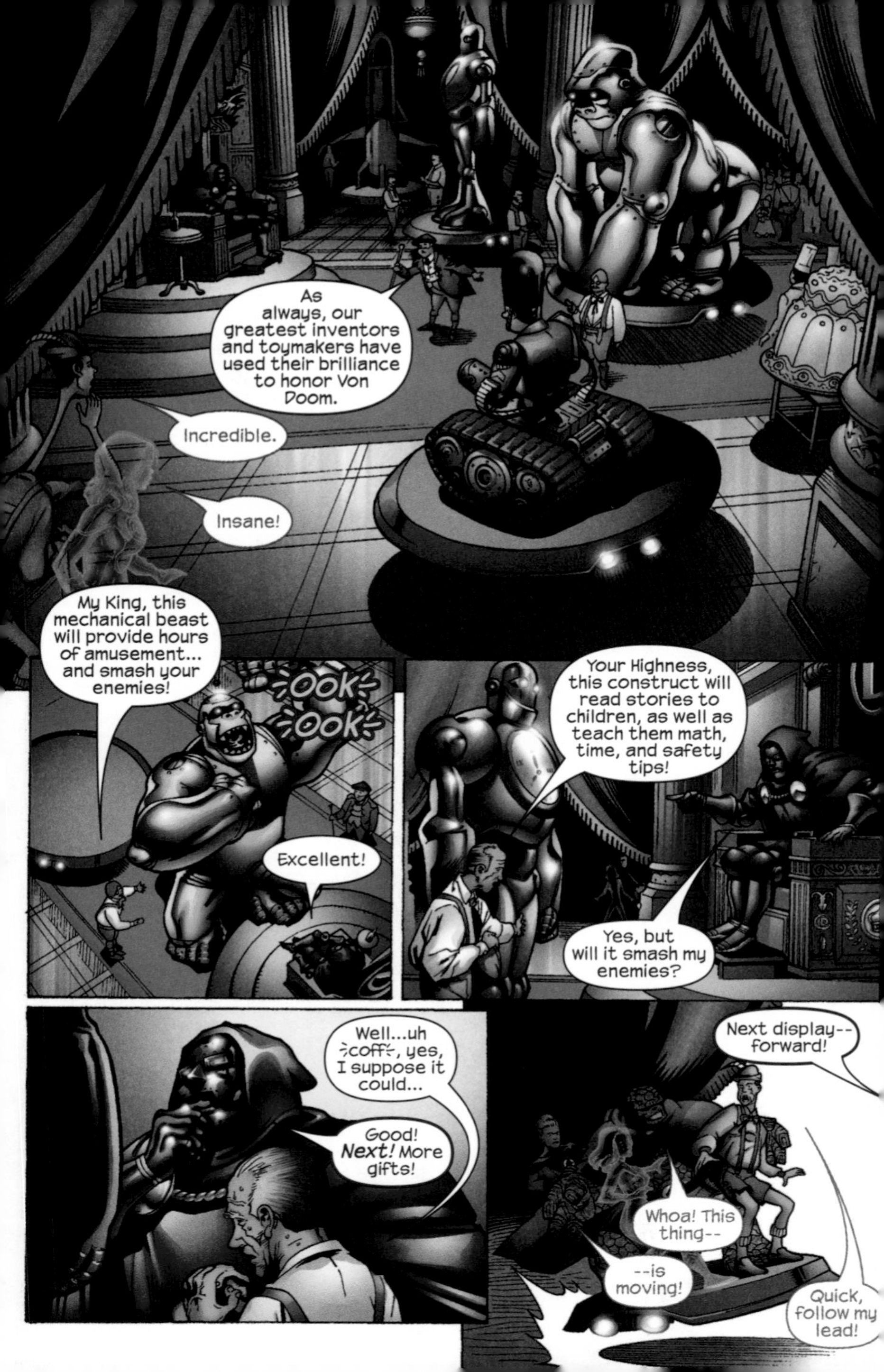
As always, our greatest inventors and toymakers have used their brilliance to honor Von Doom.
Incredible.
Insane!
My King, this mechanical beast will provide hours of amusement... and smash your enemies!
OOK OOK
Excellent!
Your Highness, this construct will read stories to children, as well as teach them math, time, and safety tips!
Yes, but will it smash my enemies?
Well...uh *coff*, yes, I suppose it could...
Good! *Next!* More gifts!
Next display--forward!
Whoa! This thing--
--is moving!
Quick, follow my lead!

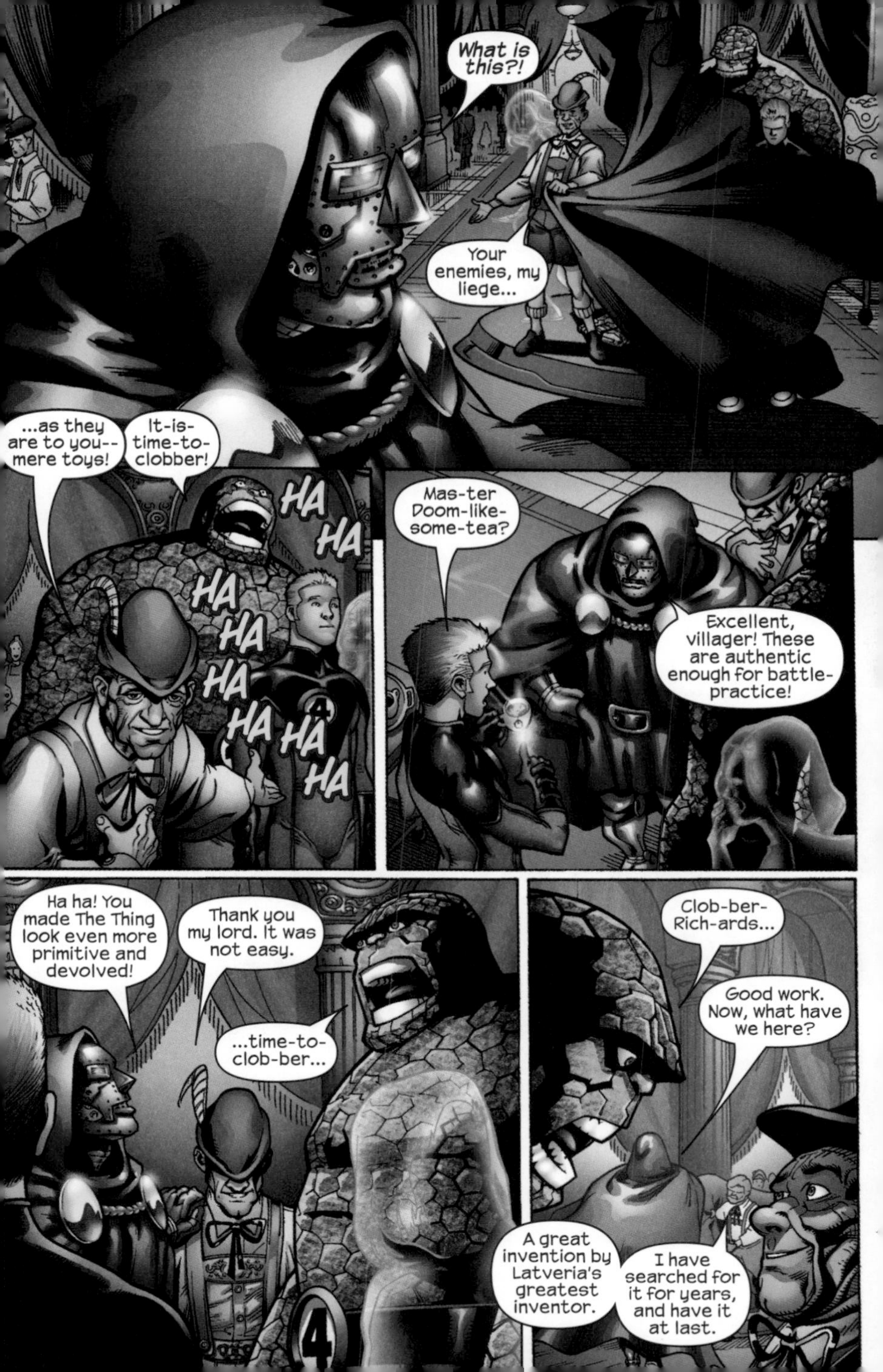
What is this?!
Your enemies, my liege...
...as they are to you-- mere toys!
It-is-time-to-clobber!
HA HA HA HA HA HA HA HA HA
Mas-ter Doom-like-some-tea?
Excellent, villager! These are authentic enough for battle-practice!
Ha ha! You made The Thing look even more primitive and devolved!
Thank you my lord. It was not easy.
...time-to-clob-ber...
Clob-ber-Rich-ards...
Good work. Now, what have we here?
A great invention by Latveria's greatest inventor.
I have searched for it for years, and have it at last.

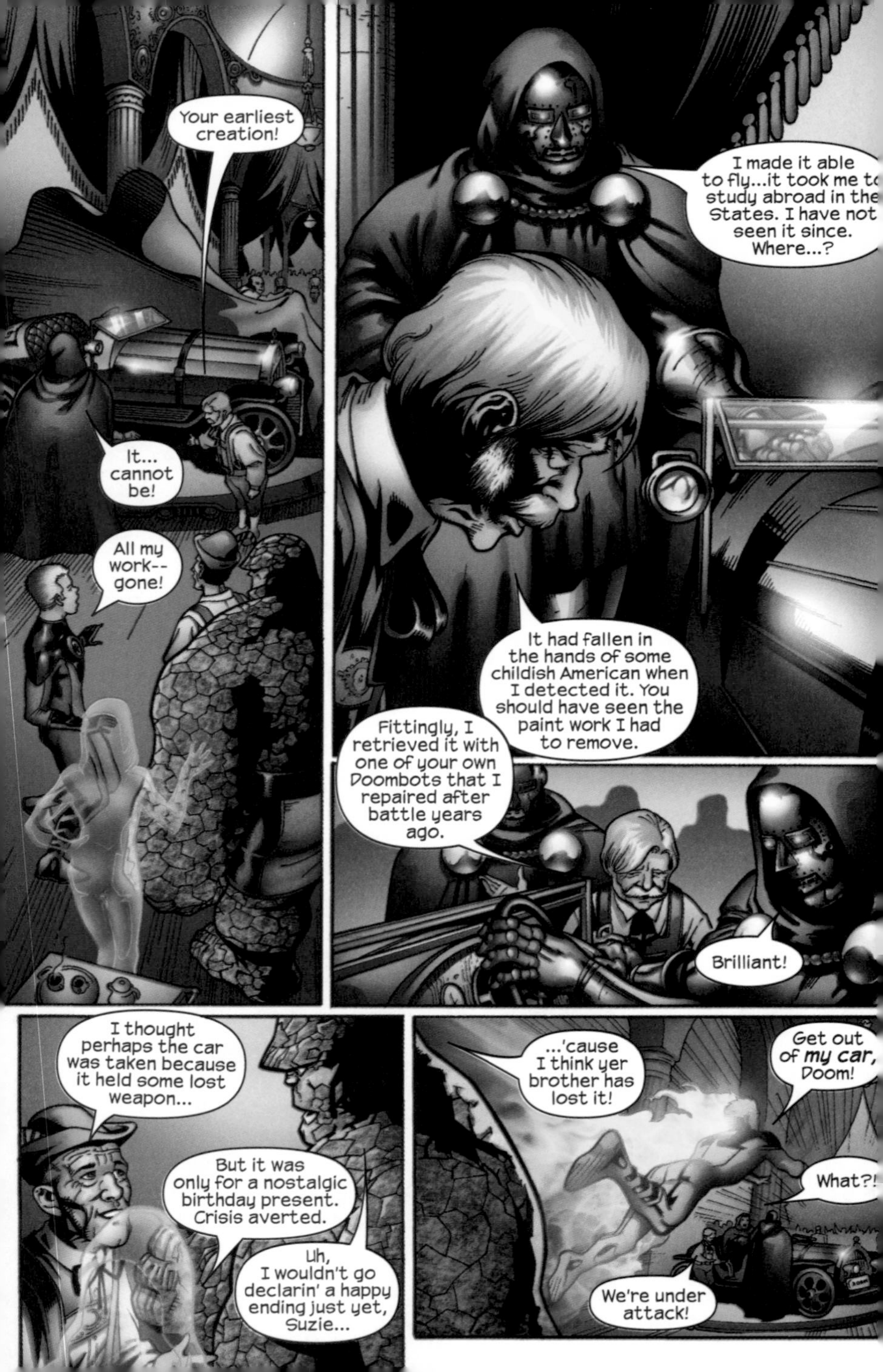

Your earliest creation!
It... cannot be!
All my work-- gone!
I made it able to fly...it took me to study abroad in the States. I have not seen it since. Where...?
It had fallen in the hands of some childish American when I detected it. You should have seen the paint work I had to remove.
Fittingly, I retrieved it with one of your own Doombots that I repaired after battle years ago.
Brilliant!
I thought perhaps the car was taken because it held some lost weapon...
But it was only for a nostalgic birthday present. Crisis averted.
Uh, I wouldn't go declarin' a happy ending just yet, Suzie...
...'cause I think yer brother has lost it!
Get out of *my car,* Doom!
What?!
We're under attack!

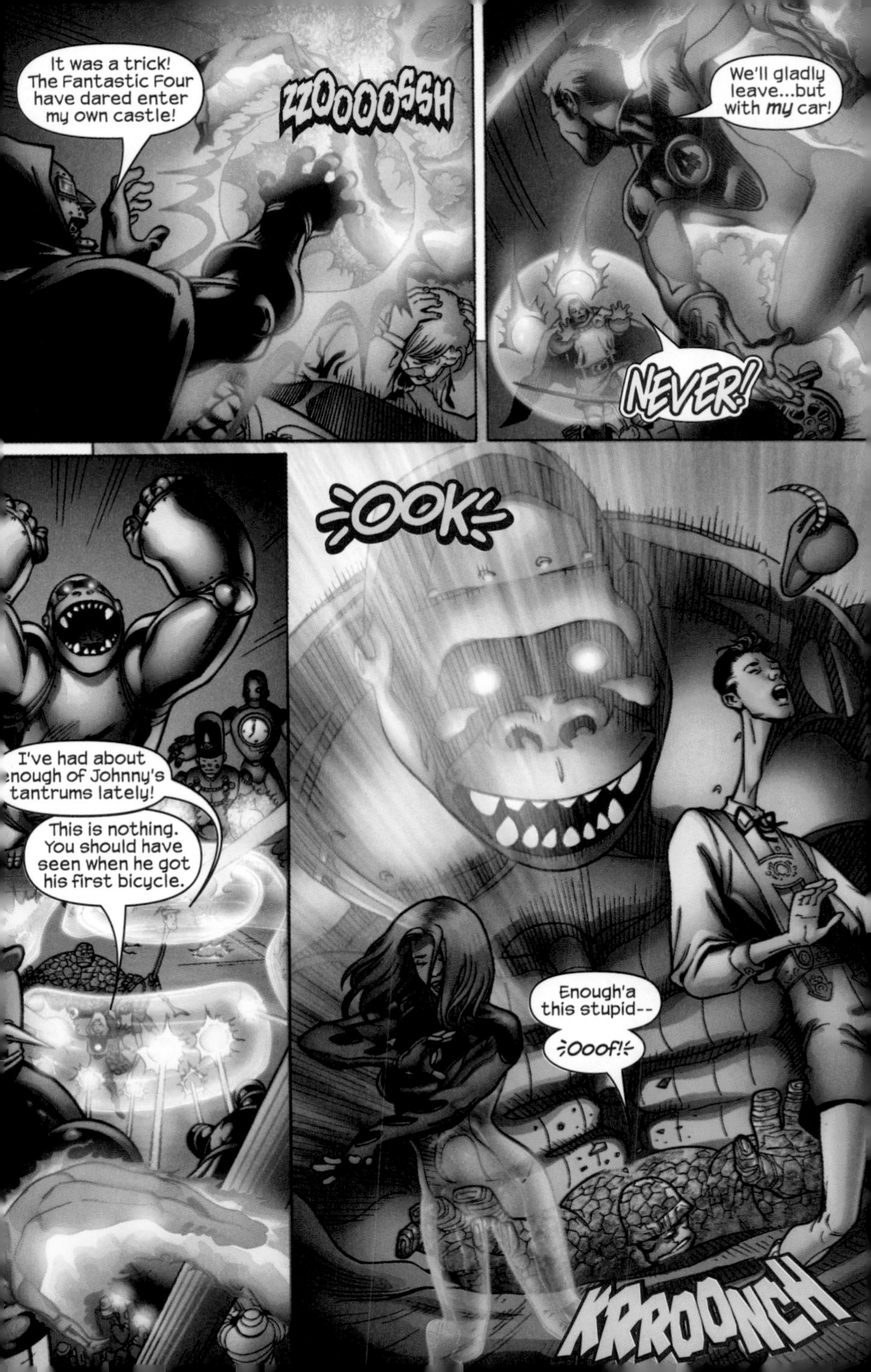

It was a trick! The Fantastic Four have dared enter my own castle!
ZZOOOOOSSH
We'll gladly leave...but with *my* car!
NEVER!
I've had about enough of Johnny's tantrums lately!
This is nothing. You should have seen when he got his first bicycle.
OOK
Enough'a this stupid--
Ooof!
KRROONCH

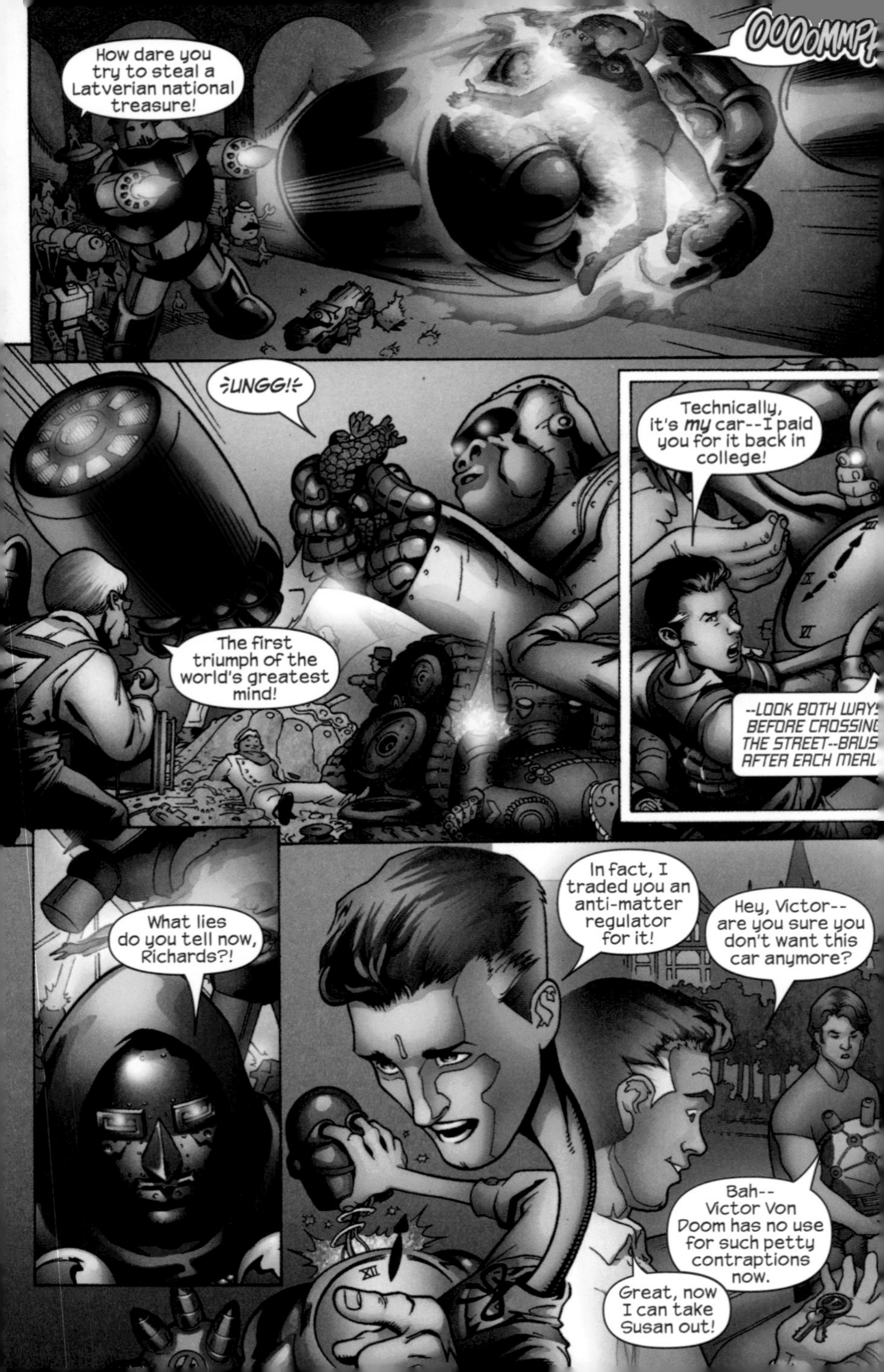
How dare you try to steal a Latverian national treasure!
OOOoMMPH
UNGG!
The first triumph of the world's greatest mind!
Technically, it's *my* car--I paid you for it back in college!
--LOOK BOTH WAYS BEFORE CROSSING THE STREET--BRUS AFTER EACH MEAL
What lies do you tell now, Richards?!
In fact, I traded you an anti-matter regulator for it!
Hey, Victor-- are you sure you don't want this car anymore?
Bah-- Victor Von Doom has no use for such petty contraptions now.
Great, now I can take Susan out!

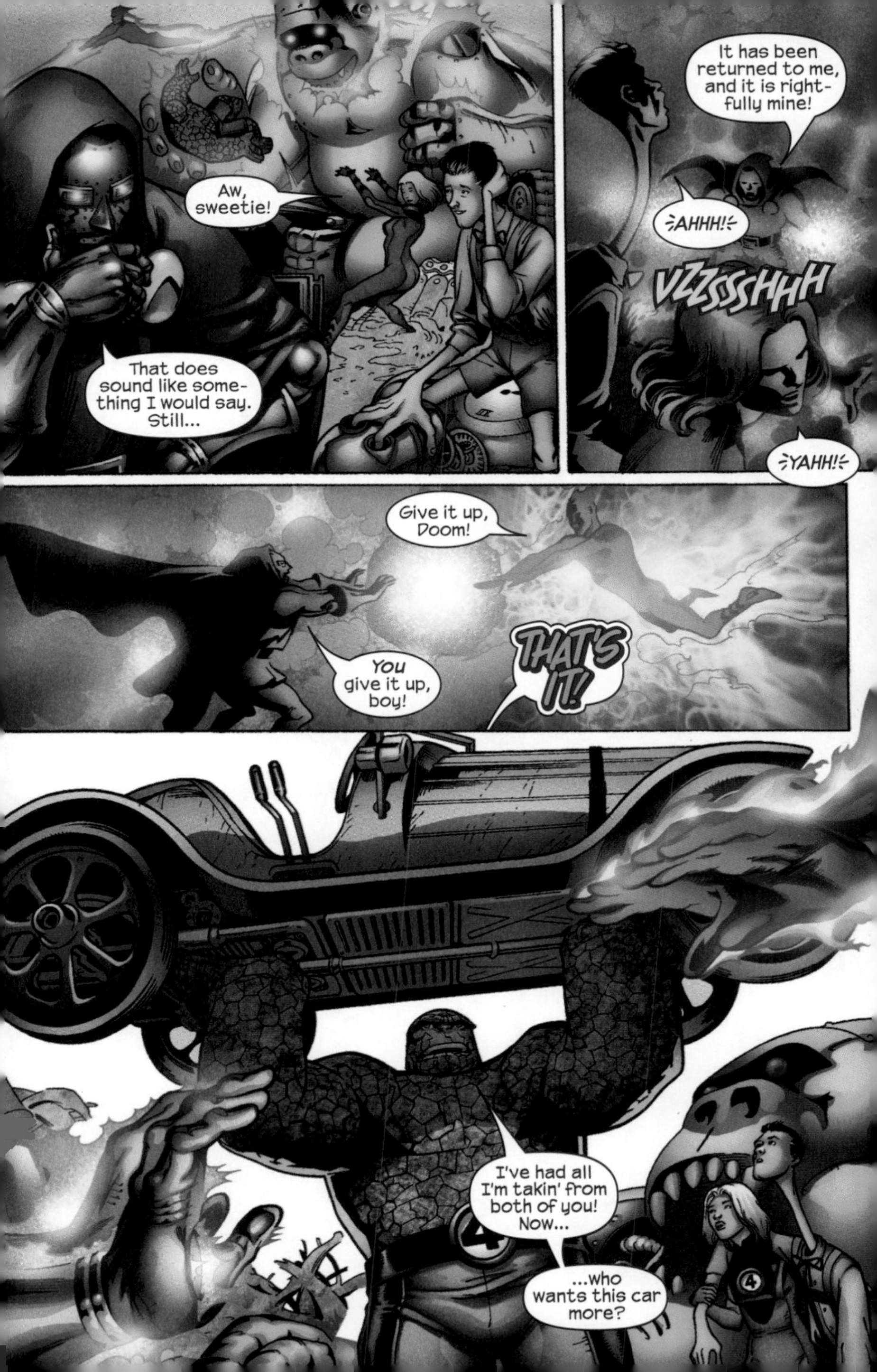
Aw, sweetie!
That does sound like something I would say. Still...
It has been returned to me, and it is rightfully mine!
AHHH!
VZZSSSHHH
YAHH!
Give it up, Doom!
You give it up, boy!
THAT'S IT!
I've had all I'm takin' from both of you! Now...
...who wants this car more?

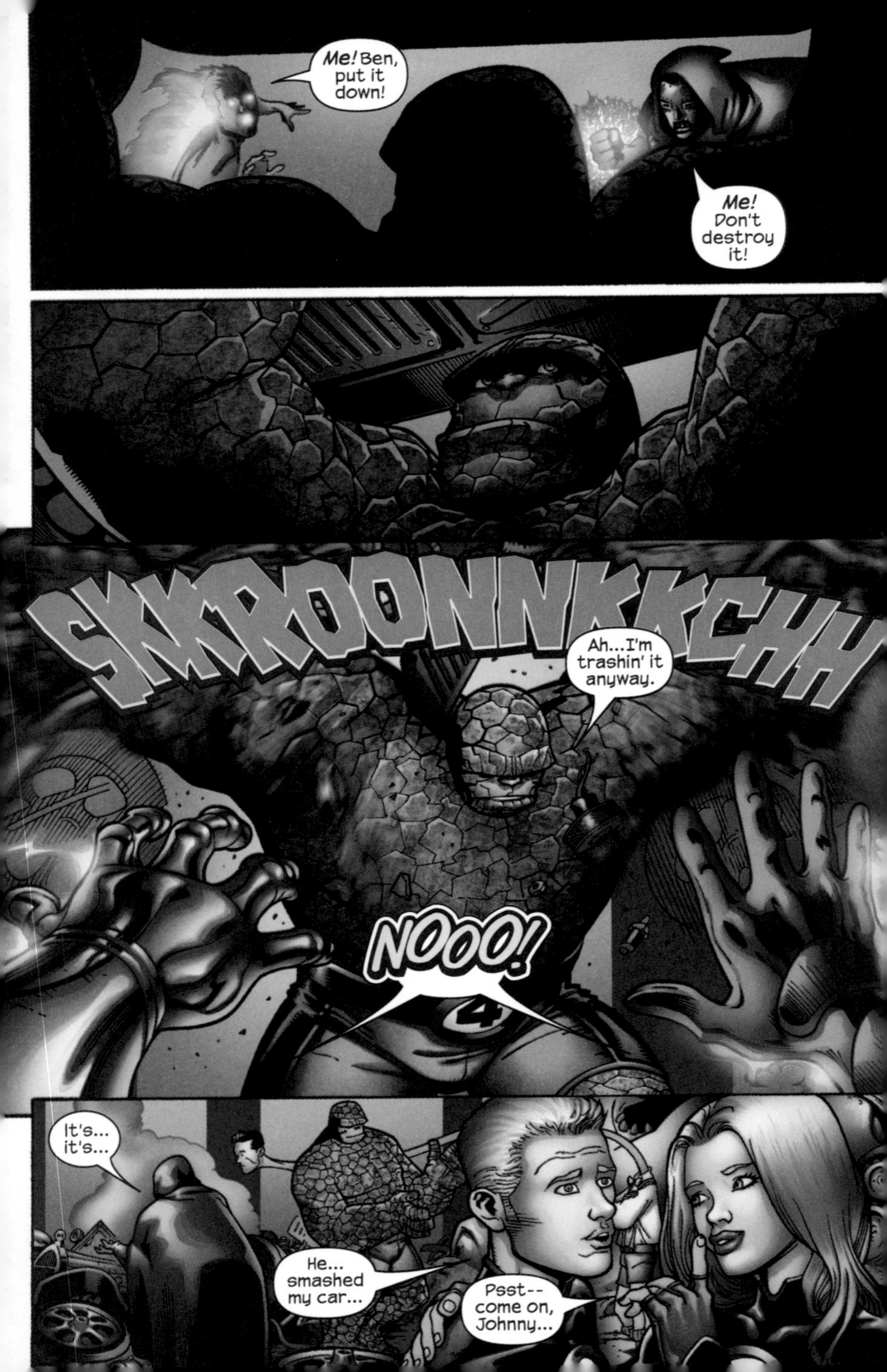
Me! Ben, put it down!
Me! Don't destroy it!
SKKROONNKKCHH
Ah...I'm trashin' it anyway.
NOOO!
It's... it's...
He... smashed my car...
Psst-- come on, Johnny...

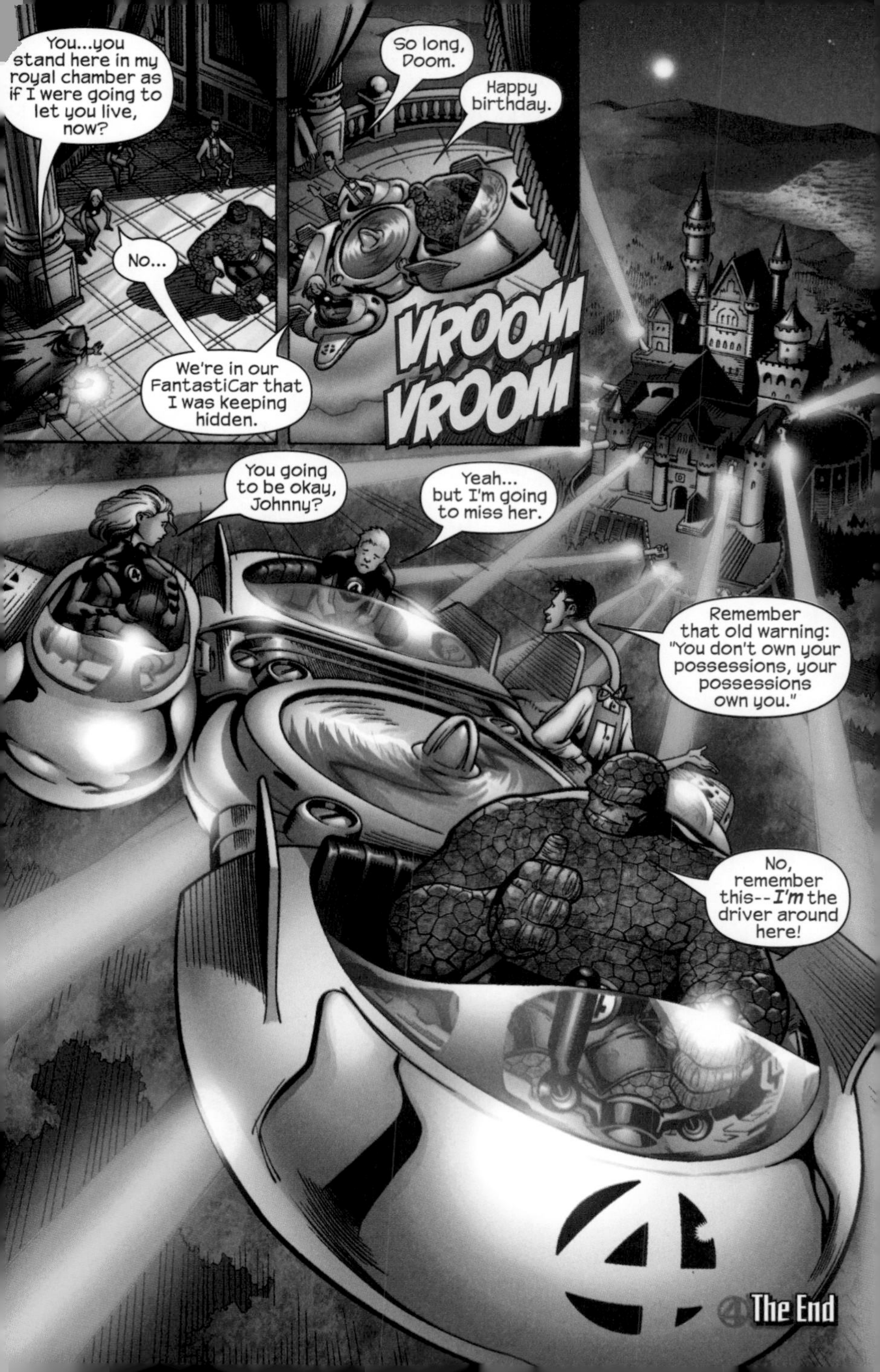
You...you stand here in my royal chamber as if I were going to let you live, now?
No...
We're in our FantastiCar that I was keeping hidden.
So long, Doom.
Happy birthday.
VROOM VROOM
You going to be okay, Johnny?
Yeah... but I'm going to miss her.
Remember that old warning: "You don't own your possessions, your possessions own you."
No, remember this--*I'm* the driver around here!
The End